I0680883

HOUSE OF DOLLS

by
Shawn Zachary

Published by FICTIONWRITERS
in association with
LULU Publications

Cover Design
by
FICTIONWRITERS

Copyright © 2006 by FictionWriters
www.fictionwriters.ws/Store.htm
FW: 622112
ISBN: 978-0-6151-3914-2

All rights reserved including the right of reproduction in
whole or in part in any form.

Acknowledgements

With sincere appreciation to
Rita Cohen
for her faithful belief in my fiction
writing endeavors, and her patience in
editing my work while coping with
my oft-time hardheadedness.

Dedicated to:

Alice Kocher/Walters

HOUSE OF DOLLS

CHAPTER I

"Matt's a good boy, but he worries me."

Lucille shook her head. "Rick. He's only ten, for heaven's sake. He's building the dollhouse for Bunny."

Rick shrugged his shoulders as he watched his only son work meticulously on a halfway finished project. "I know . . . I know. She worries me, too. But I still need to spend more time with him. Do boy things, you know." Matt's dad continued to observe for several moments, then grabbed a coat from a wall hook.

Lucille stopped doing dishes to help him with it. "You sure you don't want me to take Bunny for her treatment? You've got an awful lot to do."

* * *

Deale, Maryland; October 1954:

"Hey, dad." Matt yelled above the roar of the small outboard motor he tended. "Look at that sky out there."

Rick, rode up front rigging fishing lines. He stopped to turn and face the south. "Yeah," he shouted, as the small craft barely reached the end of the channel exiting Deale harbor -- waves beginning to rush inland denying forward progress.

Matt coughed, spitting water splashed in his face. "I thought it was supposed to miss us."

"Thought so, too. We've got to turn back." They hurriedly exchanged places.

Rick spun the boat in the water, making a dash for the shoreline, abetted by the following sea.

Rain and wind pummeled them fiercely as they struggled to gain solid ground near an old abandoned house -- both rushing inside an enclosed rear porch, finding it unlocked and accessible.

1

"Hurricane out there, and I'm not exaggerating," Rick said, removing his rain jacket and motioning for his son's.

Matt stood soaked and shivering, gazing through a row of dirt stained windows at the effects of the swirling rain and harsh gusts of wind. Their boat, once resting on shore, suddenly flew into the air landing in the water, quickly being beaten into shreds against pilings and rocks -- fishing poles and gear strewn everywhere. At the age of eleven, he had never experienced such an impact wrought by nature. "Really bad, Dad."

The house shook under the torrent.

"I know. Hope this old place holds up."

Lightning flashes lit the room brightly, exaggerating years of dust and debris covering a few pieces of furniture, old and worn.

Matt's dad disappeared and called from another room. "Come on in here. I found a kitchen with an old stove. There's still some wood. We can get warm."

A tremendous clash of thunder shook the house as if it were about to crumble. Matt stood dazed watching a strange glowing grayish light emanate from a hallway before passing through him as if he weren't there. A sudden chill, more intense than caused by the cold, rushed through Matt's body. He stumbled into the kitchen, his skin ashen in color.

"God, Matt. Are you all right?

He stuttered. "I . . . I don't . . . don't know . . .

Matt collapsed.

* * *

Deale, Maryland: January 1994 -- forty years later:

As violent as the sea may be, a rare calm in the Chesapeake Bay caused its surface to resemble a dark glass table top stretching from shore to shore -- a bay-built oyster boat daring to face the elements of the wintry day. After the craft entered Rockhold Creek, its wake slowly disappeared as if it were never there.

An old, two-story wooden house overlooking the creek not far from the Drum Point jetty evidenced years of abject neglect. Thick brush growing around the structure protruded defiantly through the deep fallen snow as if to hold it in chastisement.

At one corner of the house, a small area of dirt remained strangely uncovered by the heavily falling flakes as clumps of new plant shoots erupted from the flowerbed -- a single bright yellow jonquil blooming in their midst ignoring its impossible right to exist.

* * *

Some eighty miles away, in Nokesville, Virginia, a cemetery's gates rested open.

A barely definable roadway evidencing tire tracks snaked through snow-covered tombstones. Tree limbs stood covered with a lattice work of ice; the wind crackling through the trees and crunching footsteps heard over the packed snow; a group of bystanders gathered at grave-side.

The minister performed last rites -- his voice barely audible as he recited the Twenty-third Psalm. ". . . he leadeth me beside the still waters. He restoreth my soul; . . ."

Matt Bodine, a tall trim ruggedly-handsome man, looking drawn, tired and weary, belied his early fifties age. He stood, clean shaven, staring at his wife's flower-laden casket.

His watering eyes stubbornly held back a flow of tears as his son, Chris, placed his arm around him, turning him away from the grave. They walked quietly toward a waiting limousine -- the family following close behind.

* * *

Two Years Later:

Matt sat behind the wheel of his small sports car. Chuck, a longtime friend and former heavy-equipment employee, rode shotgun in the two-seated automobile.

"You act like you know where you're going," Chuck said, his deep raspy voice fitting his burly physical appearance.

Matt smiled, then pulled a pack of Camels from his shirt pocket. "Been a long time." He paused to light a cigarette. "Dad used to take me fishing at Deale, years ago. Sure had some fun times. If I buy the boat, it's almost ironic I could spend the rest of my life there. He always wanted to get a cottage on the water after he retired -- Deale his choice spot. He never made it to sixty-five. Damned cancer got him, Bunny, and then Catherine."

"Sorry to bust your bubble, but I think we just missed our turn. Barely noticed, but pretty sure we passed a sign back there behind some hanging tree limbs. Believe it said Deale."

"Aw, shit." Matt looked into the rearview mirror and pulled

3

to the shoulder. To be sure, he stuck his head out of his window and did a double-check. After making a tight U-turn and a left at the intersection, the sign indicated two miles remaining to their destination.

"How are the grand-kiddies doin'? Been a good while since I heard from you. Got any more since the last time we talked?"

Matt rolled his window up a little bit. "Nope, just the two." He paused to pull smoke from his cigarette. "Doubt Ellen will have any after Terry, but wouldn't surprise me if Chris and his wife had a few more." Matt chuckled. "He married a devout Catholic. Got one in the basket right now."

"That boy of yours is your spittin' guts." Chuck paused for a moment, searching for his chew. "Realize it's been a couple of years since Catherine died, but what the hell prompted you to buy a boat all of a sudden?"

"Aw, business started sagging . . . Harry offered to buy me out. Heart wasn't in it anymore. Considered myself lucky to get out with as much as I did. Figured buying a boat and living on it would be the cheapest way to go. Anyway, always loved the water and had a strange compulsion lately I really have to do this."

"Cool. . . . I guess."

"Well, here we are." Matt tamped his cigarette in the ashtray as they approached a three-way intersection -- its blinking caution light representing Deale's only connection with electronic traffic control. On one corner rested the Happy Harbor Restaurant -- the ever popular early morning meeting place for charter captains. To the left, a concrete bridge spanned Rockhold Creek.

"Damn. Used to be a wooden drawbridge. Shows just how long it's been since I was here. . . . Do me a favor and read me the directions on that paper." He pointed to the dash. "Not sure where this marina is."

Chuck scanned the notes, looked up, and poked his thumb to the right as Matt neared another intersection. After turning, Matt pulled to the side of the road as a fire truck roared from the station; sirens screaming, horns blaring.

After a short wait, the warning wail of the fire engine faded in the distance as Matt pulled from the road's shoulder and passed a variety of houses and bungalows along the narrow lane.

4

"According to this, we've gone a bit too far."

Matt completely ignored Chuck's comment and stared ahead as if in a stupor; his eyes appearing glazed.

"Hey. Beam me up Scotty. . . . You all right?"

Matt continued to disregard Chuck, acting as if he wasn't there. The car came to an abrupt stop in front of an old wooden house sitting near the end of Drum Point Road. The two story structure appeared sound, but years of neglect being evident with the front windows and door boarded over and paint flaking from its wooden-siding; the grounds sorely in need of care.

"Hey, Dude. This ain't the marina."

Matt got out of the vehicle without speaking. As if unable to control his actions, he immediately walked to one side of the building toward the rear of the structure facing the creek.

"Hey, partner. Where the hell you goin'?" Chuck asked, as he followed Matt.

"Jonquils," Matt said, in an almost mechanical manner.

Chuck came to a quick halt. "What the hell?"

At the rear corner of the house, a flower bed full of jonquils occupied a small area. Matt stood for several moments staring at them before kneeling. Gently touching one, it wilted in his fingers. He reacted instantly as if shocked by an electrical force, being knocked backward and on his behind.

"Damn it, Matt. What the hell's goin' on?"

He still didn't respond.

Chuck grabbed Matt's shoulder and shook it.

"Huh? . . . Matt managed to turn his glazed glare up at Chuck.

"What's wrong with you?"

Matt struggled to his feet in a daze. "Uhhhh . . . noth . . . nothing."

Chuck steadied him by his elbow as they walked back toward the car where Matt plumped his butt against the auto's rear -- his brow beading with sweat; his hand bluish-grey as if frostbitten.

"Jesus Christ, Matt. Mind telling me what happened?"

"I don't know. It's like . . . I just don't know."

"Well, you've sure been actin' pretty crazy. And, what the hell's wrong with your hand?

Matt stood erect staring at his clenched fist.

"Come on let's get out of here."

"One thing. How'd you know there was a garden? What're those flowers, anyway?"

"I just knew. . . . Jonquils. . . . You drive."

* * *

In less than five minutes they arrived at the marina and pulled into a parking space.

"You see a maroon Lincoln anywhere?" Matt asked rather weakly.

"Nope." Chuck nudged Matt in his leg. "Sure you're okay?"

"Yeah. I'll be fine." Perspiration continued to bead on Matt's forehead. "I still can't understand it. Something seemed to take control of me and then it let go when I touched the flower. . . . Know I've seen that place before. Just don't remember when. Must have been when I was a kid." Matt paused for a moment as if collecting his memories. "I remember getting caught in a bad storm one day. Dad and I barely made it back to shore and got inside an empty house. I remember seeing a glow and feeling numb. It might have been then. Just don't know." Matt wiped his brow on the sleeve of his shirt. He noticed his hand had returned to normal color. "I can't explain it."

"That's weird." Chuck spit juice from his chew. "By the way, who are we lookin' for?"

"Supposed to meet a guy driving a big Continental."

Matt slowly headed toward the pier to get a better look at the boats aligning the docks. Not knowing the precise location of the one advertised in the paper, he turned to see the expected vehicle as it lumbered down the dirt road and parked along side his automobile.

As much as the Continental dwarfed the small sports car, so too did its over-four-hundred-pound occupant.

"Hi. I'm Ozzie," the whale of a man said, as he struggled to get out from behind the steering wheel. "You must be Matt."

"That's right." Matt moved forward to shake Ozzie's hand. "I got here a little early."

"Oh, I thought I was late," Ozzie said, and chuckled.

"Ozzie, this is a friend who's going to check the engines out for me." Matt motioned in Chuck's direction.

Chuck stepped forward extending his hand. "Hi. Chuck

6

Mills."

"Well, Chuck. Come on. Let's go take a gander at the old tub."

"Just a minute, I need something from my car." Matt opened the door and retrieved his briefcase from behind the driver's seat.

"Hey, that's some wheels you got there," Ozzie said, then laughed loudly. "I'd need a can-opener and a barrel of grease to get in that thing."

Matt and Chuck laughed in agreement.

The three followed a long sidewalk to the pier, soon arriving at a boat bearing no name on its stern -- a forty-five-foot Owens Aruba with a very wide beam. "Come on aboard," Ozzie said, emphasizing the suggestion with a wave of his arm. "You won't believe the room inside."

Matt and Chuck boarded the craft, climbing a flight of steps leading to the aft deck. The once wood-covered bridge had been removed and replaced by a new canvas tent with its door flap open exposing the helm. Another staircase to the far right of the bridge went below to a generous salon area in the center of the boat.

"All of the furniture and appliances go with it," Ozzie said, then plopped on the sofa, occupying a large portion of it.

A galley shared part of the space off to one corner, but, most important, a full-sized refrigerator was inset into a bulkhead.

Ozzie noticed Matt's interest in it. "Work's great. . . . Not that old, either."

Two more sets of stairs were at opposite ends of the salon, one leading to the stern and the other to the bow. The fore area contained a stateroom having an upper and lower berth, plus a head and a shower. Two staterooms and a second fully-equipped head occupied the aft of the boat -- the main aft cabin stretching its width, containing a queen-size bed and more than adequate closet and storage space. The smaller stateroom also provided double berths.

It was love at first sight, but Matt struggled desperately to hide his enthusiasm as he and Chuck returned to the salon.

"Well, what do you think?" Ozzie asked, ending his guided tour administered from his seat on the couch.

"I don't think there's too much I can't handle, but it would sure take a good while to get everything done."

"Could I see the power plants?" Chuck asked.

"Sure. No problem. Gimme a hand with the rug." Ozzie grunted loudly with the effort of rising from the sofa. He leaned to grab a corner of the floor covering. Pulling it aside exposed two hatches.

Chuck disappeared into the hold.

Following further business and other trivial conversation, Matt agreed to call that evening to set up a time to have the boat surveyed. Four days later, the two negotiators drove to the Department of Natural Resources in Annapolis -- the sale finalized.

Matt's first priority: to move the boat to another marina -- one allowing him to work on the craft while in the water. He didn't have far to search, finding a perfect location adjacent to the old Drum Point house that had already began to impose its haunting influence.

CHAPTER II

Matt sat on the bow of his boat splicing a rope end as Ozzie's small outboard slowly approached, then stood offering a brief wave. "When the hell'd you get that?" he shouted over the clatter of the loud Evinrude.

"Last week. Wanna go fishin'?" Ozzie cut his engine and drifted to a forward piling near Matt's boat.

"Can't. Chuck finished the motor work and I've got to move her downstream to another marina." Matt knelt down and rolled the rope into a tight circle on the deck.

Chuck started the twin engines, and their initial roar soon settled back to a low melodic rumble.

"Damn, they sound good," Ozzie said with a huge smile.

"Thanks. . . . I've invited family down later for a ride and a cookout at the new place. It's Deale Marina. You're welcome to stop by."

Ozzie kicked his engine to life and gave a thumb's up.

* * *

Unusual to early spring, the bay teemed with activity of boaters taking advantage of the balmy weekend day.

Matt's family and a few friends sat on the bow and aft deck as a huge wake spread behind his small yacht. Chuck tended the helm while Matt got a soda for his granddaughter from the ice chest.

As they approached the inlet to Rockhold Creek, Matt took the helm, letting his six-year old grandson, Allen, steer them toward shore and into the breakwater channel. "Better let ol' Granddad take over from here," Matt whispered into Allen's ear.

Allen slid from his lap, and bounded toward the stern.

Shortly, the old house came into view. As Matt began staring

9

at it intently, he eased the throttles and pulled the engines out of gear. The boat drifted to a halt a couple hundred feet short of its mooring place. Matt sat shuddering, his forehead covered with sweat; his hands gripping the helm so tightly his knuckles turned white.

"Matt. What's wrong? You okay?" Chuck asked.

Matt didn't respond, continuing his determined gaze.

Chuck nudged him in the ribs. "Hey, guy. What the hell did you stop for?"

Matt's daughter Ellen approached. "What's wrong, Chuck?"

"I'm not sure. He looks a little pale to me. Maybe too much sun."

"I'll be okay. . . . Ellen, honey, would you get me a bottle of water out of the ice chest?"

"You don't look so good to me," Chuck said.

Ellen handed her dad the open bottle.

Matt drank generously. "It's something about that damn house."

Chuck shook his head. "You gotta be kiddin' me."

"What house?" Ellen asked.

"Nothing. Not important. I'll be okay." Matt gathered himself and maneuvered the craft into his new slip -- a spot along side the end pier, mooring parallel to the dock, its stern to the shore.

* * *

As planned, the maiden-voyage group enjoyed a cookout in the marina picnic area. While the children played, Ellen and Chuck's wife tended the barbeque grill. Matt invited a few of his new marina neighbors to join them.

By dark, everyone except Ozzie had left -- Matt having talked him into spending the night due to his slightly intoxicated condition.

He and Ozzie boarded the boat.

"I just realized today's the first time I've been on the boat since you bought it. You've done quite a bit already." Ozzie tried to squeeze his butt into a deck chair but gave up and sat on the gunnel.

"Hell. Just got started." Matt moved to the ice chest. "Want a beer?"

10

"What kind?" Ozzie asked, as if it mattered. "Just kiddin'."
He chuckled.

Matt handed a can to his big friend and decided on having a Scotch and water for himself.

"That crap will kill you."

"Yep. Probably will some day."

Ozzie changed the subject. "What's the weather supposed to be tomorrow?"

"Don't know, but can find out." Matt got up from his chair and turned on the ship-to-shore radio. Punching a button, it spurted to life and the weather station blared out reports for the DelMarVa area.

"All right," Ozzie said, elated at hearing a good forecast. Are you sure you can't make the fishing trip in the mornin'?"

"Damn, I'd love to. Just can't. After the move today, got a million things to do."

The weather report continued, ". . . lower Bay area. Winds at five to ten knots; seas at . . ."

Suddenly the radio went silent. Then, Matt heard a low murmuring sound which increased in pitch and altered into the voice of someone crying. "What the shit? What the hell was that?" Matt asked, moving to adjust the tuner.

"What's wrong?"

"You didn't hear that?"

"Hear what?" Ozzie appeared completely baffled.

Matt stammered. "You mean . . . you mean you didn't hear a woman . . . a girl crying?"

"Told you the booze would get to ya." Ozzie chuckled and shook his head. "Hey, old buddy. All I heard was the weather and some static. You really think you heard somethin'?"

"Aw, man. It ain't the booze. I must be going nuts. Sent a chill up my spine." Matt turned off the radio and shortly dismissed the incident.

After deciding to play gin rummy, one game led to another and, somewhere around two a.m., Ozzie hit the sack.

Still feeling a bit restless, Matt decided to go on deck carrying the remains of a nightcap and stood at the stern rail.

The old house appeared silhouetted against a moonlit background. Lights from a marina across the creek, a quarter-

11

mile distant, reflected on the stretch of first floor windows making them shimmer as if having a life apparently lost long ago.

As Matt turned to go below, with his back to the old house, they altered to appear as if coming from inside -- a faint indefinable translucent image materialized, then disappeared.

* * *

The following morning Ozzie left before Matt woke, but called a week later with a big surprise. He bought a twenty-two-foot bass-fisherman with a ninety-horsepower outboard. There would be plenty of fishing opportunities ahead.

* * *

By the time September rolled around, Matt's boat looked like a 'queen of the sea.' Remodeling completed, time came to relax and focus on other matters.

Matt arrived on deck from below with a mug of coffee in hand, clad in a short-sleeve shirt and shorts; his face evidencing the new growth of a beard. He moved to the stern and peered at the old house, sipping from his cup.

From the boat's bridge, Matt's view covered Herring Bay, Holland Point and a good portion of the Chesapeake. However, more intriguing -- the deserted old home on the nearby shore he had unwillingly visited on his return to Deale. Ever since that day, Matt's uneasy feeling about the property intensified -- sure that it shared some relationship with his past.

The rear of the structure faced south toward the creek with a long enclosed porch running its width. Unlike the front of the house, the rear windows remained unobstructed. There appeared to be torn curtains hanging from eight closely joined windows spanning the porch with a rear door located in the center.

During the off season, the backyard remained filled with neatly stacked crab pots awaiting summer employment. Except for the occasional roar of a water pressure hose being used, by a grey-haired old seaman cleaning them, an unusual aura hovered over the property.

As he stood, somewhat mesmerized, a faint emanation of his having stood at similar windows watching a boat being tossed and torn by a storm briefly came to him. He shook his head, coming back to focus.

Matt shivered with a sudden chill as he glared at what seemed to be yellow flowers growing in the small garden area he had earlier visited.

"You gotta be kidding me. Jonquils? This time of year?"

He sat his cup on the gunnel and retrieved a pair of binoculars from the bridge. After returning to the stern he peered in the direction of the garden finding it barren of any blooms and filled with weeds and undergrowth.

Matt's phone rang. He rushed below and pushed the speaker button. "Hello. . . . Hello. . . . Damn it. Hello."

A crackling sound came over the phone followed by a weak feminine voice, "Richard . . ." The crackling returned; then silence.

Matt glared at the phone for a moment before breaking the connection.

* * *

The early October morning evidenced another Indian Summer day as Matt swabbed his aft deck.

"Hey, old man. Ever going to stop working?" Jason called as he walked down the pier toward Matt's boat.

"Doubt so. Doesn't seem there's any end to it."

Jason represented one half of a young couple -- the other being Heather -- whom were among the few fellow boat owners at the marina invited to the cookout following Matt's arrival. Somewhere in their middle-twenties, Jason resembled a studious looking type with dark rim glasses unbefitting his true personality, and Heather, blessed with a body that just wouldn't quit -- loving to sport skimpy bikinis at any possible chance. They were good people and welcome company to Matt.

"We're going over to the Eastern Shore and Tilghman Island tomorrow. Wanna go?"

"Don't know." Matt grunted as he stuck his mop in the pail.

"Aw, come on, dude. You need a break."

Matt pulled his pipe from a pocket and lit it. "I'll think about it."

"If it's okay with you, we thought we'd come over this evening with some tapes I rented and watch a movie."

"Sounds good. What's Heather doing?"

"Taking a nap."

"How's about around seven. I'll cook up crab cakes if you

13

bring coleslaw and potato salad."

* * *

Supper went well; the night too nice to sit inside watching television. Heather insisted on doing dishes. Matt and Jason relaxed in deck chairs sitting near the aft deck stern.

"Damn, Matt. Actually feels warmer tonight than earlier today."

"You're right about that . . . and thanks for the help on rewiring the VHF." Matt took a sip of coffee.

"No problem. . . . By the way, what's with the beard?"

Matt laughed and scratched the long stubble. "Hell. Figured if I was to become an old salt, might as well look like one."

Jason drained his beer can, then crushed it in his hand. "Gonna get another and see what the little lady's up to. You ready?"

"I'm fine. But, help yourself."

Jason disappeared below.

Compelled to do so, Matt turned in his chair, then stood gazing at the old house's windows reflecting the far shore lights. Slowly they altered to a brighter stage as if they were no longer from the exterior, but emanating from inside. A swirling feminine image seemed to appear as if dancing alone beyond the span of windows. Simultaneously from the bridge the VHF's speaker exuded a lilting humming melody.

Heather gasped. "Oh, my God."

"Holy, shit," Jason mumbled.

Matt grasped the stern rail to steady himself, then spun to face Jason and Heather, his face agape with befuddlement, tinged with fear. "Jesus, God. You scared the hell outta me. Did you see that? Did you hear that?"

The VHF continued to crackle static in the background.

"I don't know what the hell I saw, but it was weird."

"I thought I saw the backdoor open slightly then close," Heather added.

Jason reached the stern. "I didn't hear anything but that damn static on the radio. What'd you turn it on for, anyway?"

"I didn't. It came on by itself."

"Shit, Matt."

"I didn't say anything earlier, but that's why I . . . we, worked

14

on the damn thing today. This kind of crap has happened before."

"I'm serious," Heather said. "I thought I saw a flash of light and the back door open and close."

Jason laughed nervously. "It was probably a spotlight from across the creek." He strained to try and get a better view. "You want to check it out Matt?"

"Yeah. Think I will. Don't like the idea of maybe a bum hanging around the marina."

"I'm with you on that."

"You know, babe, I'm really tired," Heather said. "I think I'm going to turn in early."

"We won't be long." Jason kissed Heather on the cheek as Matt reached for a flashlight.

"Okay, but be careful."

The three disembarked the boat and proceeded toward shore. Heather headed for her pier while Matt and Jason approached the house along a short path sandwiched by heavy brush.

"Damn, this is creepy," Jason said, breaking the silence.

"What do you think you saw?"

Jason's voice quivered slightly. "It was sort'a like a glowing light that seemed to flicker on and off."

"Exactly," Matt countered. "What else?"

"Then I think I saw something move inside."

"Good. I'm not nuts."

Jason stumbled and caught himself, coming up limping. "Damn that hurt."

"Come on, asshole. I don't like any of this."

Jason noticed a wooden stick and picked it up. "Like I was saying, it only lasted a few seconds. What about you?"

"Know it seems crazy, but thought I saw lights come on in that back room and a young girl dancing by herself behind the windows. That's when I heard the radio come on. Sounded like a feminine voice humming a song, or something. Not sure. Probably just a damn vagrant in there."

Jason hefted the stick he carried. "Yeah. What this is for."

As they arrived at the backyard, Matt swung his flashlight in a slow wide arch across the area.

Jason chuckled. "Think the old dude's got enough crab

pots?"

A flagstone walkway, almost swallowed by grass, stretched from the backdoor to a narrow rickety pier jutting out about a hundred feet where its far end gradually angled downward into the creek. The usable section near the shore provided mooring space for the old captain's crab and oyster boat.

"Well, let's check the door out," Matt said, as he turned the light beam toward the rear of the house.

As they neared, it appeared clearly apparent a padlock rested in place and firmly secured.

Jason tried to peer through one of the rear windows. "Guess that settles that."

"Wait a minute, I want to look around a little more." Matt went to one corner of the house and Jason to the other. Several moments later Matt returned to check on his investigating partner.

As Jason leaned over some rose bushes trying to get another peek through a side window, he flushed a rabbit that jumped across his feet. "Holy fuck," he shouted.

Matt laughed nervously. "Christ, Jason. I almost shit my pants."

Jason chuckled. "I think I did."

"Yeah. Let's split and get a drink. I need one."

"I'm for gettin' out of here, for sure, but think I'll get back to my little lady."

They started their return to the marina.

"You gotta be serious. Not like you."

"Yeah, 'fraid so. Heather goes to early mass and has to drive all the way into Marlboro to the closest Catholic church. Besides, it's going to be a long day tomorrow." They took a few steps, and, "Aw, shit. One more ain't gonna hurt."

Matt laughed and shook his head.

Two drinks later, and following additional thanks for the hospitality and meal, Jason departed.

Matt went below to take glasses before returning to the aft deck for a final smoke. He stood at the rail staring at the house as his mind seemed focused on it beyond his own intent.

As Heather had indicated earlier, he watched as a light shone from behind the porch windows and the door opened and closed.

CHAPTER III

The weekend turned out quite relaxing -- Jason and Heather also adding a pleasant surprise. The young couple announced plans for getting married and having a lawn wedding at the marina the first week of the following August. Of course, Matt received a personal invitation to attend. He did them one better and volunteered to tend bar.

Monday morning came too early. Matt heard the phone ring and rolled over in bed grabbing the receiver. "Hello," he said, sounding groggy.

Ellen's voice crackled over the wire. "Dad, is that you?"

"Uh, yeah." He paused to yawn. "What time is it?"

"Oh, I've woken you up. Sorry. I'll call back later."

"No. No. No. It's okay. Just got to bed a little late. Watched a replay of an Orioles' game on TV last night and it went into extra innings."

"Well, it's about nine-thirty. I tried to reach you a couple of times yesterday and left a message."

"Aw, baby, I'm the one that's sorry. Half the time, I never remember to check the damn thing." He paused to roll out of bed and sit on its edge. "I went over to Tilghman Island for their seafood festival yesterday with Jason and Heather." He yawned. "They're a young couple with a small cabin cruiser across from me on the next dock. You met them at the cookout."

"You're right. I remember. Sound's like you had fun. I'm really happy you're enjoying yourself. You deserve it."

Matt could almost see her smiling as she said it.

"I just wanted to remind you about Terry's birthday party Wednesday evening."

"Wouldn't miss it for the world." Matt grunted as he tried to remove one of his socks left on from the previous eve.

"Okay, Daddy. See you then. Love you. Bye."

Matt placed the phone in its cradle. He stood and stretched his arms over his head, as much as allowed under the low ceiling of the aft cabin. After grabbing a fresh towel and wrapping it around his neck, he went up the short stairway and flicked on the coffee maker. He turned on his heels and bounced back down the steps and adjusted the shower faucets to the desired setting. The steaming water beat against his face and body. It felt great. He felt great.

* * *

The summer passed in a flash -- another boating season almost gone. Matt was beginning to resemble an 'old salt,' for sure. He had given up cigarettes, and sporting a short 'salt-and-pepper' beard, with a pipe clenched between his teeth, no one would accuse him of ever having been a landlubber.

After dressing in a pair of jeans and a pullover turtleneck, he sat on the aft deck sipping his coffee from a huge mug. The morning brought a slight chill in the air, making him feel really alive. The drone from the old seaman's pressure hose beckoned gulls swooping down to get the smallest morsels of decayed bait from the crab pots. Combined with the smell of salt water in the air, the scene cast a perfect mood.

Matt packed his pipe, lit it, and, with cup in hand, disembarked and strolled up the pier. He slowly approached the old house, biding time until the preoccupied worker, garbed in chest-high wading boots, took a break.

"Good morning," Matt said, as he neared.

"Mornin," the seaman said, without looking up -- adjusting a valve on the compressor.

"I'm Matt Bodine. I've got that big Owens over there," he quickly added.

"Know you do." He growled under his breath as his wrench slipped off the fitting. "Don't mean to be rude. I'm Captain Joe."

Matt knew better than to initiate a handshake and left the amenity up to the local. Other than standing erect and stretching his back, Captain Joe made no overt gesture.

"I've really been fascinated by your old house."

"Ain't mine. Got that one next door." Captain Joe motioned

with his thumb over his shoulder toward a modern brick home about a hundred yards distant.

"Is this property for sale?"

"Don't know. Ain't never seen a sign on it." The Captain pulled a short cigar butt from his shirt pocket and clenched it between his teeth. "Got a match?"

"Sure." Matt moved forward and handed him a pack. "Keep them."

"Thanks." Pausing to light the butt, Captain Joe puffed hard before getting it lit. "Damn thing got a little damp. Wonder why?" He chuckled.

The minor witticism constituted a crack in the icy chill commonly found among the local gentry. "I'm really interested in the property."

"Well, goes back a long way. I was still a young pup, . . . 'round nineteen-thirty, maybe thirty-one. Strange group, they was. Me bein' just a boy, you know. Never paid much attention to them. Didn't have no boys. Kept to themselves all the time. Been vacant ever since."

Matt remained enthralled and didn't dare interrupt.

Captain Joe eased himself to sit atop a nearby tree stump. "Seems they had a daughter I don't remember much about. Do know the ma died; then the girl died; then the old man, I reckon. Anyway, like I said, 'cept for a few vagrants every now and agin, it's been deserted since the early thirties." He paused long enough to relight the butt. "After all them years, figured I might as well use the backyard and pier. Nobody seems to care, and it keeps bums from hangin' 'round." His cigar fizzled again and he scraped away the charred end with his finger nail, sticking what remained behind his lower lip. "Well, time's wastin'." He groaned, rising from the stump.

"Yeah. Thanks a lot for the information. Sorry I took so much of your time."

"Pay it no mind," the graying Captain said, reaching down for the end of his hose. As he walked toward the pier, he called out an afterthought. "Guess their kin could still own it, I reckon. Don't remember their last name."

The loud hum of the pressurized water again filled the air.

Matt couldn't resist taking a peek inside the house and peered

19

through the rear windows. The room appeared practically barren except for an old table, rocking chair, and a chest against the far wall. Cobwebs and thick layers of dust covered everything. Access to the side windows proved impossible due to unattended rose bushes and wild berry thorns. The front door remained boarded, and the other downstairs windows completely covered from the inside.

Suddenly Matt was stunned at a brief mental flashback of having been inside the premises with his father. As if automatically drawn, he immediately went to the small corner garden area once filled with jonquils, now barren of flowers, weeds or brush, knelt to one knee, and softly ran his hand across the soil.

Content for the moment, Matt returned to his boat hearing the phone ringing as he boarded.

"Yeah," he said, a bit winded from trying to get there before the machine answered.

"Mr. Bodine. This is the harbor police calling. We understand you've been having wild orgies aboard your vessel."

Matt laughed. "What the hell do you want, Ozzie?"

"Nothin', really. Just wanted to see how you were doin'."

"Good. As a matter of fact, great."

"Hadn't heard from you in a good while. Over the cold shivers, I hope?"

"Yep, all gone. But, let's not get into that."

"You sure sound like you're in a good mood. Wanna go fishin this evenin'? Harvey said he wanted to try his new motor out."

"Awful choppy down here. Noticed several charters coming in early."

Get the weather station on the horn and see what they say."

Matt carried the phone over to the ship-to-shore and pushed a couple of buttons. "Wait a minute. I'm going to put this on the speaker phone."

In the middle of a not-too-favorable report, the volume faded and low murmurs came from the speaker. As times before, the faint whisper suddenly turned into whimpers and the sobbing of a child. Amidst the low cries, Matt clearly heard the voice call, "Richard."

"Damn, Ozzie. What the hell's going on?"

"What? What do you mean?"

"Don't tell me you didn't hear that."

"Hear what? All I heard was your losin' the channel. You must be gettin' a weak signal."

"You mean you didn't hear someone crying. And, the name Richard. It sounded like a kid. Maybe a young girl." Matt expressed frustration. "And, this time I haven't had a damn drop to drink."

A long pause took place before Ozzie responded. "Do you hear anything, now?"

"No. No. In fact, the thing's gone off by itself. I didn't turn it off, Ozzie."

"Will it turn back on?"

Matt pushed the switch and the radio immediately spewed out a conversation taking place between the Coast Guard and another vessel. He changed the channel and the weather report again sounded through the speaker. "That's crazy, Ozzie. Really crazy. This is about the fifth or sixth time it's happened. You've been listening twice and you never heard it either time."

"Well, I can hear the weather right now and it doesn't sound too good."

"I don't know what the hell's going on, Ozzie. I've had unexplained interference on my TV ever since I moved here and, just recently, beginning to get a lot of static occasionally on this phone." At that moment, repeated clicking over the instrument indicated Ozzie receiving another call. "You better take it. Talk to you later."

"I will. But, I'd check the radio out. There's probably a loose connection or somethin'."

The conversation ended, Matt pushed the phone speaker button and moved to turn off the weather forecast. Again, the same thing happened. Matt shivered as an eerie sensation traversed throughout his body.

CHAPTER IV

Weeks passed, fall arrived, and the radio long since rewired with no further incident. Considering the problem solved and all of the major repairs complete, Matt found time to enjoy himself socializing with marina friends and having a great deal of success fishing for stripers. Jason and Heather's wedding went off without a hitch and Ozzie helped Matt with the bartending. The season all but over, Matt gained a good bit of work winterizing boats, through a number of contacts previously made, making enough profit to carry him over the winter season without tapping into his savings.

He virtually ignored the old house since his visit with Captain Joe, until a surge of inclement weather caused several days of mist and heavy fog. An accompanying exceptionally high-tide dictated he check his land lines. After donning a rain jacket, he stepped onto the aft deck and immediately noticed an unusual phenomenon.

Lights from the marina across the creek were totally obliterated by the dense haze, but a flickering glow appeared from a downstairs window in the old house and the back door seemed to be ajar.

As Matt left the boat and walked along the dock toward shore, the light continued gleaming. Logically, he thought, if it were a reflection, at some point during his movement it should have disappeared, even for a moment -- but, it didn't. Deciding not to go any further, he returned to check the lines. After boarding his boat again, he noticed the light gone and the door closed.

Matt spent a restless night experiencing intermittent sleep. The morning brought a strong determination to investigate the old place. His mind whirled with possibilities -- the most obvious, as before, a vagrant being in the house. Matt heard Captain Joe leaving before daybreak to tend his crab lines, knowing he wouldn't return until the afternoon. There was no urgency, as far as time mattered, but his need to know overpowered rationale. Not having any idea of what to expect, he armed himself with a crow bar for protection, and to use on the door if needed.

The walk to the old house seemed longer than usual -- dreading what might be found. Upon reaching the rear of the property, he quickly noticed the door latch undone and the lock lying on the ground. Anything or anybody could be inside, he thought.

On opening the door, his first instinct cried for him to call out to whoever might be present.

"Hey. Who's in here?"

The words came loud and clear and seemed to echo in his head. The fact no one responded made little difference.

Although, still feeling uneasy, he reasoned, there had been plenty of time for someone to have spent the night and already vacated the place.

Typical of many homes built on the water, the porch-like area was somewhat comparable to a modern day family room affording a good view of the creek. Cautiously continuing his investigation, he found a dining room, a kitchen with a wood burning stove, and a living room across the front of the house. A stairway to the second floor was in the center of the home and, as Matt stood at the bottom of the steps, a strange sensation welled throughout his body.

As if drawn up the stairs, on the upper floor, he found a large master bedroom with two smaller rooms adjoining the hallway. No toilet nor bathroom facilities could be found, and the smallest of the areas appeared to have served as a storage room. The remnants of an old wooden bed remained in the second bedroom, minus springs and mattress. The only other thing Matt noticed appeared to be a small closet in a far corner with the door hanging crooked off its hinges. Compelled to look inside, he detected nothing out of the ordinary.

A double-check while departing the house provided no evidence at all of any recent intruders. After closing the backdoor, he replaced the padlock, intentionally leaving it disengaged and returned to his boat.

* * *

Since Thanksgiving Day resulted in a combined family affair, Matt decided to spend Christmas alone. He dropped off gifts ahead of time, and called many of his old friends to express holiday wishes. However, a surprise Christmas Eve visit knocked him off his heels.

"Ho, ho, ho. Merry Christmas. . . . Merry Christmas," Matt heard someone shout, accompanied by a pounding on the side of his boat, as he sat stretched out dozing in front of the TV.

He jumped to his feet, scampering up the stairs and onto the bridge. "Well, I'll be damned," he said. "Come on aboard, Jason. Merry Christmas. . . . Hi Heather."

Heather climbed on board and embraced him with a big hug. "Matt, this is a good friend of ours, Kitty," she said, turning away to refer to a third party arriving on deck.

Not having first noticed her presence, the surprise changed to mild shock at hearing the name. It was a stunning reminder of a pet nickname for his wife.

"Hello, Matt. Happy holidays," the rather slim and attractive light-toned Afro-American woman said, offering her hand in friendship.

Matt responded, finding her grasp to be warm and not reflecting the cold of the evening. "Hi. Welcome aboard."

They all went below. Matt helped Kitty remove her coat, and he and Jason carried everyone's garments to the aft cabin.

"Wow, Matt. You've really got it looking good," Jason said, observing the lower area.

"Asshole. Thank God, I had everything cleaned up. Who's the lovely lady?"

"She's a neighbor. Kitty lost her husband a while ago and didn't want to see her spend the holidays alone. Hope you don't mind."

"Course not. Come on, let's get a beer or something."

The two rejoined the ladies and Matt quickly took drink orders. Conversation jumped from one subject to another, but nothing of a personal nature.

Jason and Heather were among the very few boaters at the

25

marina who would spend time on their craft during the winter season. Although rarely taking it out, they tremendously enjoyed overnighters and weekend stays.

During the course of the evening, Matt learned they planned to spend the week, until New Year's Eve; however, Kitty had to get back home by Christmas night.

Around one o'clock, an attempt to return to their own boat was foiled by the weather. An ice storm left the docks so slippery it would have been foolish to attempt leaving. Matt had more than enough room. Jason and Heather slept in the aft cabin; Kitty took the fore compartment, and he, being the gracious host, sprawled on the couch.

In the morning, Matt awoke to the sound of a door closing in the forward area. Immediately sitting up and getting to his feet, he pulled on his pants and a sweat shirt, just in time to see Kitty poking her head around a partition.

"Merry Christmas," Matt said. "Come on up."

Kitty came around the corner clad in Matt's pajama top. "Merry Christmas," she said. "I hope I didn't wake you." She yawned, covering her mouth with the back of her hand.

Kitty had worn her hair in a tight bun the night before and now long dark brown strands hung just below her shoulders. She was a stately, extremely attractive woman. Matt judged her to be about ten years younger than he, in her late thirties to early forties, and only a few inches shorter than himself.

"Coffee?"

"Yes, Please. A little milk for this Kitty. No sugar."

Matt smiled at her witticism as he placed two cups on the table, one on each side. They took seats opposite one another. "Sleep okay?"

Smiling, she said, "Oh, yes. I've never slept on a boat before. It was heavenly."

"That's good. Really glad you enjoyed it," he said, fumbling for something better to say. "Would you feel more comfortable if I offered you my robe?"

"I'm all right. It's nice and cozy. It's surprising how warm and homey a boat can be." Matt took a long sip from his cup before speaking. Kitty beat him to it. "How long have you lived aboard?"

"A little over eight months. I bought the boat a good while after my wife passed away and started living aboard while I did most of the work on it."

"You've done a wonderful job. It's beautiful." Kitty gently shoved her cup toward Matt. "Do you have some more?"

"All you can drink." He smiled and got up from the table. Shortly returning with the pot, Matt filled both cups and placed a tin of homemade cookies in front of her. "My daughter made these," he said, sitting down.

She slowly removed the top and gasped at the delectable array of Christmas goodies.

"How did you know my weakness?" She giggled.

Her smile, and especially her presence, brought a warm inner glow to Matt. Something he hadn't experienced in a long time.

Unaware he was staring at her, "Penny for your thoughts," she said, interrupting his stupor.

"Uh, I'm sorry. It's just . . . not used to having such lovely company."

"Me, too," she said, with a grin, and a bit of blush. "Heather said you're a hermit. Are you?"

Matt started laughing and shaking his head. "Never thought of it like that," he said, chuckling, "but she's probably right. Haven't socialized very much, and certainly haven't spent any time alone in a woman's presence since Catherine."

"That's a beautiful name. She was your wife?"

"Yeah. We were very close." He paused to freshen both of their cups. "I used to occasionally call her Catty. That's why I acted a bit funny when we were introduced last night."

Kitty expressed an understanding smile. "I was afraid you might have been set back by my ethnic background."

"Oh, my God, no. The thought never entered my mind."

Kitty expressed a reassured smile and paused to sip some coffee. "I lost my husband not long ago in an automobile accident. I can truly empathize with you. It's not easy to adjust after such a sudden tragedy."

"Oh, I'm sorry. That's really got to be difficult. My wife had a prolonged illness. At least with Catherine I had the chance to spend time with her before she passed."

They both sat quietly for several moments, as if lost in

separate thought.

"So, what do you do to keep busy?" Matt asked, breaking the silence, and the mood.

"I'm a professor of psychology at George Mason University," she said, looking up to meet his eyes.

"Wow. I didn't realize I was entertaining such a learned guest," he said jokingly, returning her gaze with a grin.

She smiled. "Well, I don't know about that. . . . And, so, what do you do?"

"Fish, fish, and more fishing." He laughed. "Naw, I used to have a small construction contracting business until it almost went belly-up. Tired of the rat race, I moved down here, rebuilt the boat, pick up odd jobs here and there, and decided to become a recluse. Voila, here I am."

Kitty laughed heartedly for the first time.

It pleased him.

"What's all the racket going on?" Jason asked, groaning and stumbling up the stairway. "Can't anybody get some shuteye around here?"

"Listen to that," Matt said, directing his remark to Kitty while turning to confront his drowsy friend, clad only in boxer shorts. "It's eleven o'clock and the day's almost gone."

Jason squinted his eyes, gazing at the wall clock. It was closer to nine-thirty. "Bull." His response came as he pulled a can of diet soda from the refrigerator, popped the top, and consumed almost all of its contents in a single gulp.

Heather surfaced a short time later and the two ladies fixed a large breakfast for all.

The weather improved and the sun began to make its appearance through scattered clouds. Jason left long enough to return with a change of clothes for his group. The gals took showers in the aft head, while the guys used the one in the forward compartment.

After driving to Annapolis, they spent the afternoon touring the downtown harbor and window shopping along Main Street -- having dinner afterward at a waterside restaurant before driving back.

It had been a wonderful day. Matt hated to see it end and having to say goodbye to Kitty.

"Everything has been so wonderful. I really enjoyed myself and think you're a pretty terrific guy." Kitty leaned forward and kissed Matt on his cheek.

Matt blushed, feeling almost like a schoolboy. "You be careful driving home. . . . Call me when you get there."

Kitty waved as she pulled away.

Matt stood watching until he could no longer see her car.

* * *

The rear door of the old house opened. A light flickered against the lower rear windows as the haunting sound of a girl moaning and her wailing cry echoed throughout the house.

The door slammed shut.

CHAPTER V

Several days later the weather improved a great deal. Matt busily worked on the dock's electrical panel as Jason arrived. "Need any help?" he asked.

"Naw. Just putting in a new breaker. . . . There, that does it." Matt picked up an empty package and stretched his back. "Want some coffee?"

"Nope. We're getting ready to leave." Jason slapped Matt on the back. "You sure made a hell of an impression on Kitty."

"What makes you say that?"

"She was on the phone with Heather when I left my boat. What did you do to her?"

"Nothing. Got no idea what you're talking about."

"Well, she thinks you're handsome, sharp, sexy. . . . I don't see any of that myself." He laughed.

Matt chuckled in return. "Screw you." He pulled his pipe from his jacket pocket.

"No. No kidding. You did make her day. This is the first time I've seen her show any signs of life since her old man died. Anyway, I wanted to ask you if you'd like to come to a New Year's Eve party tonight? It's going to be at my parents." Jason paused for a moment as he blew his nose into some tissue. "They've got a mansion in Great Falls," he facetiously added.

"I don't know," Matt said. "Figured on just hanging out here. Not much into traveling on holidays."

"Kitty's gonna be there."

* * *

The evening proved unseasonably warm. Matt's car pulled into the driveway approaching a huge contemporary home with numerous automobiles parked nearby, spread throughout the

31

wooded area. After locating a space, he exited the vehicle and arrived at the front entrance, ringing it's doorbell.

Short moments later Jason responded. "You rang?"

"Hey, Lurch. What's happening?"

"Come on in. Join the party. Your smooch-woochie's here."

Matt's eyes got almost as big as saucers. He had never seen a private home with such a massive living room area. The circular fireplace in its center mirrored its reflection in a floor-to-ceiling glass wall of windows of the cathedral high-ceilinged room -- the site breathtaking.

"Well, don't just stand there," Jason said, interrupting Matt's stupor. "Let's get a drink."

Matt followed him toward the bar as his eyes searched the mass of attendees in hopes of spotting Kitty. She noticed him first and waved -- Matt acknowledging her across the room with a big smile and a nod.

After getting their drinks, the two joined the women as Jason's parents arrived -- introductions made, and an evening of fun commenced.

"Isn't this place just beautiful," Kitty said.

"It knocked me off my feet when I walked in. Sorry I couldn't get here earlier." Matt sipped his drink and took Kitty's hand in his. "I'm dying to see what's out back. Wanna go?"

"I sure do," she said, with a smile and a squeeze of his hand.

They found the exit to the outside rear deck. As the door closed behind them, the sounds from inside became muffled. After strolling to the large stilted deck's edge, they stood against the railing and peered through the leaf-barren trees. The full moon glistened across the rushing water of the Potomac, in close harmony with the rock group's CD music faintly heard from inside.

Matt stood with his arm around Kitty's shoulders. He looked at his watch. "Better go inside. It's almost midnight."

Kitty smiled, placed her arm around his waist, and they rejoined the gala proceedings.

Taking Kitty's hand again, Matt led her to the dance floor and they had just began their rendition of the 'twist' when the music ended and a gigantic TV image appeared from one side of the room.

32

The New Year's countdown began, and ended, with Matt and Kitty in a deep embrace and everyone cheering loudly.

"Happy New Year, Kitten."

A tear welled in Kitty's eye. "No one's ever called me that before."

Matt gently pulled her closer and they kissed for the second time.

"Hey. Cut that out. It's my turn," Heather said, with faked jealousy in her voice. She planted a juicy one on Matt's lips and then giggled.

Jason did the same with Kitty.

They all laughed.

* * *

In the distance, the Deale church bell echoed the arrival of the New Year. The old house became vibrant with a bright light shining though the rear porch windows. The ghostly figure of a young girl glided across the floor as if dancing to a lilting tune.

Suddenly, the house darkened.

The gaiety of earlier moments altered to a wail of grief, permeating the night.

* * *

Kitty expressed prolonged regrets at having been so unavailable following New Year's Eve. However, they talked several times since, trying unsuccessfully to maneuver around her busy second semester and lecturing schedules. A standing invitation remained open for her visit whenever convenient.

In the following days, Matt exuded a new found energy in being alive -- everyday matters faced with zeal and quickly dispatched. Jason called to tease Matt, but also added reassurance Kitty was truthful about being preoccupied. Heather happened to be taking one of her night classes and related how impressed Kitty had been with both he and his boat.

Snow began falling heavily on the afternoon of his birthday. The forecast called for eight to ten inches before ending. While driving to the local stores before it got any worse, Matt shopped for a few staples and made a quick stop at the liquor drive-in for tobacco, beer and a few different selections of booze. By the time he got back to the boat, it was slippery going. Safely making it aboard, he slid off his boots, leaving them just outside the cabin door on the canvas-covered bridge. The warmth of the salon a welcome change as he put away the supplies.

Using a buck glass, he poured in a generous portion of Scotch, adding a dash of water. When finished, he turned on the stereo, already tuned to his favorite semi-classical station, and slumped in his special chair wriggling his toes near the kerosene heater. He felt content to just relax and enjoy the soft music, but the phone rang for the first of many times in a row.

Ozzie called, then Ellen, his son Chris., and finally Chuck. Thanking everyone for remembering his special occasion, he had no more placed the receiver in the cradle and it rang again.

"Hello."

"Happy birthday." Kitty sounded melodic in her greeting.

"Hey." Matt's reaction was inspired by recognizing her voice. "Thanks. But, how did you know it was my birthday?"

"You know me. A little psycho-telepathy here, . . . a little ESP there." She laughed at her own humor. Matt joined in. "Heather told me," she finally admitted. "So, how are you doing? It's been about a week since we spoke."

"Everything's great, especially after hearing from you. "And, it has been way too long since we talked. What you been up to?"

Kitty sounded tired. "Still knee deep in work, but I do enjoy it."

Suddenly, severe static appeared on the phone line.

"You work too hard."

"I can hardly hear you. Are you still there?"

Matt strained his voice. "I don't know what's wrong. This happens a lot. I'm on the galley phone. I'm going to put you on hold and get the other one. Maybe that's the problem."

Matt took a quick peek out of the window and the old house appeared uneventful.

After taking a seat in his recliner and pressing the speaker button, before he could say anything, he heard the crying and sobbing of someone on the line -- the static gone.

"Damn, Kitty. Did you hear that?

"What? I heard you pick up the other phone."

Matt gulped his drink down; his hands trembling.

"What's the matter?" Kitty asked.

"Uh, . . . Nothing. I'm fine. Thought I heard something

34

weird on the phone. Probably imagination."

"Well, at least the interference is gone."

"Thanks for that. Can you wait a second? Need to fix another drink."

"Sure."

Matt approached a port window and peered at the old house. It still remained unrevealing.

"I'm back."

"Good. I was getting lonely." Kitty giggled.

"What you need is a break. I'll even drive over and pick you up, if you'll say yes."

"In this snow storm? You're crazy." She laughed. "But, it's a nice thought."

"You think I'm kidding, don't you? It hasn't really started here."

"No. That's the problem. I know you're serious," she said, and quickly added, "tell you what. If the streets are okay, I'll drive down tomorrow evening and stay over through Saturday."

Matt was elated and couldn't suppress his enthusiasm until he got a sudden chill as his VHF radio on the bridge spurted to life. "Can you hold on again for a minute. I'll be right back."

As Matt arrived at the radio, it turned itself off. He unzipped the tent-flap and stared at the old house. Its open door slowly closed as it began to snow heavily.

* * *

After saying goodbye he could hardly sit still. He stayed busy by cleaning everything in sight, whether it needed it or not, working well into the evening before realizing it to be after dark. Matt tried looking out of the window, but the tinted glass didn't allow much of a view of the night exterior. He pulled on his coat and boots, went above to stand on the bridge, and lit his pipe.

He moved from beneath the canvas cover onto the aft deck, making a swooping survey of the surroundings, and marveling at the effects of the white blanket already covering the boats, piers and ground. Matt turned in the direction of the shore where a light, more brilliant than seen before, glistened from the lower windows of the old house.

He mumbled, "There's no way that can be a light reflection."

As if compelled, he retrieved a flashlight from the bridge, left the boat, carefully gaining his footing on the dock. He trudged up the snow-covered pier, finding its soft texture not as hard to manipulate as imagined. Soon reaching the shore, he immediately made his way to the property's backyard.

Matt came to a quick halt some twenty-feet from the house. The light still shone brightly inside -- a set of footprints leading away from the backdoor for a short distance without showing signs of any return. They stopped in the middle of nowhere. Matt looked up and found himself confronted by what appeared to be a faint ghostly mist peering at him from inside.

He staggered backwards and gasped in amazement. "Awww, God."

Seconds later, the image dissolved and the light was gone.

While taking the flashlight from his pocket, he moved to the window where he had seen the figure and aimed its beam inside. Nothing seemed changed, with no evidence of any water on the floor that probably would have been present had someone entered from outside. He shuddered in reaction.

"Oh, Jesus," he mumbled softly. "What the hell's going on?"

Full of apprehension, and some fear, Matt hurried back to his boat, but after reaching the aft deck couldn't make himself go inside. The window's light flickered again and a figure seemed to be gliding back and forth inside the room again as if waltzing to music.

That evening proved the most disturbing night of his life. He hardly slept, anticipating what he might find on the morrow. Finally falling into deep sleep around six a.m., Matt awoke at nine. While lying in bed he dreaded rising, but sensed an urgency to return to the house. Confused and unsure about his plans, better judgment dictated he should leave well enough alone. Nevertheless, after a shower and his mind somewhat cleared, he dressed in warm clothing and had a hot cup of coffee before attempting the adventure.

Matt stepped onto the aft deck to greet a clear sky -- the temperature almost balmy, and typical of the erratic weather patterns of the region. In consideration of Kitty coming that evening, he took time to clear a path down the dock to the shore.

Another boat owner arrived to tend to his craft located not far from Matt's. "Good morning, Matt. Sure is a hell of a lot of snow."

"Hi, Sully. Haven't seen you in a while."

"Too, damn busy lately. Just thought I'd come down and check things out. Thanks for keeping and eye on my boat."

"No problem" Matt said. "Glad to do it."

"Well, best get to it. Catch ya later." Sully began clearing snow along his finger-pier.

"Got'cha. Later." Matt stuck the blade of his shovel into a pile of snow when he reached shore, and walked toward the aging structure. Upon entering its backyard, his footprints from the night before were clearly apparent and deeply etched in the covered ground while those he had seen coming from the house no longer existed. He also noticed the padlock gone.

Matt felt a combination of curiosity countered by hesitation, but pushed the door open and went inside. There was an aroma he couldn't distinguish -- best described as a pungently sweet odor.

As he investigated the first floor, as previously done, an unseen force began controlling his movement drawing him to the staircase. He proceeded up the steps, without knowing why, walking directly into the small bedroom containing the old bed. Drawn to the closet, Matt stood in its doorway gazing around the inside as if in a daze. His eyes eventually focused on the floor and detected loose boards in a far corner. He knelt to pull them upward. They gave rather easily, revealing a small wooden box. He carefully grasped the delicate item, rose, and immediately left the building. After closing the backdoor, he paused. There was no doubting it. He heard a soft wailing cry.

Matt rushed back to his boat and placed the box on the counter. He removed his outer clothing, then opened it.

The phone rang.

"Hello."

"Richard, . . . help me . . ."

He trembled, almost dropping the phone receiver.

* * *

Matt attempted to put the experience out of his mind, spending the rest of the day preparing for Kitty's visit. As hard as he tried, his head swirled in turmoil measuring the pros and cons of mentioning anything about the strange happenings to her.

Ozzie's reaction, and his not being able to hear the crying over the radio, added cause for deliberation. However, Kitty was a psychologist. But did this have anything to do with psychology? Would she think him crazy? He really didn't know how to handle the situation, but desperately had to share it, or else go mad.

CHAPTER VI

Kitty called around six saying she had been detained, but just leaving. Matt judged her arrival time, and even though the air had chilled, sat on the bridge anxiously waiting to see her car pull into the lot.

"Welcome to the great outdoors," Matt called, jogging through the snow to greet her.

Kitty grinned from ear-to-ear as she got out of her vehicle. "Good. You can help me." She handed Matt a round tin container. "I baked an angel food cake."

"Oh, into spirits, too, huh?"

She laughed and shook her head in a teasing, but positive manner. "Better not drop it. It might turn into devil's food."

While laughing and almost falling in the snow, and taking time-out to throw snowballs at each other, they finally made it to the boat, immediately going below where Kitty warmed her hands above the heater. Matt busied himself taking her personal things to the aft cabin and returned to find her at the bar pouring two snifters of brandy.

Kitty turned to face him, placing one of the glasses in his hand. "I thought this deserved a toast, as well as a little warming to the belly," she said, smiling. "To a wonderful evening."

Touching glasses, they both sipped the biting liquid while gazing into each other's eyes.

"Well. Now, it's my turn. Here's to the most intriguing and wonderful person I've had the pleasure to meet," Matt said, repeating the toast gesture as Kitty clearly blushed her acceptance.

Matt broke the mood of the moment, suddenly feeling uncomfortable. "First order of business is to show you around

39

my boat. You didn't get to see much of it before."

"I'd love that."

"Can't have you opening a wrong door and finding some skeleton inside."

Kitty laughed as they headed below to the aft area.

Matt stopped at the small cabin to the starboard. "I use this as a little work room."

Kitty peeked inside. Matt's dollhouse sat on a card table with tools and materials lying about -- the model more than half-finished.

"Oh, my. Who's that for?" Kitty asked.

"I started it years ago for my sister. Now, it's for my granddaughter. Give's me something to do in my spare time."

"You are sooooo talented."

Kitty smiled. Matt grinned.

"You've used the shower and head already," he said, pointing to his right, "and here's the aft cabin sleeping quarters."

Kitty took a few steps inside. "This is wonderful. It's almost unbelievable."

"You'll be sleeping here tonight."

They returned to the salon.

"Hungry?"

"Starved," she said with gusto.

"You better be. I've worked and slaved all day just to please you."

"Ooohh, you're really trying to make me purr, aren't you? She smiled devilishly.

"Something like that." He grinned. "Hope you like seafood."

"Love it. Except raw oysters."

"Oh, yeah. Christmas Day. . . . Annapolis. I remember." He chuckled.

Matt placed baking potatoes wrapped in wet paper towels in the microwave, and a cookie sheet covered with foil containing striped bass in the broiler. He opened a cabinet drawer to get a pair of hot pads while staring at the wooden box. He picked it up and shoved it inside as far in the back as he could to avoid seeing it again.

Allowing Kitty to set the table was the extent he let her be involved.

40

Matt turned on his favorite radio station.

Kitty expressed her perfect approval of his taste as she settled into his reclining chair watching him complete his determined task. "Uhmmm, that smells so good." She couldn't resist commenting on the succulent aroma filling the room. "What are we having?"

"French-fried sea slugs."

"Ha, ha. Aren't we clever."

* * *

Outside, the wind had risen, swirling the snow.

Lights from inside the old house's first floor rear windows flickered wildly on and off.

* * *

The meal proved fantastic -- shrimp cocktail, asparagus spears, and baked potato stuffed with crabmeat bathed in hollandaise sauce -- the main entree, seasoned rockfish sautéed in lemon butter -- the coup d'etat, an almost endless supply of white zinfandel wine.

Kitty groaned after her last bite. "Ooooh, you're trying to kill me."

Matt beamed with great satisfaction. "We've still got your cake."

"Oh, be quiet. You really do want to get rid of me, don't you?" She laughed, and faked more pain.

"Not really. Just testing." Matt rose while removing their empty plates.

"Let me help," Kitty said, attempting to get up.

"Sit still. And, that's an order." Shunning her protests, Matt cleared the table and returned to take her by the hand. "Now. I want you to come over here, sit down in my favorite chair, and relax. I noticed you've taken a liking to it already." He grinned. "Here's your wine." He sat her down and immediately refilled her glass to the rim. "You can take a nap, or we can jabber while I do the dishes. It's up to you."

By the time the sink was full of steaming soapy water, Matt turned to find her fast asleep. Smiling and extremely happy, he washed and dried the dishes, putting them away in the process.

After taking a seat on the couch, he stretched his legs and leaned his head backward gazing at Kitty as she slept. Matt's mind went into another of its rampages, trying to sort the mixture of emotions, happenings, and unexplained phenomena experienced. He found it almost impossible to separate thoughts of Catherine from those of Kitty.

Although everything about them was completely different, he reasoned his subconscious need to compare was related to physical attraction. Beyond his youthful years, Kitty posed the only deep sexual stimulus he had ever experienced other than his wife. He cursed himself for feeling guilty about desiring another woman, and wondered if the self-imposed chastisement would ever end.

Unaware he had dozed into semi-unconsciousness, the phone ringing snapped him to respond. Literally leaping to his feet, he snatched the receiver from its cradle as Kitty barely stirred.

"Hello."

Matt heard a slight pause and the sound of a click. He shook his head, looked at the phone, and hung it up while triggering the coffee maker on. He noticed the hot pads still lying on the counter, opened the drawer to put them away, and gasped.

The box had changed its position from the back to the front of the compartment. He grabbed it in desperation and shoved to a far corner of the sink top.

"Matt, I'm sorry I fell asleep."

Matt reacted in an unnerved manner. "Aw, shit."

"Excuse me?"

He hurriedly apologized. "God, I'm sorry. Not used to having anyone around. You startled me. A little edgy I guess. I dozed off, too. . . . Coffee?"

Kitty rose from the chair, and forced her way into his arms.

* * *

The old house's windows glowed with light. Inside, the youthful ghostly image danced by herself as if holding someone in her embrace.

* * *

Matt attempted to pull away.

Kitty quickly denied his move and forced herself back into his arms. "Please don't stop holding me. At least, not now."

"I don't know what the hell's wrong with me," he whispered. "Half the time I act like a brainwashed kid trying to cling to an

42

irretrievable past."

"I know, . . . I know," she said, pressing harder against his chest.

Holding each other for an extended period of time, they slowly related to the soft music sifting through the room. The semi-classical station had reverted to a program of romantic selections from the sixties and seventies, and Sam Cooke's mellow tones added to the mood. Beginning to glide to the sounds, their movements were with profound synchronization. Never taking her head from his shoulder until the music and dance ended, Matt gently lifted her head and kissed a tear streaming down her cheek.

* * *

Inside the old house, the ghostly image of a young girl, now dressed in fine flowing lace, continued gliding while humming a lilting tune -- the lovely melody soon altering to cries of despair.

* * *

The morning brought a renewed vibrancy. Matt awoke to the aroma of coffee and bacon sifting through the boat. As he left the fore cabin, he stole a peak into the galley area finding Kitty busily fixing breakfast and still dressed in her nightie. He ducked into the head, brushed his teeth, combed his hair, and did it a second time all over before slipping into his robe. After climbing the short stairway, he was able to approach Kitty without being detected. "Good morning," he whispered in her ear as he grasped her around the waist.

"Oh, God." She gasped while spinning on her heels. "This time, you scared the hell out of me."

"Great. Then, there's no more evil spirits in your lovely body."

"You've got that right. But, there's not much blood left either."

A small trickle seeped from her thumb. "Oh, babe, I'm sorry," he said, putting her finger to his lips. "I really am sorry."

"Oh, shut up," Kitty said, pushing him away at arms length and then pulling him forward to cover his mouth with hers.

The kiss was long and meaningful. Matt felt a collapse of every existing emotional barrier. "Wanna try that again for another million years?"

"Sure. But it may take a few trips through reincarnation." Kitty attacked his lips for the second time.

"Damn," Matt said, with exasperation. "Why in the hell didn't we sleep together last night?"

"Because our mothers taught us, 'never on a first date.'"

"You call last night a date? We just laid around like a couple of lumps."

"I know." Kitty slyly smiled while filling two plates with eggs, bacon and hash browns made from scratch. "Let's eat," she said, handing a serving to Matt.

Very little was said as they sat down to the morning meal. Matt felt sensitive, believing he had spoiled what began as a wonderful weekend. Damn his moralistic attitudes, he thought. Was he doomed to ruin the rest of his life?

"A penny for your thoughts," Kitty said, interrupting the silence. "I think I've said that before."

Matt stopped sipping his coffee. "Damn, it," he said, slamming down his fork and quickly rising from his seat. "To hell with mothers' lessons. I ain't a kid no more, and you're one hellava . . ." He literally scooped Kitty into his arms and carried her to the aft cabin, almost stumbling down the stairs.

"You damned fool," she said, giggling, while trying to steady their descent by bracing her hands against the bulkheads. "Let me down," she facetiously demanded.

Matt paid no attention, placing her on the bed. He removed his robe while leaning to embrace her lips.

Kitty spread her negligee as Matt moved to lie beside her. The moment was there. They took advantage of each and every second. Months, and even years, of frustration surfaced in a resounding fulfillment of lost hopes and mutual satisfaction.

* * *

As the snow fell at an even greater rate, the rear door of the old house opened and the ghostly image of the young girl appeared in the doorway weeping.

* * *

"Don't know if you remember, or not, but we never finished breakfast," Matt said, in a faked manner of concern. "If we do this on a regular basis, I'm going to need a whole lot of Wheaties."

Kitty punched him in the ribs and squeezed his chest even tighter. "I've never felt so complete."

"Me, too. Want seconds?" he asked, jumping up to dodge a wicked blow from her improvised swing.

"You wish," she said, laughing and wriggling her naked body in a suggestive and provocative manner. "If you want me, you know when and where to call."

Matt retreated to the head and turned on the shower. He paused only long enough to adjust the temperature of the water flow, stepped inside, and was surprised to find Kitty following him. After lathering their bodies with soap, he caressed her small but firm breasts and moved his hands down under her torso to her lower limbs, bringing them to rest between her thighs. Wrapping her arms around his neck, she sent her tongue deep into his mouth as he pressed her hips against the wall until entering her body. Pounding beads of water echoed the sound of mutual ecstasy -- their sexual union continuing long after gratification.

"That's a great way to start a day," Matt said, drying his chest.

Kitty grinned. "You bet. We should do it more often."

Taking her in his arms, he used his towel to dry her back. Not needing additional words, Matt lightly kissed her forehead and left the room.

Both emerging about the same time, Matt warmed the unfinished breakfast in the microwave and they completed the meal. A different atmosphere prevailing, the two sat side-by-side, occasionally feeding each other a morsel.

"That was great," Matt said, with sincerity.

"What, the sex or the food?"

"The meal, of course."

Kitty stuck her tongue out at him.

Matt laughed. "Seriously, I need to penetrate your mind for a change, not your body."

"If this is to be a professional diagnosis, I'll need another cup of coffee."

"Well. . . . All right. It's a small price to pay." Matt refilled both cups, tainted them the way they should be, and the two moved to the sofa.

"Okay. What's this conversation going to be about?"

"Another woman . . . maybe. To tell you the truth, I'm not

too sure."

Kitty's expression suddenly soured.

Matt was shocked at what he had said. It came out all wrong and certainly put in a way to cause her reaction. "Aw, God, Doc. It's not what you think. This isn't any real woman. I'm not sure. . . . It could be a child. Hell, I'm just not sure, period."

Easily detecting the torment Matt was experiencing, Kitty moved slightly away from his side and turned to better face him. She took his hand in hers and gently squeezed it, sending a sign of encouragement.

Matt gathered himself and raised her hand to his lips, tenderly kissing her fingers.

"Wow," he sighed, pausing briefly before trying to start over. "It all began quite a while back. In fact, the first night I moved into this damn marina. A buddy of mine, Ozzie, spent the night and was supposed to go fishing the next day. That evening he asked me to get the weather on the ship-to-shore radio." Matt hesitated as he adjusted his seated position and pointed to the device across the room. "I've got one on the bridge, too. There's a marine weather channel that's on around the clock. In the middle of the report, the station faded and I heard this faint but discernible sound as if it was a child, or maybe a young woman, crying."

"And, Ozzie didn't hear it?"

Matt got a puzzled look on his face.

"You said, I heard," she explained.

"Oh, yeah, I did. Anyway, didn't give it much thought until it happened again. It's been at least five or six times the same thing . . . and the other day I had Ozzie on the speaker phone and it was the same as before. Ozzie made jokes about my drinking too much, . . . and suggested losing the station was either a weak signal or bad wiring."

"What you heard during the ensuing times, was it any clearer or different in any manner?"

"Yeah. Maybe a little bit. Can't be really sure, though." Matt felt fidgety and got up to stretch his legs. "I completely rewired the thing and didn't have any problems for a long while. Not until after I paid a visit to the old house over there on the shore."

Kitty's eyes brightened. "The one with the crab pots in the backyard?"

Matt shook his head in agreement. "At night, the lights from the marina across the creek bounce off the windows making it look like they're coming from inside. Only reflections, I thought, but one evening there was so much haze you couldn't even see the far shore, let alone the lights, and there was still a flickering glow in the damn window."

Continuing to relate his story in great detail, he told her about being drawn to the property during his first visit to Deale; talking to Captain Joe; the prints in the snow; the images of a youthful figure inside; the older spirit appearing at the garden, and his first investigation through the house.

For the most part Kitty sat spellbound, making no comment, only asking an occasional question.

"Yesterday morning was the last time I went to the house. When I got there, the only remaining footprints were mine from the night before. Inside, a weird faint aroma drifted through every room. I Got to the bottom of the stairs and it was like something took over my body. Next thing I knew I found myself kneeling in the small upstairs bedroom closet." Matt retrieved the wooden box from the counter. "I raised some loose floorboards and found this." He handed it to Kitty.

Carefully opening it, there was a fancy comb, some ribbon, a photo of a lad with 'love, Richard' written on the back, and a diary. On the first page was a name and a date: Sarah — October 3, 1929.

CHAPTER VII

Matt awoke holding Kitty in his arms. Lying still, so as not to wake her, he smiled with the feeling of great satisfaction; the warmth of her body molding to his creating a needed sense of emotional security.

She originally planned on only spending the one night, but they stayed up late into the morning hours reading the entries found in the diary and discussing the other phenomena. Having wanted to immediately visit the old house, Matt convinced her it would be best to wait until Captain Joe was out to sea.

During the evening, Matt had tested the weather channel numerous times with no unusual results and their observations of the old house indicated nothing more than the normal reflections of light in the windows. Kitty had drawn no conclusions nor offered any comment regarding the situation. More important, she had an open mind and a strong curiosity to investigate.

Matt carefully moved away from Kitty, hoping not to wake her. She rolled to her other side and snuggled her pillow.

Quietly, he grabbed his robe, proceeded to get a cup of coffee, then decided to spend some time working on the dollhouse.

As he placed a new interior wall partition in place, he shuddered as a sudden chill passed through his body. He quickly spun in his chair to observe what appeared to be a misty form dissipating just beyond the doorway.

Matt jumped up and looked beyond the door jamb to his left and then the right, observing nothing unusual. He shook his head, considering it his imagination playing tricks, and peeked into the aft cabin.

Kitty stirred.

Matt sat on the bed, leaning over to kiss her forehead.

"Uummmm, you're awake," she said, nestling her cheek and rubbing her nose against his hand. "Good morning."

"Good morning, sleepy head." Matt swung his legs up to lie down beside her.

"I love sleeping on this boat, but with you in the bed it's even better." She ran her fingers across his stomach.

He flinched. "That tickles."

She giggled.

"Well, Doc. "Are you ready for the big day?"

"Yes," she said, in an exuberant manner, quickly sitting up in bed. "I don't know when I've ever been so excited."

Matt grabbed her shoulders, pulling her down to lie on top and embraced her lips. "God, you've got bad breath." He chuckled, in a devilish manner.

She bit his lip.

"Ouch." He pushed her to the side and rolled out of bed, first to his knees and then jumping to his feet, stubbing his toe in the process.

"Serves you right."

The playfulness in their new relationship did a great deal to solidify a growing bond. Every moment together seemed to expand their mutual compatibility.

After showering and having breakfast, Matt checked to see if Captain Joe had gone. "The old man's left. Not that it really matters, but rather not raise questions."

Providing Kitty with an extra scarf, a skull cap, and a pair of his gloves dwarfing her hands, they made their way to the old house. Arm in arm, with each step, her grip seemed to tighten in anticipation of what was to come.

On their arrival at the backdoor, Matt came to a quick halt. "See. This is what I've been telling you," he said, noticing the earlier missing padlock being in place and pointing it out to Kitty.

"Maybe the old man put . . ." Kitty stopped in mid-sentence.

Matt knew what she was thinking. There were no footprints in the snow coming from the direction Captain Joe would have taken.

After pushing the door open, they went inside. Other than an expected musty smell, no other unusual odor was present. They toured every inch of the house -- including showing her where he found the diary. The two continued to investigate each nook and cranny. There seemed to nothing out of the ordinary. After returning to where they entered, they left the house and Matt yanked the door shut.

Before releasing the knob, he reopened it and walked back inside. Without uttering a word, he proceeded to the foot of the staircase and stopped. Kitty followed close behind. Halfway up the stairs, a small rag doll sat on one of the steps.

"Oh, my God," Kitty muttered, gasping and clenching her hands over her mouth.

Matt knew if there had been any doubts in Kitty's mind, they surely were quickly dispelled. As the two walked back to the boat, she cradled the doll beneath her coat against her breast.

After removing their wraps, although the hour was still early, Matt poured two glasses of brandy. Handing one to Kitty, he gulped his own in a single swallow and turned to get another.

He faced the galley sink, leaning with one hand on the counter and the other rubbing his forehead. He started shivering.

Kitty moved against his back, wrapping her arms around his waist. Pressing her cheek between his shoulder blades, she remained until he stopped trembling. "I . . . I wouldn't have believed it, if I hadn't seen it." She struggled making the statement.

Gently pulling away from him, she moved to touch the doll placed on top of Sarah's wooden box sitting on a shelf. "What I know about paranormal activity wouldn't fill a thimble, but from what little I do know, I'm sure this is highly unusual. There's been story after story of psychic phenomena. To experience it yourself . . ." She stopped without completing her statement, and only shook her head, gazing at the doll. She picked it up and gently pushed a small amount of stuffing protruding from a narrow slit in its belly.

Matt tried to joke. "Well, I guess I'm not crazy after all."

"That you're not," Kitty said, replacing the doll to its place and moving to take a seat on the couch.

Matt handed her a cup of coffee.

She took a careful sip of the steaming liquid. "Everything has happened so fast, my mind's in a whirl. It's like a thousand points of light flashing on and off without having any pattern. I just need time to think."

"Would you like to be alone?"

"Not really, but I think it's the best idea. If I stay, I'd still have to leave early this evening. Maybe the long drive will help. I really need to get in touch with a friend of mine."

"I understand, Doc. Truly, I do. And, don't you worry about me. I'll be fine."

Kitty afforded a big grin. She rose from the couch, gathered her belongings, purposely leaving her negligee lying across the bed. "If you let anyone else wear it, I'll wring your neck," she said, taunting a reaction from Matt.

He simply crossed his heart with a finger and stuck his right hand up vowing a solemn oath, and asked, "What about Jason?"

* * *

Kitty called later that evening assuring Matt she felt a lot better. The initial impact of the happening had subsided and appeared much more able to confront it in rational terms. She also indicated having spoke to her friend who was very learned in paranormal matters. The two agreed the events to be a manifestation of something very powerful emanating from the spiritual world. Matt felt even better after learning Kitty considered it important enough to take a leave of absence to make a further investigation.

At Kitty's suggestion, and with added incentive, Matt spent the next week checking every possible source in the county to find out anything he could about the property and the owners. Simultaneously, Kitty had her hands full in making hasty arrangements to cover her teaching and lecturing responsibilities. They both agreed not to call each other through the short period. There would be plenty of time together during the next several weeks.

* * *

Seeing Kitty arrive the following Sunday afternoon made Matt feel like a little kid. He ran to greet her in the parking lot, tripped over a tree root and fell, ripping his pants and skinning his knee in the process. Kitty was laughing hysterically when he reached her.

"It ain't so funny," he said, limping and rubbing his leg.

She hunched over holding her stomach with tears rolling down her cheeks. She was barely able to speak. "You . . . you . . . looked so . . . falling like that."

A mental flashback of the act brought Matt to his knees, and even more laughter from Kitty. Her mood so infectious, Matt began to react in the same manner.

Eventually regaining a little bit of decorum, the two hugged, and Matt loaded a dock cart with her luggage. By the time they got back on the boat they had returned to a normal level of sanity, and standing in the middle of the bridge, they embraced.

"Oooh, I missed you." Kitty moaned, adding a big squeeze.

"Me, too, to you, too, Doc," Matt eagerly replied.

Kitty smiled. "We better get this down below. There's some stuff for the freezer."

After getting things put away, Matt sat on the edge of the bed staring into the closet as Kitty busily made a fresh pot of coffee. Seeing her clothes hanging next to his brought a warm sensation and contented feeling. He jumped up and joined her in the galley.

"Anything exciting since I was here?"

"Nope. Intentionally avoided going over or even paying any attention to the place." He stuck his finger into a block of cream cheese she was opening and licked his finger.

"Stop that."

"After we have a bite, I'll run a phone cord into the small aft cabin. It'll make a good office for you.

"What about your dollhouse?"

"No problem. Almost finished with the hard part. I'll work on it out here on the booth table. Plenty of room."

Kitty nodded her approval, then picked up the rag doll sitting on top of the wooden box still resting on a shelf. "Maybe I should check this out at the university lab. Although, it appears it's homemade from old flour sacks. . . . Oh, well. She gently returned it to its spot.

"I was able to find some interesting info though."

"What?"

"For starters," Matt said, "I found out the last name of the guy who owns the place."

"Great. Let's get to it," she said, carrying a package of bagels and the cheese to the table. "You get the coffee."

Matt fixed two mugs of the steaming liquid as Kitty retrieved her brief case and placed it next to the table. Matt got his own pad of notes from a nearby drawer. They both sat down.

"Hi, Doc."

"Hi," Kitty said, looking up with a smile and then quickly returning to search through her papers.

"I just like to say that. It's a lot better than goodbye," he sheepishly explained.

"You're nuts. But, I love it."

"Okay, what have we got here?" Matt said, with a sigh, while scanning his notes. "Well, I called the county property tax division, and over the phone I didn't get a lot of help. Without a name or other property identification information I'd have to go to Annapolis and try to search for myself. I checked with all the local real estate companies and got the same answer each time. None dated that far back, and their consensus . . . it would have more than likely been a private transaction." Matt paused to spread cheese on a piece of bagel and handed it to Kitty.

"Thanks, hon." She didn't even bother to look up and kept fiddling with papers.

"Then I got really lucky. I learned that back in the twenties and thirties, a community group of Deale citizens had visions of a growing business and population expansion. They started a local newspaper which functioned for a number of years before going under.

"And? . . ."

After that, their records were shuffled from here-to-there and, now, archived at the local library. I busted my butt over there and located some names of the members of the community group. I took the list and checked it against the local phone directory, and Bingo, came up with three still living."

Kitty looked up briefly, smiled, and went back to her work.

"I'm sorry. I guess I'm just excited. I've never done anything like this. My mouth keeps running like it's got diarrhea, and nothing's really coming out."

Kitty leaned back and laughed. "I'm the one who should be sorry. Go on, I'll pay closer attention."

"Anyway, to hell with the details, I found out the family's name was Colison. To be exact, the old man's name was

Jeremiah Andrew Colison, and the house is still titled in his name."

Kitty's eyes brightened.

"And, that brings up another point." Matt handed Kitty his half of the bagel.

"Thanks, hon. And what's that?"

"If he's dead, why would the property still be titled in his name? You'd think somewhere along the line, a relative, or at least someone would have taken it over. If not them, even the county or the state."

"One thing for sure, it's obvious someone's had to pay the property taxes over the years."

Matt nodded. "Makes sense." He stuck the butter knife into the cheese and licked the blade. "Anyway, I checked out the nearby churches dating back to the thirties and came up with a blank."

"What about the cemeteries?" Kitty asked.

Just getting to that. After covering the churches, with no luck, an old seaman I've worked with a few times mentioned several private grave sites being around the area. Wanna go for a walk?"

* * *

After visiting grave sites near the marina, they strolled down a country lane coming upon and old farm. On the far side of a huge field, a deserted house sat in the distance with a small unkempt grave yard nearby.

Matt spread the strands of rusting barbed wire allowing them to enter the property. They trudged through tall weeds, arriving at the first of a number of headstones dotting the area.

The two meandered in different directions.

"Hey. Over here," Matt called loudly.

Kitty rushed to his side.

Matt pointed. Before his feet stood two tombstones -- one marked, Mary Margaret Colison, 1907 - 1933; the other, Sarah Elizabeth Colison, 1920 - 1934.

Kitty couldn't control her excitement. "Oh, Matt. Do you know what this means? There's a wealth of information here."

Matt scratched his head. "How you figure that?" He stooped down and pulled tall grass away from the stones.

"Her mother was only thirteen when Sarah was born? What's more, Sarah was just fourteen when she died, only a year later than her mother."

"So what? What difference does that make?"

Kitty knelt beside him. "Stop to think about it. There's an unsettled spirit of a young girl in that house who died at the age of sixteen." Kitty gently brushed away some dirt from the face of Sarah's tombstone.

"So."

Kitty rose to her feet. "I sense something's really wrong. Call it women's intuition. But the year between her mother's death and Sarah's seems to have been an extremely troubled time for her." Kitty offered Matt her hand and pulled him up. "This is fantastic. I can't wait to get back to the boat. I want to read more of the diary. Maybe we can figure out how the doll and everything ties in."

"That's great, but you're missing something important. A third stone for the old man."

"God, you're right." Kitty began counting on her fingers. "Let's see. . . . Yes. It's more than possible he's alive."

"But where is he? And why abandon his property?"

* * *

Matt and Kitty arrived at Deale Marina, walking hand-in-hand.

"You weren't able to find any other family in your search?" Kitty asked. "Nothing about Richard?"

"Nope. Nada. But, it doesn't mean they're not around. Still paths to explore, but it'd be a lot easier if the damn locals weren't so standoffish and biased."

"It's because of me, isn't it?" Kitty asked meekly.

"No. . . . Well, maybe a bit. These people down here still live in the dark ages most of the time. They just don't adjust to outsiders of any color."

"I want to go inside that house again," Kitty said profoundly.

"You think that's a good idea? I'd rather not."

* * *

Matt closed the rear door behind them. "Looking for something particular?"

"Not really. I just want to get a better feel of the house. One

56

of my psychic friends suggested I might consider using some sound recorders.

"Cool. Maybe we can catch the ghost having a party."

Kitty frowned. "That doesn't deserve a comment."

"By the way, in the beginning I was afraid you'd think I was nuts if I told you about all this. Instead, you seem to know an awful lot about spirits . . . , you know, . . . what you're doing, and all . . ."

"A little bit, but not what you may think. Psychology and parapsychology sometimes overlap. We may have a patient who appears to be disoriented . . . and most are . . . but once in a while it may go beyond that. In other words, demonic-possession, . . . like the movie the Exorcist, or something of a lesser degree."

"You gotta be kidding me."

"Nope." Kitty smiled and shook her head.

They moved through the backroom and into the kitchen as she continued. "According to a psychic friend, what's so unusual is for a haunting to extend beyond these walls," she said, looking around the room, "the radio; the phone; footprints in the snow. . . . The appearance of the doll really knocked me for a loop. You can't imagine how extraordinary it is. I've been told the manifestation of a physical object happening as it did is virtually unheard of. It borders on being a miracle in itself. When you found the box, it just didn't appear out of seemingly nowhere. It probably rested for years where you found it." Kitty moved into the front living area. "I'm not sure what we're getting into."

Matt became more serious. "What? What do you mean? It's just a ghost. . . . Or, maybe two ghosts."

Kitty took him by his arm. "Sometimes, dealing with these type of situations can be dangerous. Not so much physically, but mentally."

Matt didn't respond to her statement. "Come on. Let's get the hell out of here."

* * *

Kitty removed her jacket and tossed it over the arm of the couch while Matt poured a couple of cokes over ice.

"It's obvious someone from the other side is trying to contact you. Why you? I have no idea."

"Well, they sure seem to have my phone number." Matt

stared at the doll sitting on top of the box, grabbed it, and shoved it into a drawer. "I'm getting tired of the damn thing staring at me."

"Phew. You are a bit edgy." Kitty opened the drawer and removed the diary, before putting the box back. She sat on the couch.

"Sorry. I don't like things I don't understand."

Kitty thumbed through the pages. "Maybe it's because you're more clairvoyant than you realize, possessing a spiritual wavelength compatible with whoever is trying to reach out. In any case, you definitely seem to be the contact."

"So, in essence, what you're saying is some ghost has a problem and is trying to get me to help it out?" Matt said, smiling to cover his concern.

Kitty grinned in return. "Yeah, something like that." She finished her drink and handed the glass to Matt. "Could I have another?"

"Sure." Matt got up and moved to the refrigerator. "How are we supposed to know what's bothering this ghost, uh, spirit, I mean?" Matt returned to the couch with Kitty's soda.

"Before getting into that, you've got to make a decision as to whether you want to turn away and forget the whole thing or pursue it further."

"Is that possible? Will the spirit stop interfering with the radio and leave me alone?"

"To tell you the truth, I really don't think so. It may have already gone too far. The spirit seems to have slowly increased its ability to expose itself to you, from what you've told me. It's a great deal like the growth of a child and the expansion of abilities." Kitty reached down into her case and brandished a pack of cigarettes.

"I didn't know you smoked," Matt said, showing minor surprise.

"Do sometimes. Usually when I get stressed."

Matt turned in his seat retrieving an ashtray from a shelf behind him.

Kitty continued. "I believe the spirit's determined to pursue you, and its cause. If that's the case, its efforts will only intensify over time."

"Doesn't look like I've got much choice, then." Matt reached for Kitty's cigarettes and took one.

Kitty gave him a 'for-shame' glare.

"Just breaking an old New Year's resolution." He paused to light up. "Well, the way I look at it, Sarah's gone a long way to try and hook me in. I say Sarah, because everything so far points to her as being the spirit."

"You're probably right. But, for the sake of argument, it could be her mother."

"Hadn't thought about that." Matt paused to drag from his cigarette, looked at it, and then dubbed it out in the ashtray. "Well, I'm going to call 'it' Sarah. Just easier for me to refer to a person rather than an it, a spirit, . . . or a ghost."

Kitty smiled. "Sarah it is."

"What do you really think about all this?"

"I think it's fascinating and intriguing. Celeste, . . . she's a psychic friend, . . . feels this could lead to become one of the most provocative paranormal events ever recorded. I don't want you to be disillusioned. I . . . we, stand to possibly gain a great deal from this. But, that's not the main reason. More than anything I want to be with you, to help you, and not let you go through it alone."

Matt reached and grasped her hand, bringing it to his lips. "I know. But this is getting way over my head. Have you ever heard of a pair of ghosts at the same time?"

"Not really. But like I've said before, this surely isn't my specific area of expertise. I'm just along for the ride, so to speak. But, I do have excellent contacts with several psychics across the country, one of whom I trust a great deal. I mentioned her a few minutes ago . . . Celeste. She's in New York City. I attended one of her seminars during college. I really think we should both meet with her soon."

Matt hesitated for a moment, then said, "You say when, Doc. You're the boss."

"And, I don't want you to go near that house until after we've seen her."

"Here's to Sarah," Matt said, offering a toast and finishing his drink.

Kitty didn't join him.

CHAPTER VIII

Without wind, the evening became tolerably cool. Both Matt and Kitty, spent from the afternoon of mental strain, decided to go out for dinner. The walk to the restaurant soaking in fresh air did a lot of good.

Nothing was said during the meal regarding the old house; conversation primarily covering their lives as children and general upbringing.

"Carol," Matt called and motioned to his waitress. "When you get a chance."

"Sure, hon. I'll be there in a second."

"I like this place," Kitty said. "You seem to know so many of the people."

"Came here a lot, but got tired of eating alone."

Kitty smiled her understanding.

"All right, love. Here you are," Carol said, handing a menu to Kitty. "He doesn't need one." She grinned and started to leave.

"Don't go 'way." Matt stopped her retreat. "I want you to meet my lady friend. Carol, this is Kitty, and vice-versa."

"Hello, Carol."

"Hi, Kitty, pleased to meet you." Carol smiled with a nod of her head. "You've got a peach of a guy here as your friend."

"Thank you. I agree." Kitty grinned with her response.

"By the way," Carol said, "I hear you've been asking around about people named Colison. My mother told me she knew them."

Matt and Kitty showed immediate surprise and enthusiasm.

"I don't have time to chat right now. I'll catch you after dinner."

* * *

61

As Kitty and Matt continued having their meal, the old house remained dark and foreboding as the moonlight glistened across the surroundings. A flickering light began to slowly increase in intensity from the rear lower windows, and a spiritual transformation started taking place.

The enclosed porch slowly took its form of yesteryear in a ghostly image. There were no cobwebs nor dust. The furniture sat in place and a small vase of fresh Jonquils adorned the table. At one end of the room, the faint form of an older woman, clad in an ankle length dress and bonnet, rocked gently while knitting.

The elderly spirit rose and moved to the table, stopping to smell the flowers, then continued to enter the kitchen which was also in its past, but surreal state. At the wood-fired stove, she placed a tea kettle on one of the burners, and the transition of ghostly images disappeared.

* * *

Matt and Kitty finished their dinner as Carol joined them, carrying her own mug of coffee.

"What a night," Carol said, as she took a seat.

"Rough one, huh?" Matt asked.

"Yeah, oh, yeah." Carol sipped from her cup.

"I don't know how you do it," Kitty said.

"Believe me, deary. If there was another way, that's what I'd be doing." Carol smiled and took another sip. "Anyway, like I mentioned earlier, Mother's still alive and, at ninety-five, doing quite well. She's really alert and knows more about Deale than just about anyone in the area. I've got no idea how she heard about it, but she knew you were looking for the Colison family." Carol reached inside her apron, retrieved a pack of cigarettes and lit one. "She said she knew the name and remembered them being the only Amish people ever in Deale. If you'd like to talk to her, you can." Carol laughed. "That is, if you can get a word in edgewise. Once she gets going she's hard to stop."

"Carol, that's fantastic. You don't know what it means to me. Kitty and I would love to meet her."

"I've got the day off tomorrow, why don't you stop by in the morning around ten? We're the fifth house on the right from here on Deale Drive."

Spending the rest of the evening filled with great anticipation,

Kitty and Matt stayed up late discussing their sudden good fortune. On the morn, they decided to have breakfast at the Harbor before visiting Carol's mother.

Arriving at the house, they parked in the driveway and approached the front door.

Carol answered the bell. "Good morning."

"Hope you don't mind us being a little tardy? We were up late last night," Matt said.

"No. Not at all. Please. Come on in."

Carol led Matt and Kitty through the front to a family room in the rear of the modest home. An aged woman sat in a rocker near a fireplace with a shawl over her shoulders and another covering her lap and legs.

"Mother. These are the friends I told you about."

"I know. You're Kitty and Matt. I'm Birdie. She rubbed her hands over the shawl straightening out wrinkles. "Well, sit down. Make yourself comfortable."

Carol stood in an interior doorway as Matt and Kitty took seats on a couch across from Birdie.

"Can I get you anything to drink?" Carol asked.

Matt looked at Kitty. She shook her head negatively. "No, thanks. We're fine."

"I'll take a beer," Birdie said. "And, mind you. No glass."

Matt and Kitty smiled at each other.

"I can even remember things happenin' before I was four years old. You just ask me anythin' you want."

Kitty provided an encouraging smile. "First, we want to thank you for seeing us. Please let us know if you get tired."

"Tired? Who me? Ain't enough I can do around here to make me tired. Just enough to keep me bored. But, talk. I sure can do that."

Matt and Kitty grinned.

"Carol said you knew the Colison family. What can you tell us?" Matt asked.

"Yep. Knew the mother and daughter. Mary Margaret and Sarah. That daughter, she was a sweet young'un. The father, don't remember the first name, don't know as I ever knew it. He was a mean old bastard.

Carol returned with her Mother's bottle of beer.

63

"Amish they was. Wore them long dresses and aprons with bonnets. The father, whatever his name, dressed in black and wore one of those big brim type hats. He had a beard. Yep, I remember. A long beard. He was really mean."

"Why do you say that? What did he do?" Kitty asked.

"He didn't want Mary Margaret or Sarah makin' friends with nobody." Birdie tipped the bottle to her lips. "Don't go thinkin' I'm a boozer. I drink three beers a day. One in the mornin', one in the afternoon, and the other at night 'fore I go to bed. Usually have tomato juice with my beer in the mornin'."

Matt smiled. "Did Mary Margaret or Sarah have any close friends at all besides you?"

"We weren't friends. Lawdy, no. My best girlfriend, Sally Mae, knew them pretty well. What I know about the Colisons, I heard from her. Sally Mae's son, Richard, had a crush on Sarah."

Matt and Kitty appeared elated.

"Oh, Matt." Kitty pressed her hand against his knee.

"Richard. Can you tell us anymore about him?" Matt asked.

Birdie sipped some more beer. "Sarah liked him, too."

"What happened to Richard?" Kitty asked.

"He got hurt. Had an accident as I recall. About the time Sarah died." Birdie squirmed in her rocker and tested her beer once again. "He was in the hospital for a long while. Before he got out, Sally Mae took sick and died." Birdie paused and gazed at Kitty and Matt. "You sure you don't want a beer?"

"No, thanks." Matt laughed.

"Rumor was he became stupid after the accident. You know, brain damaged. Last thing I heard he was still alive and workin' in Solomon's Island at a boatyard."

"Do you know how Sarah died?" Matt asked.

"Same way Richard had his accident. They was both out on the jetty and he slipped on the rocks. Sarah fell in and drown. Richard hit his head. Folks told it, he was tryin' to save her."

"Just one last question. What was Sally Mae's last name?"

"Johnson."

Matt scooted to the front edge of the couch seat. "I apologize. I've got one last question, too. Did Sally Mae ever mention where the Colisons came from when they moved here?

"Lancaster, Pennsylvania."

64

Matt and Kitty rose at the same time.

"We can't express how much help you've been and how much we've enjoyed talking to you," Kitty said.

"You don't have to leave, do you?"

Matt smiled broadly. "Yes. But, I'd like to buy you a beer sometime."

Birdie laughed. "Think I wouldn't take you up on that? I could teach you a thing or two, young man."

All goodbyes said, and promises of a return visit made, Matt and Kitty departed and headed for the marina.

"Well, there's one thing I'm more certain of than ever. The father holds the answer. He knows the why to all of this."

"What if he's not alive?" Matt asked.

"He's alive. He's got to be. Sarah's father seems to be the only possible source to keep the spirit going since Richard appears out of the question because of his problem. For some reason I just feel her father knows the answer." Kitty paused and stared out of the passenger window. "You're simply a tool. The spirit knows that and is pushing you toward finding him."

* * *

Matt packed a small valise and utility bag, including enough apparel to last a few days. Kitty had gone ahead to her apartment to do the same. The psychic they planned to see lived in the Bronx. The trip could easily be made, up and back, in the same day, but they were enthused with the idea of doing a tour of the town while having the chance. Never having been in the 'Big Apple,' Matt looked forward to the break from the boat and small town isolation.

Logically opting to travel by plane, they arrived at the airport about an hour prior to noon departure. Their bags checked-in, they went to the bar to await the boarding call.

"I'm excited," Kitty said, exposing a bit of the little girl deep inside.

"Me, too. But hate the hell out of flying. Would have much rather gone by train, or for that matter by bus."

"You didn't tell me that," she said, with concern. "God, you've never flown before. Have you?"

"Nope." His answer was short and sweet.

"Oh, gee, I hope you don't get airsick."

"Who, me? You've got to be kidding. As much as I'm on the water."

Kitty smiled, and then laughed. "It's a wee bit different. But I'll be there to take care of you if anything goes wrong."

"Like what, a plane crash?"

"No, silly." She laughed even harder. "In case you've got to puke."

Matt laughed.

"What would you like?" the waiter asked.

"I don't care, but make it a triple." Matt said.

The young man smiled. "First time flying, huh?"

"We'll have two Scotch and waters," Kitty interrupted, shaking her head in disbelief.

The waiter left chuckling to himself.

"I'm sorry," Matt said in a whimper. "I'm a baby."

"I know you are," she said, soothingly. "Now, now, don't cry."

Matt winked and chuckled.

Suddenly, it occurred to her. "You're putting me on, aren't you?"

He confessed. "I almost had my pilot's license when I was in my thirties."

"Ohooo, I could almost kill you," she said, with all seriousness, and then burst into laughter.

"Got'cha."

* * *

Visiting New York in the middle of winter left much to be desired -- the streets full of slush and the traffic even more unbearable. Traveling into town via taxi, they arrived at the Lexington Hotel around three-thirty. It had literally taken longer to make the trip from Kennedy Airport, than it did to fly from D.C.

There were certainly more luxurious places to stay, but the accommodations sufficed. Matt earlier insisted the excursion be at his expense and the Lexington's rates better suited the budget. Whatever he decided, was okay with Kitty.

Not being able to see the psychic until the following morning, they spent the remainder of the day trudging through the messy streets and strolling down Broadway. Their wandering winding up near Radio City, the two zealous tourists couldn't resist seeing the show. It was dark by the time they got out, and jabbering about how much they enjoyed the Rockettes, a nearby restaurant proved a welcomed stop. Although the prices were exorbitant, the meal rated higher.

Tired after the long day, Matt suggested they catch a cab to the hotel.

"This isn't working," Matt said. "Feel like a short trek?"

"Yes. I'm cold. Let's go."

On a semi-deserted street, a youth suddenly jumped from the shadows threatening them with a knife.

"Hey, asshole. Gimme your money or I'll cut ya bad."

Matt's face contorted menacingly into that of an almost grotesque monster, his eyes altering to exude a glare causing Kitty to tremble and the mugger to retreat in fear.

Kitty screamed. "Matt, are . . . are you all right?" she stammered, as she shook his arm.

"Uh, . . . uh, wha . . .? Yeah. . . . What happened?" Matt hunched over trying to gather himself.

"I don't know," she said, still shaking from the experience. "Let's just get out of here."

CHAPTER IX

The hotel doorman summoned a cab -- the hack thrilled with being hired for the morning. Kitty handled the fee negotiations, proving herself a hard bargainer. However, the driver wasn't particularly impressed with their destination -- the lower end of the Bronx far from being the most popular or visited part of the boroughs.

They eventually arrived in a district dotted with warehouses and a line of row houses across from a network of railroad tracks.

After further demanding the cab driver wait, with the promise of an extra gratuity, they entered one of the buildings.

With the door closed behind them, it was pitch black -- no lights in the hallway.

"Damn, I can't see a thing. Have you ever been here before?" Matt asked, displaying some frustration.

"Yes, I have," Kitty said. "Just knock on the door."

"What door?"

"The one right in front of you, dummy." She giggled.

Matt glanced at his feet and saw a shimmer of light at the foot of an apparent door. "Oh, that one." Matt gave it a good series of raps with his knuckles.

Several moments passed before a response. Finally, the door opened. A short chubby baldheaded male greeted them..

"Hi, Chet," Kitty said. "Madame Celeste is expecting us."

"Hello, Doctor Smallwood, it's nice to see you again."

They followed Chet inside and down a long hallway to a waiting room.

"Who was that? It looked like someone out of the 'Adam's Family." Matt shook his head.

Kitty gave him a dirty look.

69

Matt seemed amazed and in disbelief of the environment. The small cubicle was filled with crucifixion symbols, statues of Joseph and the Blessed Mother, along with numerous other religious artifacts. "What in the hell have you gotten me into?" he whispered.

"Shush."

Taking seats beside each other among a number of other waiting clients, all appearing weird to Matt for one reason or another. They sat silent without anyone in the room saying a thing.

"Holy hell," Matt finally mumbled under his breath.

"Be quiet."

"Madame will see you, now," Chet said, appearing in the doorway.

Kitty quickly rose to her feet and tugged at Matt's arm, following their leader back up the hall.

"Damn, Doc. Those people back there didn't even blink when we got to see her before they did," Matt said, confused by the events.

"Don't worry about it."

At a spot near where they originally entered, Kitty and Matt were led up a flight of stairs to the second floor and arrived in a luxuriously furnished living room. A split-second later, a graying matronly woman dressed in a simple cotton dress, but gaudily bedecked in costume jewelry, entered the room.

"Oh, it's so marvelous to see you, my dearest Kitty," the newcomer said, rushing to take Kitty into her arms in a big embrace.

Kitty reciprocated. "Celeste, this is Matt."

"Hello, Matthew, I'm glad you've come. Please. Sit down and make yourselves comfortable."

They all took a seat -- Kitty and Matt side-by-side on the couch -- Celeste across from them in an overstuffed chair.

"Relax, and don't be so rigid." The Madame directed her remark at Matt.

"I'm sorry . . ."

"Don't be sorry," she said, with determination. "You may be apologetic at anytime you wish, but never, ever, be sorry."

He didn't totally grasp the logic; however, he guessed it made some sense.

"Madame . . ."

"That's the second mistake," she said, interrupting what he was about to say. "To my friends, I'm simply Celeste. The title was created for commercial purposes."

"Oh. I hadn't thought about the money end of it," Matt said, more sarcastically than intended.

Celeste smiled. "Quite the contrary." As if reading his mind, she continued. "Those waiting people you just left downstairs are here for another purpose. A type of pilgrimage as a point of fact."

Matt felt embarrassed, and wondered why Kitty hadn't aided him in his plight.

"I have more money than I could ever spend in my lifetime. My riches were not gained by my gift of perception. They came through inheritance. Funds earned using my talents are turned over to the church to help the poor and needy. I was drawn to this place in the early forties. In the yard behind this house there is a shrine of the 'blessed mother' awaiting a miracle to reoccur. Admittedly, it is long overdue, but I will wait for whatever time it takes. As you've undoubtedly noticed, I have many religious symbols and artifacts in my home. I am Catholic, and I am of God."

Matt was speechless and sat mesmerized.

"You have had contact with the other side," she continued, "and are correct in being apprehensive and afraid. There is a power in your experienced manifestation stronger than any I have ever known. The spirit is crying out for you to save it and rid its agony. I cannot tell you why, but of one thing I am sure. You will never be left alone unless you respond to the need. I also sense an urgency in settling the matter quickly. But this I must warn you. Resist the evil with all of your strength, yet the spirit means no real personal harm. It is your mind that is vulnerable. You have already experienced this only last night. The force that saved you in the streets was not of your own. It was the impellent power of the spirit that has connected with you, protecting you from harm so that you may fulfill the needed task." Celeste slumped in her chair.

"My God, she's had a heart attack," Matt said, jumping to his feet.

"No, no." Kitty touched his arm to soothe his concern. "She spoke from being in a trance. She'll be okay." Kitty stood and took him by the hand, leading him from the room.

On the way out they passed Chet and he bade them goodbye.

As the two reached the outside, Matt sighed with relief at finding the taxi still sitting at the curb.

The cabbie sighed relief as they got into the backseat, evidently happy he hadn't lost his fare.

"How did she do that?" Matt asked.

Kitty gave Matt a puzzled look. "Do what."

"Knowing about the spirit, and everything else?"

"Psychic ability."

"Aw, bull," Matt retorted. "You called her."

Kitty's temper flared. "Where have you been? We haven't been apart since we got here and I didn't even talk to her when I made the appointment with Chet. With all you've already experienced, do you still have doubts?"

Matt paused, feeling guilty. "No. I guess I'm just confused."

Kitty grasped Matt's hand. "I know. But Celeste is very knowledgeable about these things. Do you think you can accept what she said?"

"Yeah, I'll try. Where do we go from here?"

* * *

It was great to be back on familiar turf, even if it was Kitty's apartment. She had excellent taste in decor, but nothing spectacular about the complex in which she lived. Matt tried to steer clear for the most part as she pored over books and stayed engrossed in her work. Although comforted by his presence, she seemed to understand when he became restless and decided to return to the boat. After promising her research wouldn't take much longer, Matt departed confused and full of endless questions without answers. He had been impressed with the psychic even though not understanding all she said. However, her warning had been clear. And that concerned him. What did she mean by mental control?

Equal to the fun parts of the trip, he felt a bit hurt at being pushed aside by Kitty's dedication to her research -- too damn professional, he thought. But, why in the hell not? She was only trying to help him. He cursed himself for his negative attitude.

Getting back to the marina provided some peace of mind. Not wanting to cause an interruption, he decided not to attempt contacting her until she called first. Strictly out of desperation, he dialed Ozzie's number.

"Hello." The familiar voice on the other end of the line sounded refreshing.

"What say, big buddy?"

"Damn, Matt. I thought you were all but disappeared."

"Still chugging along. How've you been?"

"Gettin' older. I'm trying to catch up with you," he said, chuckling. "Heard any good crying on the radio, lately?"

"If you only knew." Matt responded in exasperation without thinking.

"Knew what?" Ozzie acted concerned.

"Forget I said anything."

"No. You sound like you're troubled. Lay it on my shoulder."

"I'm serious, Ozzie. I'm not sure what's been going on and, half the time, what I'm even talking about."

"Man, you're coming through like gibberish. Stop the double-talk and fill me in."

"Well, you brought it up a few minutes ago when you made the joke about the radio. I'm sure all of it has something to do with the old house sitting on the shore."

"Wow. Don't tell me you've been seein' ghosts and all that bullshit."

"Damn it, Ozzie, I didn't want to get into this and I don't need your snide remarks. I've got friends working on the matter and I just got back from New York after meeting with a psychic. My mind's all screwed-up."

"Sorry you called. We better talk some other time," Ozzie said in defense.

"I apologize, too. It's a bad time. Talk to you later."

After hanging up the phone, Matt realized he had deferred from saying he was sorry. An eerie sensation passed though his veins.

As a diversion, he switched on the television. ESPN carried a fight-special showing excerpts from past Olympic matches. Matt was never much on boxing, but sports in general were a great attraction. He dozed.

Waking up shortly after midnight, his neck ached from having spent the hours slumped in the chair. Being hungrier than needing more immediate sleep, he decided to raid the refrigerator. He found leftover bagels, but no cream cheese, and improvised with peanut butter and jelly. Enforced with a glass of milk, Matt returned to sit in front of the television.

After sifting through the channels using his remote, he settled into the middle of an old movie. Not having filled the kerosene heater, the room gradually became increasingly cool. He waited for a commercial break, retrieved a canister from the bridge, and added fuel to the unit bringing it to full capacity. Shortly, the warmth revived.

The program ended; the clock indicating it was a few minutes before midnight. Feeling some more shuteye wouldn't be a bad idea, Matt started downstairs and realized he hadn't sat the fuel can back outside. He slipped on his dock shoes and returned the container to its proper spot on the bridge. Curious about the weather, he unzipped the canvas entrance and poked his head through to test the night air. Immediately he was confronted face to face by a shimmering figure close enough to touch. "Aw, my God," he shouted, staggering backwards.

"Matt. It's me, Heather. It's just me," she repeated.

Bending over with his hands on his knees, he gasped trying to catch his breath and get his heart rate back to normal.

"Oh, I'm so sorry. I didn't mean to scare you." Heather moved forward to place her hand on his shoulder.

"Uh, I . . . I'll . . . be fine." He struggled in getting the words together, while straightening to an upright stance. A low chuckle altered into an uncomfortable laugh.

"You better get inside. You're freezing without a coat.

They went below.

Heather immediately turned the heater up a notch and Matt stood warming his hands. "I feel terrible."

Matt's adrenalin began to calm and the shaking subsided. Slowly, his mental faculties regained order and it made sense something had to be wrong for Heather to be there. "What brings you out this fine night?" he asked, attempting to sound jovial.

74

"Jason's in Philadelphia on business and, I'm so far behind in my studies, I came down to get away from the phone and try to cram."

Matt smiled and continued rubbing his hands.

"I had no idea how late it was and wanted to take a shower at the bathhouse before going to bed. When I got back to the boat, I'd locked myself out. I didn't know what to do. I saw your lights on, so I came over here and tried to knock on the back of your boat, but you didn't hear me. I shouldn't have come aboard like I did." Heather's fragile emotions made her eyes well with tears.

"Come on, now. It's not all that bad," Matt said softly, placing his arm around her shoulders and adding a little squeeze of reassurance. "Here." He handed her a handful of tissues.

Drying her eyes, she walked to sit on the couch.

"Hon. You don't owe me any kind of an apology. I'm just glad to be here to help. If anything, I should apologize for upsetting you."

"Please, don't," she pleaded. "It was my . . ."

Matt interrupted her. "No, it's all right. I don't want to seem mysterious, but there's plenty of time to explain in the morning. It's late and we're both tired. You take the aft cabin, I'll sleep up front." He winked.

"Thank you, Matt. Good night."

"Sleep well." He disappeared around the corner.

* * *

Before Heather left the following morning she lauded him with thanks for helping her get aboard her boat. Matt then set out to do his chores of the day.

He was low on just about everything and needed to make several different stops. After visiting the local Laundromat, he went for groceries and to fill up with gas while his clothes dried.

All chores completed, he headed for the local library in hopes of finding some nearby Colison and Johnson relatives. Other than the post office, it was Deale's only physical identity with government. Searching the computer files proved hopeless and he sought assistance from the information desk.

Matt located a document prepared by a sixth-grade class in the late forties he found rather unique and historically accurate regarding the Deale area, but unresponsive to his needs.

Although, a number of old-standing family names were mentioned, nothing surfaced making any connection of importance. However, in a section devoted to religious background, it made mention of different small sects existing, including the Jehovah and Adventist, among others, but no Amish.

Matt continued his research back on the boat by attacking the phone book. There was no listing for Colison, although the name spelled with a double 'l' seemed quite popular. Things could have been worse, he thought.

The phone rang, breaking his concentration.

"Hello."

"Hi."

Just what he needed, Kitty's melodic greeting. "Doc. Damn, it's good to hear your voice."

She laughed, and mimicked his favorite phrase, "Me, too, to you, too."

"I've missed you," he said, making a kissing sound against the receiver.

"Well, not for much longer. I'm on my way."

With the click of the receiver, he could barely control his exuberance.

Thanking the deity for having gotten the shopping done, the boat still needed a going over. In a mad rush, linens were changed, the clean clothes placed in their proper place, and a thorough vacuuming completed throughout the vessel. After taking a couple of steaks from the freezer, he carefully laid a bottle of wine on top of other frozen items for a quick chill. Promising himself not to forget it was there, he made a mental menu for an impromptu dinner.

Matt gathered the papers and phone books and wiped the table, counters and shelves with a damp rag.

Time passed so quickly Kitty's footsteps could be heard on the bridge before realizing she had arrived. He rushed up the steps and threw his arms around her. They dwelled in a long embrace. "Whew," Kitty wittingly remarked, "if that's for openers, I don't know if I can handle what comes later."

"We'll find out, won't we?" Matt pinched her on the butt as

he turned to go down stairs.

"Ouch, but not so fast. There's more in the car."

"I'll get it," he said, insisting she go below.

Matt couldn't believe what she had brought. In excess of the usual luggage, there were three boxes of books, office supplies, video and audio equipment, and a personal computer and printer. "Moving in?" he asked, and laughed. "I hope," he added in a whisper.

"I heard that." She smiled. "We can set the computer up in the small stateroom, if it's okay? I forgot to tell you there's a collapsible table in my trunk if you need it."

"Say no more. I'm on my way."

It took quite a while to get things in order. Kitty needed the computer to telecommunicate with a network of libraries at various universities across the country, and to access some special software programs. Since a phone hookup was required for using the modem, installing a jack seemed more logical than the long exposed cord already in existence. After getting what was needed from the hardware, the project didn't take long to complete.

Up and running, Kitty fascinated Matt by providing a brief demonstration of accessing a local university library. Rather impressed, to say the least, the two joked about the effects of computers in the workplace. Other than getting a big laugh over Heather's ghostly appearance, they made a pact to avoid anything involving spirits, except those coming in a bottle.

The evening was wonderful -- dinner, a TV movie, soft music, and a romantic interlude lasting well into the night.

CHAPTER X

Always an early riser, Matt carefully tried not to disturb Kitty. He gathered his clothes and slipped upstairs to get dressed. After switching on the coffee pot, catching the morning news seemed a good idea.

It was strange how life patterns could change, he thought. Not very long ago there was a time when the morning newspaper was a must -- being near sacrilege should the paper boy miss a delivery.

He fixed a cup of the hot brew, then sat at the table fiddling with the dollhouse.

At nine o'clock, running the channels resulted in stopping on the Montel Williams Show -- his guests being psychics. He considered waking Kitty, but second thoughts led to deciding there probably would be nothing she hadn't seen or previously encountered. It was the correct decision -- the program proved boring and getting a little fresh air much more self-satisfying. Donning a coat and boots, he went for a stroll around the marina.

All of the snow had melted, except for remote spots denied exposure to the sun. Intentionally walking in a direction away from the old house, meeting the only other live-aboard boater consequentially led to a brief chat about the weather and other vague marina matters. The two promised a get-together at a later date. Matt watched as the old-timer waddled down his pier, stopping to check all of the dock connections before climbing aboard his craft. The air was crisp, and it felt good to be outside.

"Oh, Matt." He heard Heather call, turning to see her approach. "I was just heading up to take a shower and wanted to thank you again for the other night." She carried a canvas bag and towels.

"You're welcome," he replied, acknowledging her appreciation. "You in a rush this morning?"

"Well, . . . not really."

"Good. Kitty came down yesterday. Why don't you stop by for breakfast? She's still sawing logs."

"That would be nice. I'd love it."

"And just come on aboard. You don't have to knock," he said, starting to laugh.

"I will," she called back, halfway to the bathhouse.

Matt scurried to the boat and realized he had ingredients to make a gourmet meal. However, thinking it best to wake Kitty to give her the chance to freshen up before breakfast, he found her already in the head.

Drawing a small glass of cold water from the galley, with great stealth, he pulled aside a corner of the shower curtain and tossed the liquid inside.

"Oooooo," she screamed. "Damn, you. I'll get you for that." She laughed. "Pay backs are hell," she added.

"Hurry up. We're going to have company."

Matt's galley duty nearly completed, Kitty surfaced from below at the precise moment Heather arrived from above. "What a surprise," Kitty said, moving to embrace Heather. "How have you been?"

"Fine. And, you?"

"Everything's wonderful," Kitty answered; her broad smile emphasizing the point.

"You look great, and happier than I've ever seen you before."

Kitty moved to put her arms around Matt's waist. "Guess why?"

Heather smiled and slipped off her coat. "Missed you at class."

"How's the substitute professor doing?"

"All right, but he's boring . . . not like you."

Kitty slightly blushed with the compliment.

Matt interrupted their exchange. "Soup's on."

The ladies were shocked when presented eggs-benedict served with asparagus sprinkled with back fin crabmeat. Matt popped a bottle of bubbly and made it a festive champagne brunch.

80

As they ate, Kitty initiated conversation with Heather about the reason for her leave of absence, divulging only that the old house seemed to have intrigue and a meager possibility of spiritual influence. Kitty fibbed she was writing a book dealing with the impact of physic phenomena in psychology, then asked Heather to assist in the project and earn extra credits in the process. Not hesitating to accept the offer, before she left, Kitty provided her with a list of research duties.

"What do you think?" Matt asked, as they settled down after saying goodbyes.

"She'll do fine. I can use the help, but really don't want her overly involved, nor to know the whole of it."

"Good idea. But, before we get into what you've been doing, I'd like to fill you in on a couple of things." He handed Kitty several pages of notes.

"You have been busy," she said.

"Yeah, but not getting anywhere," he added. "I guess the next best thing to do is track down birth records over in Annapolis."

Kitty opened her briefcase and sat it on the table as Matt took a seat on the couch.

"Now it's my turn," she said, becoming very serious. "Everything I've learned has reinforced my first opinion. I've spoken at length with Celeste since our meeting, as well as a number of her other associates. They all concur. We're in the middle of an extraordinarily rare phenomenon. Kitty paused for a moment to look in her purse. "You've already been greatly affected by this unbelievably strong force," she nervously continued, finally retrieving a pack of cigarettes and lighter.

"This is getting neat." Matt tried to joke and ease her mood.

"It's not at all funny," she harshly reacted, lighting the wrong end of a filtered stick of tobacco, then firing up another. "You still don't remember anything about the incident in New York, or that Celeste knew about it without being told."

"What do you mean?" Matt shifted his position, becoming more concerned.

"We were almost robbed trying to get back to the hotel."

"Awww, come on, now, Doc."

"It's true." Kitty almost shouted the statement. "The expression that came over your face, and the menacing glare in your eyes, not only frightened him away, it scared the hell out of me, too. I honestly sensed you could have subjected him to severe harm without even touching him." She jabbed the half-finished smoke into the ashtray. "Honey," she said, and paused, finding it difficult to continue. "At that moment, you were possessed."

Matt leaned forward, bracing his elbows against his knees and placing his hands on each side of his head.

Kitty moved to kneel before him. "Celeste mentioned the happening to you and it went right over your head. You knew, or remembered nothing about it." She rubbed her hand soothingly along his thigh. "What you experienced was a brief spiritual possessive interference."

"God, what's happening?"

"I don't know, but we're going to find out. Come on, you need a drink. Me, too." They stood for a long time in front of the bar holding each other before filling their glasses. "Well." Kitty sighed. "What should we do next?"

"You're the Doc." Matt's answer was purely defensive.

"Yeah, that I am," she hesitantly agreed. "But I wish I could be more sure of myself in all of this. . . . We could ride over to Annapolis and check birth records, or go over Sarah's diary again."

"I'm not much on traveling right now," he said, suddenly feeling very tired.

"So. That settles that," she responded very cheerfully. "Where's the box at?"

"Still in the cabinet over there."

"Oh." She turned and moved to the custom-built unit on the port wall. Opening the drawer, she began to tremble and whimper. Matt rushed to look inside. The doll sat braced against the wooden box with a tear streaming down its cheek, the stuffing again protruding from it's middle.

* * *

Days sped by shortening the abbreviated month of February. At the urging of the university, Kitty returned to school earlier than planned. Matt missed her hands-on support, but attempted to carry the load, doing a lot of leg work by himself. Gaining information from birth records proved useless. He concluded

Sarah could have been born at home without having any legal documentation.

Well aware the Hughesville area of Maryland held a large contingency of Amish, Matt decided to investigate a possible connection and used the pretense of wanting to buy the Deale property, and not being able to locate its owner. First inquiries were made at the Saturday Amish Market. From there he gained information leading to a meeting with one of the more important and knowledgeable elders of the group. As helpful as the old bearded gentleman tried to be, no ties within his community to the name Colison existed. Before ending their conversation, Matt received an elder's name in Pennsylvania as a viable alternative.

Matt called Kitty at the university and got her voice mail. "Hi, Doc, just me. Wanted to let you know I'm heading up to Lancaster on a tip and from what Birdie mentioned earlier to see if I can locate any Colisons. I'll try to call you later from there. Miss ya."

* * *

Matt arrived at Lancaster in the late part of the day. Rush hour was maddening due to heavy highway construction. After finding the tourist information center closed, he opted on a nearby motel to spend the night.

He knew nothing about the Mennonites or Amish religion, or tradition, and felt taking an organized bus tour to be wise before trudging in and making an ass out of himself. There were a number of brochures available in the lobby and numerous trips from which to choose. He made a reservation for a ten-thirty excursion the following morn.

Matt dozed off in the middle of an HBO movie.

* * *

The digital alarm clock read one-thirty a.m. in the darkened cabin with Kitty sound asleep in Matt's bed.

* * *

The rear windows of Sarah's house glowed with intensity. The back door opened as Sarah's spirit appeared in the doorway. She raised her arms above her head, then sensually rubbed her hands up and down her body.

* * *

Matt laid on his back, perspiration beading on his forehead.

He began to writhe in bed. As an eerie light brightened the room, Matt's unconscious distress heightened.

Suddenly, the light dissipated.

Matt sat upright, shuddering from a chill -- his body in a cold sweat -- the bed soaking wet.

Feeling the need for immediate warmth, he got into a steaming shower and profusely lathered his body until suds filled the bottom of the tub. After stepping from behind the shower curtain, Matt began to dry with a towel, uncontrollably rubbing himself until almost raw.

"What the hell's happening to me?" he pleaded while wrenching open the bathroom door and rushing to retrieve a bottle of Scotch from his luggage. He wrenched off the cap, then turned it up against his lips, swallowing several gulps before slamming it down on the dresser. As he stared into the mirror, a reflected misty image began to vibrate and ever so slightly fade. Suddenly, it stopped.

"Good Jesus," he said imploringly, his hands grasping the sides of his head.

* * *

Still uneasy from the previous night's experience, Matt boarded the bus -- almost filled near to capacity by the time he arrived. Their tour guide, a younger lady, probably in her thirties and in recent day Mennonite dress, introduced herself and began by explaining the included itinerary.

Matt having slept late and missing a chance for breakfast, not that he had been in the mood for it, carried a fresh cup of coffee. The window seats taken, he was forced to sit on the aisle next to a young teenage lad. Sipping the hot liquid burnt his lips and he spit a few drops in his lap. The kid looked at him with total distaste.

They toured the nearby countryside viewing many Mennonite and Amish farms and the antiquated mannerisms practiced by the lasting followers of Jakob Ammann. The guide explained the Amish to be a group remaining true to old orthodox Mennonite beliefs. Other Mennonites deviated and came to accept certain modern conveniences.

However, there still remained quite a few taboos seeming to be rather contradictory. A modern Mennonite family might have a car in the driveway, a tractor to till the fields, and electricity in their homes, but a phone was totally forbidden. Yet, pay booths were commonly placed near driveways leading to prosperous farms. Many more comparisons of the two distinct groups were given, and a wine-tasting stop a welcome break. Matt became fascinated by a vintage of apple wine prompting him to buy several bottles to take home.

As a final point of interest, everyone was promised the chance to meet and speak with an orthodox Amish family -- an occasion supposedly considered a rare opportunity. As the bus slowed to a stop along a highway in front of a mediocre farm, the guide suggested the group exit and stand on the shoulder of the road. She also insisted cameras be left in the bus in lieu of religious belief.

In the distance, a young girl emerged from a doorway carrying something in her arms. After approaching the tourists, she began a rehearsed speech apologizing that her father was in the fields and the mother taken ill, then immediately started promoting the sale of handmade potholders, waist aprons, and Xeroxed copies of an authentic Amish cookbook.

The lass, having completed her outdoor sales, boarded the bus following the last tour bus passenger.

"My family thanks all of you for your kindness. If no one else wishes to purchase any more goods, I shall be leaving."

Matt stood and moved forward as if in a daze. "Sarah?"

The young girl expressed surprise. "Yes. How did you know my name?"

Matt regained some rationale. "I . . . I guess I just thought you looked like a Sarah." He awkwardly smiled.

"Would you like to buy something?"

"Yes, . . . please. I'll take one of those booklets you have."

"Oh, the recipes."

Following the transaction, Sarah exited the bus and hurried up the road to her home.

Damn, can't anything be sacred anymore, Matt thought. It was clear the roadside stop proved to be nothing more than a tourist gimmick promotion by the tour company with the Amish family making a buck in the process. But, on the plus side, the recipes she described sounded tantalizing.

The driver closed the bus doors and, the tour soon over, dropped Matt off at the motel. It was just after two o'clock and he felt famished.

Ages had passed since eating at a fast-food joint. Thrilled with the chance, he went across the street to order a double cheeseburger, French fries and a chocolate shake at McDonald's. As he ate, it became uncomfortable to sit on the rolled up mini-publication in his back pocket and he pulled it out, laying it on the table.

Truly enjoying every bite taken, his mind rested in relief from turmoil while suppressing a welcomed but embarrassing burp into a napkin. He hoped no one had noticed as he stuffed the cookbook back in his slacks, returning to the motel.

Tired from the lack of sound rest, Matt stretched across one of the beds and began to doze, only to again be disturbed by the object in his pants. He disgustedly threw it on the floor.

Unable to sleep, he felt compelled to get up and stepped on the crumpled book. Picking it up and glancing at the introductory page, it was signed 'By, Ruth Elizabeth Colison.'

Initial excitement with the discovery was dampened by sensing something had goaded his attention to the book ever since he bought it.

Unsuccessful in contacting Kitty, the event brought to mind her warning about the powers of spiritual intervention. Maybe there was also a reason he couldn't contact her. Episodes of all the unexplainable things that had happened rushed though his brain. He fought the feeling of losing control.

Matt settled his nerves with a double Scotch which helped regain a semblance of stability. Eventually able to focus on current matters, rather than attempting immediate direct contact with the Colison family, he dialed the Tourist Information Center. They referred him to a group known as the 'Elders for Amish Hospitality.' Matt called them. Arranging a next day appointment was the only available choice.

86

CHAPTER XI

Relieved at getting through the night without further incident, Matt continued to be dismayed by not being able to reach Kitty the following morning. Although repeatedly leaving the motel number on her machine, she hadn't returned the call.

Matt showered, had a quick breakfast, and arrived for his scheduled meeting. A rather sexy receptionist asked him to wait for a moment and then ushered him into a lavishly furnished office to meet the elder in charge.

"I see you're surprised with the environment," the elder commented while shaking hands. "My name is Peter. Please sit down." Matt took a seat in a chair facing a huge executive desk while his robust bearded rival returned to sit on the opposite side. "What can I do for you, Mr. Bodine?"

"Please excuse my ignorance of your culture," Matt said, "but I'd like to gain information regarding a family by the name of Colison. I've been trying to buy property in Maryland and haven't been able to locate the owner."

The elder said nothing in response and only peered at Matt over his reading glasses.

"My wife passed away not long ago and, having the need for seclusion, I've really identified with the old house. It means a lot to me." Matt described Deale and expressed a desire to restore the long vacant home. "I bought this yesterday during a tourist trip." Matt slightly rose to lay the cookbook on the desk, opened to the first page.

Not bothering to look at it, the elder replied. "I'm familiar with it. The Colison families have been in this area for quite a number of years. Most are of the old beliefs, but there have been defections in the past to the newer Mennonite concepts. And, even to the outside world," he added.

"Do you think I could speak with them?" Matt anxiously asked.

"Yes, I'm sure it can be arranged. But, you must realize many of the orthodox look upon those who stray to either be dead or never having existed in the first place."

Matt nodded his head indicating his understanding.

"Contact my secretary sometime around early afternoon. She'll let you know the arrangements. If you need further assistance, I'll be happy to meet with you again."

Expressing his deep appreciation, Matt left the office feeling rather chipper. He had a little over an hour to wait and hoped his visit would be possible before the end of the day. After returning to the motel, there was still no success in reaching Kitty and trying to catch her at the university wasn't considered.

Matt called the Amish office at one o'clock, received directions, and told to be at the Colison farm at four p.m. He timed it perfectly, parked on the highway shoulder respecting their distaste for modern travel, and walked the long dirt road to the house.

Greeted at the front door by the young girl who had sold him the cookbook, Matt was ushered through the living room and into a huge kitchen. An elder, somewhat less than his own age, sat at the far end of a table surrounded by eight chairs -- one on each end and three on each side. The eldest of the daughters moved to take a place next to her two sisters.

"Be seated." The long-bearded man gestured with his hand to the unoccupied chair opposite the girl.

Matt was surprised and didn't know what to do. As if by instinct, he took his seat, sitting beside their two sons. Nothing had been said about being invited for dinner.

The lady of the house finished placing the last of many bowls on the table and returned to the oven.

"Mother." With the single word, spoken as a command, she moved to take her seat as the father rose from his chair. "Precious Lord, bless this house and the food we partake. Amen!" He sat down. "Eat!"

The mother got up and returned to the stove, retrieving a basket of hot bread. The children followed their father's lead and began scooping gobs of food on their plates, passing the bowls in a clockwise fashion when finished. Matt did the same.

The meal was delicious, and nothing store bought. Home churned butter melted into the freshly baked rolls creating a taste of sheer delight. Matt hadn't realized his hunger and the elder and his wife grinned their satisfaction with his hearty appetite. Not a word was spoken at the table.

Oddly, the entire family finished near the same time. Matt lowered his own fork and started to place it on his plate.

"Eat. Eat," the elder repeated, with a nod of his head and motioning Matt to continue by waving his hand. No one moved until he had cleaned his platter. The father stood and walked toward the front of the house. "Come," he said, as he passed by Matt.

Matt was beginning to wonder if his host was able to make a complete sentence. Saying "thank you" to the wife as he left the table, she returned an appreciative smile.

He followed the elder of the house through the doorway into the living room. It was like those seen on the tour -- sparse of furniture and everything a product of the community.

The elder stoked a stack of burning logs and moved two high-backed wooden chairs from their positions against the wall, setting them in front of the fireplace to face each other a few feet apart.

"My name is Joshua and you are Matthew. That is a very good name. Do you smoke?" he asked, pulling two cigars from his breast pocket.

"Thank you." Matt accepted his offer and followed his lead.
"Did you grow the tobacco?" Matt asked, trying to become part of the conversation.

"No. It comes from a community in Maryland near where you live."

"Oh. Hughesville?"

Joshua nodded his affirmation. "What work do you do?"

"Uh, I used to build homes, but now I work on fishing boats and sometimes do repair jobs."

"Both a fisherman and carpenter as well. I can sense you are a dedicated and good man, Matthew. You have children?" he asked.

89

"Yes. A son and a daughter. I have two grandchildren, also."

"I am not so fortunate, as yet. But, the day will come."

"Joshua. My wife . . . "

"I know," he interrupted. "Your wife has passed and I share in your sorrow, but you ask me to talk of things rather left forgotten."

Matt didn't know what to say and could detect an expression of concern and indecision etched in the elder's face.

"In my great-great-grandfather's time, he had a brother Joseph, whom, among other things, shamed our family by taking a woman from your world. He became unacceptable and banished from our order. His name never to be spoken in any household." Joshua paused to relight his cigar in the fireplace. "I should not speak of it now, but as I have aged it has become more important to understand the things in life we cannot change. As an inquisitive youth, there were many whispered stories about him becoming a devil and having many wives."

Joshua rose and began pacing the floor. "Relatives of Joseph remain in this area. The maiden name is Fletcher. It is not good to talk more of this. Now, you must leave."

Matt's coat hung on a hook near the front door. Putting it on, he profusely extended his thanks to Joshua as he left.

"God be with you in your plight, Matthew," he heard him call as he walked down the road.

It was well after dark by the time he got back to the motel. Finally reaching Kitty, she denied having received any messages, other than the one telling her of his trip before he left. She did comment there had been an unusual number of hang-ups possibly connected to the time of his calls. They both agreed it was rather strange. Matt brought her up-to-date on recent events and told of his plans for more records research prior to returning. He intentionally didn't mention the midnight experience. They agreed to meet at the boat on Saturday.

The following morning brought rain and Matt found himself running out of fresh clothes. Going out long enough to buy underwear, socks and a white shirt, he returned to dress for the day.

Based on previous experiences, official birth records dating back before the turn of the century were difficult to find and frequently nonexistent. A return to see the Amish administrator, Peter, appeared the logical thing to do. Granted an almost immediate audience, Matt learned news traveled fast even without telephones. It was amazing how well informed the elder was about his meeting with Joshua.

After apologizing for having withheld information during Matt's first visit, Peter explained Joshua's reaction and feelings had to be ascertained before personally becoming involved. He gave Matt the name and phone number of the great-great-granddaughter of Joseph Colison: Rebecca Ann Fletcher. Attempts to contact her before leaving the area failed.

The ride home seemed long and boring, but worth having made the trip. Matt found an unexpected and pleasant surprise seeing Kitty's car in the parking lot when he returned late Friday evening. Not bothering to unload his things, he hurried to the boat. Both acted like they hadn't seen each other for months. There was an initial long embrace, culminating in the aft cabin and eventually leading to needed sleep.

* * *

Matt awoke not finding Kitty in bed. Still groggy, he could hear her shuffling around in the galley and was unable to discern the time based on the amount of daylight engulfing the room. Looking at his wrist did no good. The watch lay on top of his pants sprawled on the floor. He reasoned the hour to be a lot later than he usually slept. Continuing to enjoy the comfort of his own bed, and the solitude offered by the water environment, Matt dwelled in deep thought about his blossoming relationship with Kitty.

"All right, sleepyhead, time to rise and shine," Kitty called down the steps. "Breakfast's ready."

Matt rolled out of bed, put on his robe, and went upstairs.

"Boy, you were tired," she said.

"What time is it?"

Kitty looked at the clock on the microwave. Eleven-thirty."

"Holy cow. I've never slept this late in my life."

"You must have needed it." Kitty turned to hand him a glass of orange juice. She made a gesture with her hand. "Sit. Eat."

Matt started laughing.

"What's so funny?" Kitty asked, smiling.

91

"You sound just like an Amish elder I met."

Kitty joined him at the table and Matt told her about the Colison family and all of the other details.

"So, this great-great-granddaughter, . . . What's her name?"

"Rebecca Ann Fletcher," Matt answered.

"So, Rebecca won't be back at home for another few weeks?"

"Yep. Her aunt said she was visiting friends in Florida and promised to have her call when she gets back. Damn, I'm anxious to talk to her."

"I just hope she can help."

"Me, too," Matt concurred. "Sure would be nice to find Sarah's father alive. Do you really think he could have an idea of what's been happening?"

"I kind of doubt he'd be aware of any spiritual phenomena, but learning more about Sarah and her mother and how they died would sure help. I really think both of their deaths hold the key to all of this." Kitty rose and started removing dishes from the table.

"Then there could be two ghosts?"

"Possibly, but I still don't think so. Celeste insists it's not."

"Learned anymore from the diary?"

"Other than sensing from Sarah's writings she was somewhat illiterate for her age, and had a crush on a boy named Richard, the diary's entries don't provide very much detail. However, she did refer to the doll in most of her later entries as Baby Sarah. At one point she made a plea that if her mother was there she could fix it. I guess she's referring to the doll's stomach being torn. . . . It seemed to be her confidante and only friend she had to share her feelings. All in all, I'd say she was a lonely and somehow suppressed teenager even for her generation. Possibly even learning disabled."

"Yeah, it does reflect Sarah's pretty strict upbringing. That would be consistent with an Amish background," Matt replied.

Kitty agreed. "True. And, there's something more. I don't know if you really paid close attention to the dates of the entries, but the last one was a little over a week before she died. It more or less confirms Birdie's story about her having had an accident of some type."

"Why's that?"

"Nothing eerie. Simple deduction. Nothing indicates she was ill, or anywhere earlier in the diary, as well."

"Can you see any of it adding up to what's been happening?"

"Nothing specific," Kitty said. "Want some more coffee?"

"Please."

Kitty fixed two fresh cups and joined Matt at the table. "Well," she started. "It's about time to get down to the nitty-gritty. I'll probably sound a little like a college professor, so forgive me," she said and laughed. "Anyway, above all else, logic dictates there has to be a reason for a haunting. I only use that term for the lack of a better word, but I don't want to get ahead of myself, so we'll get into that in a few minutes," she said. "Now remember, this is from an amateurs point of view, plus some input from Celeste and a few others. Psychics practice in a lot of ways. Some use astrology, cards, tea leaves, read palms, or whatever. Many simply predict from visions or the aura of their subject, while others use direct contact with the spiritual world."

Kitty paused to sip her drink, using a napkin to dab a few drops spilt on the table. "A common concept regarding spiritualism is the human being is made up of three life forms: the physical; the spirit, or the soul if you prefer; and the ego."

"The ego," Matt asked?

"Let me try to explain it this way," she said. "The spirit only needs the physical body to exist in this world and perform as we do every day. We eat, sleep, drink and defecate to sate the body not the spirit. When we die, it's only a physical death. The spirit shortly leaves the body, but a period of spiritual sleep takes place before it rises and begins to adjust to its next plane. The ego, which is comprised of desires and characteristics of the personality, is slowly shed as no longer needed. Each plane of the spiritual world represents a step in preparation for the one that follows, ultimately leading to the highest which is absolute purification and the possibility of being in the presence of The Almighty. It's in this adjustment where difficulties may occur."

Kitty was feeling tense and sought a cigarette. "Damn, I know I've got some. . . . Here they are." She sounded relieved.

"Need a light?" Matt asked.

"I've got one." She returned to sit down.

"As you were saying," Matt said, urging her on.

"I'm sorry if I'm getting technical, but I feel you should have an overall view of the subject."

"I appreciate it, Doc. It's a topic I know nothing about."

"Anyway, I was saying the spirit may be troubled for some reason and have difficulty making the transition, thereby caught between the planes. The problem could be as simple as not being able to accept death and refusing to go on. Then again, it could be the result of being confused or distraught over having confronted something very extraordinary during earth life."

"So, you feel Sarah's spirit is caught up in a state of limbo and causing these things to happen."

"Not all together. There's certainly evidence to substantiate it as a strong probability, but without direct spiritual contact it's difficult to be sure."

Matt reached to put out the smoldering residue from her cigarette in the ash tray.

"I'm sorry," she said.

"No harm done." Matt smiled.

"Well, to get on with it, seeing lights or an image and being led to find the diary can be considered, more or less, within normal bounds of spiritual phenomena. As I've indicated before, the crying on the radio, the doll, and then the tear, are extremely unusual. We've also assumed it's Sarah and not the mother."

"But, the diary and the doll, plus a child crying, doesn't that lean in favor of it being Sarah's spirit?"

"Possibly," Kitty said. "But both things could have been significant to the mother, as well. She might have bought the diary, and made the doll for Sarah." Kitty paused for a moment. "Or, the doll could have even been the mother's from childhood and passed on to her daughter."

"Damn, . . . one hell of a lot to consider, isn't there?" Matt stood up and stretched. "What's it like outside?"

"It's supposed to be in the low sixties this afternoon," she said.

"Come here and give me a big hug before we go for a walk." He smiled as she moved into his arms. "Aw, Doc. You make me feel so good when you're around. Think I could take it full-time."

She laughed softly, pressing even closer to his body. "A stroll sounds like a great idea," she said. "Let's go."

Matt settled on a thick pullover sweater and got one of his windbreaker jackets for Kitty. Hand in hand they left the marina and headed in the direction of Deale Beach.

The temperature seemed even warmer than predicted. It wasn't long before the outer garments were discarded, each tying their own around the waist.

Deale's beach was aligned with homes -- a public pier running well out into the water. They walked to its end and leaned against the rail. Matt pointed out various landmarks and where things were, including some unable to be seen.

"What's that long row of rocks over there?" Kitty asked, pointing to her right.

"That's a breakwater, . . . Drum Point Jetty, to be exact. The channel coming out of the creek is really narrow and it helps keep the waves from beating boats aground," Matt explained. "The area through here is known as Herring Bay and that's Drum Point."

"Oh. Isn't that where Birdie said Sarah and Richard had their accidents? How do you get to it?"

"What, the jetty? I'll show you on the way back, but that's for another day." He laughed. "I'm getting pooped."

"Poor little thing." She lovingly poked his ribs. "You walk more than this when you play golf."

"No, I don't. I ride a cart."

"Shame on you," she said. "All right, let's get back. You sure you don't want me to jog and get my car and come pick you up?"

"I'll get you for that," he said, as she ran away toward the shore.

Keeping his promise and pointing out how to reach the breakwater, they stopped at a mom and pop type pizzeria for something cold to drink on the return trip.

"This has really been fun," Kitty said, as they approached the dock.

Matt let her walk in front.

"It wasn't so bad after all, was it?" She laughed and turned around to get his reaction.

He wasn't there.

"What in . . ." Kitty looked to see Matt walking toward the old house. Jogging back up the pier, she called out asking him to wait.

Matt ignored her and kept walking. Suddenly, he stopped. "Matt. What are you doing? Matt. Are you all right? Matt," she half-screamed, shaking him by his arm.

"Uh, . . . what?" he said, coming out of his stupor.

"I asked if you're okay?" she said, moving to a position in front of him and gazing into his eyes.

"I . . . I was just going to talk with the old lady who was working in the flower garden over there. Didn't you see, her?"

"Tell me what happened."

"I noticed her when we started to walk down the dock and wanted to find out who she was. She was picking some yellow flowers. I lost sight of her for a second when I walked past the big tree. When I looked again, she was gone."

"Matt, there is no garden, . . . no flowers. It must have been an apparition."

"I'm going in the house," he said with determination.

"I'll go with you."

"No. Just wait here. I have a feeling it's something I should do alone."

"Okay," she reluctantly agreed. "But, if you're not out in five minutes, I'm coming in."

Matt proceeded to the backdoor finding it ajar. He looked through the doorway -- nothing seeming unusual. However, moving inside was like stepping through a time-portal. The door closed behind him.

The room appeared clean and serene, furnished in a manner indicating Amish influence. Contrasting, however, were pink flowered curtains covering the two long rows of windows. On the table rested a kerosene lamp and a vase filled with fresh jonquils. Everything in sight was neatly kept. A high-backed wooden rocker sat in a far corner, next to it a small wicker basket filled with knitting and yarn. At the opposite end, the same dresser remained against the wall, but in perfect condition.

Disturbed by a squeaking sound, he turned to see an old woman now sitting in the chair. Matt was spellbound and couldn't move. She rocked slowly back and forth, embroidering and humming a barely audible tune, oblivious of his presence. She leaned over to replace her sewing in the basket, then rose from the chair and moved to the table, so near to where he stood he could have reached out and touched her. He distinctly caught a soft aroma as she passed.

Rearranging the flowers, she spoke. "Oh, aren't they so lovely?"

"Yes, they are," Matt answered.

She started humming again and turned holding one of the flowers against her breast. From the vacant look in her eyes, Matt could sense she still didn't know he was there -- her words meant only for herself. At a slow pace, she walked through the doorway leading into the kitchen.

Instinctively Matt followed. However, when he stepped into the next room it was covered with dust and in the condition as of current time -- the old lady gone. On his return to the back room, it, too, had transformed to present day.

Immediately leaving the house, he walked straight for Kitty.

"I thought you were going to check the inside," she said as he neared.

Matt didn't speak. He just looked at her and began to tremble.

CHAPTER XII

Back aboard, Matt sat on the couch as Kitty wrapped a blanket around him to combat his feverish chill. After pouring some hot tea, she moved to sit beside him on the sofa's arm. Taking the cup, he began drinking in short rapid sips before handing it back to her. "Here, have some," he said without looking up.

She took the mug, but not his suggestion. "Feel better?"

"A bit."

"Matt, I know something happened, but it's hard to imagine whatever it was. You went into the house for less than ten seconds and came right out."

"There was an old . . ." He stopped in mid-sentence. "What?" he asked, looking up at her, startled at her comment. "My God, Doc. It seemed like I was in there forever." He paused for a moment to motion for his tea. "Before I went in everything seemed normal, but inside, I was in another time." Matt explained everything vividly remembered, sipping between each detail.

Kitty patiently waited until he had finished.

"Could I have some water?" he asked, giving the mug back to Kitty.

"Sure, babe," she said. "God, it's hard to see you like this. I know how frightening it must have been."

"That's what's strange. I didn't feel endangered at anytime. Maybe some apprehension in the very beginning, but never scared."

Kitty handed him his ice-filled drink.

"After I left the house, I felt completely drained. It was like all of my energies had been sucked out of me." He took a generous swallow. "Felt so damn cold."

"That happens frequently in making spiritual contact from what I understand," she said, "especially in early occurrences."

"Are you saying this won't be the last time?"

Kitty appeared to know he sought encouragement. However, it wasn't forthcoming. "Far from it," she reluctantly responded.

Matt sat staring into his glass as he swirled the liquid.

"Honey, you just don't seem to be able to understand how powerful this influence is. The spirit's obviously not going to give up easily. It's apparently gone a long ways in identifying with you. . . . And only you," she emphasized. "It's trying to take over a part of you."

He squirmed in his seat.

"This is a troubled being, desperately needing help," she continued. "You've got to realize it."

Matt exuded irritation and confusion. "If she's so anxious to use me, why did she act like I didn't exist?"

"It's like I said before. There could be several reasons for what happened. The spirit could be confused or even afraid. Or, more than likely, it's having difficulty in breeching the gap between her world and ours." Kitty thought for a moment. "I feel the spirit's trying everything it can to get through but it's having as much difficulties as you are in dealing with it."

"You keep referring to the ghost as it, or the spirit."

"Just a force of habit." Kitty smiled. "I guess it's a subconscious defense mechanism to avoid allowing a more personal identification. And after all, we still don't know who or what it is."

"Well, at least we know it's a she, and it's apparently the mother and not Sarah." Matt finally got rid of the blanket and went to the bar to fix a drink for himself. "Want one?"

"Please. I could use it, now."

"Why don't we just crawl into the bottle and forget about it?"

Kitty laughed. "Make it Grand Marnier and you've got a deal."

Matt joined Kitty at the table with two snifters. "So what's your opinion . . . about it being the mother, I mean?"

"That's the most obvious deduction since the spirit has manifested itself in an older form, but I would be surprised,"

Kitty said.

"Me, too, . . . I think. Everything seemed to point to the girl. Especially the crying I heard on the radio. But it only lasted a few seconds each time. Is it possible Sarah's spirit could age itself at will?"

"From what I understand, absolutely. In fact, although Celeste disagrees, while other of her associates feel otherwise, there could be two active spirits. Sarah's mother could be present attempting to help Sarah."

"That sure makes me feel better. I may have two to cope with after all," Matt said. He paused to digest his thoughts. "Hungry?" he asked.

"A little bit.

Matt got up, tossed a loaf of dark bread to her, and made a couple of trips to and from the refrigerator carrying deli-meats and condiments. "I just wish I could go over there, sit down and talk to her, and get it over with." After taking his seat at the table he began piling up a sandwich.

"I know," Kitty said sympathetically. "At least for now, you've got to wait on the spirit. It's running the show."

"You said, for now," he countered. "You mean I might be able to eventually initiate a contact."

"It's possible." Kitty took a bite of potato salad. "Mediums do it all of the time."

"I sure as hell ain't no medium." He laughed.

"Everybody's got perceptive senses, whether they know it or not. It's already proven you're exceptional. The only problem is you don't have any idea how to use them."

"That's great. You think I'll ever get the hang of it?"

Kitty smiled. "It's not important. What's necessary is for you learn to be in control of your mind and emotions, no matter what's happening. If we handle it correctly, there should be a way to put the spirit to rest. But, God, Matt, you can't allow yourself to become so involved you become part of it."

* * *

Although only two days passed, calling at almost every opportunity, Kitty kept in close touch after leaving Sunday evening. All had been quiet, even though making it a point to be constantly observant of the old house. He was walking on pins and needles and wanted something to happen.

Matt sat at the table working on the dollhouse but couldn't keep his mind on it. Every time he looked at it brought back memories and the loss of his sister, Bunny. He decided to get a breath of fresh air and went topside.

The weather continued to be unseasonably warm allowing comfortable access to the outdoors. While watching the old crab boater checking over his pots, he decided to pay a visit. "Good morning, Captain," Matt called, nearing the backyard.

The grey bearded gent seemed surprised when he looked up.   "M⟨

"Great weather, huh?" Matt said, not having anything better to say.

"Pretty good, I reckon," Captain Joe grunted, shoving a stack of crab pots aside.

"How's the oysters been this season?"

"Could'a been better. Could'a been worse."

Damn, Matt thought, what the hell do you have to do to communicate with these people?

Captain Joe smiled. "Wife says you've been showin' a lot of interest in the place."

His unsolicited remark took Matt by surprise. "Uh, yeah. I've taken a real liking to it. Used to be in the construction business and thinking about buying the property and fixing it up," he lied.

"Uummph! Awful lot to fix."

"I've seen worse." Matt tried desperately to parry with the wise old man. "Have you ever noticed anything odd, . . . you know, unusual about the house?"

Captain Joe disappeared behind a group of pots and surfaced at the other end. "Nope. Nothin 'cept it's an eyesore."

Matt started to walk away.

"You serious about buyin' the place?"

"Yes, sir, I am."

He eyed Matt, evidently searching for truth in his response. "Well, you did a fair job on your boat, reckon you'd do the same on the house." He paused to stick a cigar butt between his teeth. "Like I said a while ago, I was a real young'un back then. Talked to my older brother, Will. Said the girl died and a short time later the old man closed it up and took off. Never seen him after that."

"Did he say how she died?"

"Nope. But I understand it was pretty sudden. Will remembers seein' her from time-to-time. Said he spied on 'em once in awhile. Told me she snuck off to the woods to meet some boy when the old man wasn't around."

"Your brother, uh, Will, he doesn't remember the boy's name?"

"Don't know."

"Could you find out if he does?"

"Can't. Will died a couple of weeks ago."

"I'm sor . . ." He couldn't get the word out.

"It's okay. You have a good day. I gotta lot to do." Captain Joe turned and walked toward his house. He stopped in mid-stride. "Hey. Thought jest occurred. I gotta get out tomorrow mornin' and my helper's feelin' poorly. Wonderin' if you'd like to try your hand at oysterin' fer a day?"

Matt was totally shocked. "Uh, . . . uh, yeah. Sounds okay. But I've never done it before."

Captain Joe grinned. "Well, guess you're in fer a real treat."

Following the conversation, Matt felt beaten by the war of wits. He took a seat on a tree stump, faced the creek, and lit his pipe. Watching the sun reflect over the rippled water had a tranquil effect. As he became more relaxed, his mind drifted in thought, finding it inconceivable three years had passed since Catherine's death.

Although wonderful memories lingered, the once restraining emotional bonds carried beyond her grave were gone. There was no denial Kitty did much to fill a deep void. But the timing of her introduction into his life brought questionable coincidence. The combination of his experienced phenomena and her amateur involvement with the paranormal prompted suspicions of being something more than a meeting by chance.

Could this spiritual entity possess the power to cause such a happening? He would have to ask Kitty. Matt stood and stretched his limbs relieving the last of his tension.

As he turned toward the house, the old woman was again tending her garden. Heeding earlier warnings, he convinced himself to stay calm and deliberate in his response. "Hello. It's a beautiful day," Matt called to her. Not getting an answer, he walked slowly until stopping several feet short of the flower bed. "It's a beautiful day," he repeated.

The old lady continued humming, busily pulling weeds from a patch of Jonquils, completely unaware of his presence. She selected a handful of the largest blooms, then rose and walked directly to the rear entrance. Matt followed her through the backdoor, but she was no longer there -- the only thing remaining, an aroma of freshly picked flowers countering the musty atmosphere of the house.

Unconvinced the apparition was over, he went from room to room hoping to find her elsewhere. Disappointed, he returned to the boat and fixed a fresh pot of coffee.

The phone rang. "Hello."

"Could I speak with Sarah, please?"

A rush of adrenalin surged through his body. "Who the hell is this?" Matt demanded. "What kind of sick joke are you trying to pull?"

"Sorry . . . , I'm sorry. I must have dialed wrong."

Click.

Matt reeled from the unsettling blow. Replacing the receiver in its cradle, he moved to the sink and splashed water on his face. "Damn" he muttered, drying his forehead with paper towels. He had to keep his cool. It was just a wrong number.

With a cup of coffee in hand, he felt the need to be outside. Sitting on the aft deck proved restful and entertaining. Several teenagers played football on a nearby lot, prompting smiles in remembering younger days. He leaned back enjoying the sun, and slowly nodded into a shallow state of sleep.

"Richard. . . . I love you."

Matt reacted like having been slapped awake, snapping to an upright seated position. He strained to focus his eyes in the bright light expecting to see whoever had spoken. No one was there. He had to have been dreaming, he thought. Turning his attention to the house, the old woman again stood at her garden. As he watched from a distance, she eventually returned inside -- the vision gone.

The apparition repeated itself several more times. However, he noted each manifestation occurred only after he became preoccupied by something else. Not once did it materialize while consciously waiting for it to happen. He eventually went below.

The ship's clock indicated it to be slightly after three and Matt's stomach growled its disapproval at having been ignored. He placed some deli-meat and cheese between slices of rye bread and, accompanied with a bottle of beer, switched on the TV. Engrossed in an afternoon quiz-show, he finished the sandwich while beating most of the contestants with answers. The beer hit the spot and during commercials he went to the fridge for another.

Anxious to return to the game, something urged him to look out of the port windows. In a fleeting glance he thought he saw a young girl standing in the doorway of the old house. Having only limited vision of the building, Matt raced upstairs to the aft deck to get a better look. The old woman was again tending her flowers.

* * *

The wind blew briskly in the early dark hours preceding dawn as Matt joined Captain Joe on his boat.

Unnoticed, as they pulled from shore, the ghostly image of a young girl appeared in the open doorway of the old house, caressing a bouquet of jonquils while clutching them to her breast.

"Bit gusty this morning," Matt said, straining his voice above the roar of the engine and rush of the wind.

"Yep, Gonna be a doozy out there fer a while." The old seaman paused long enough to stick a chaw behind his cheek. "Don't mean ta speak outta school, and sure ain't none of my business, but you and that lady friend you got are the talk of the town."

"They can go to hell as far as I'm concerned," Matt countered, almost screaming above the noise.

"Figured you'd say that. Don't matter none to me. Jest thought ya might like to know."

The oyster boat reached the end of the channel confronting three-foot waves beating against the bow.

"We going to be able to do any dredging with it like this?"

"She should calm down a bit by the time we gets to the beds."

A sudden huge wave hit the small boat broadside -- the sea rushing across the deck sweeping Matt overboard.

"Oh, my Gawd," Captain Joe yelled. He quickly turned the boat into the waves and watched as a life preserver mounted on the side of the cabin detached itself and spiraled in Matt's direction. Shocked by what he'd seen, he shortly came to his senses and rushed to help Matt back aboard.

Matt knelt on the deck, coughing up water.

* * *

Kitty sat at her computer, hearing footsteps on the bridge above her head. She rushed to the salon to greet Matt.

Having removed his outerwear above, Matt stood at the foot of the salon steps dripping a large puddle on the floor.

"Is it raining that hard outside? . . . What happened to you?"

CHAPTER XIII

Thursday morning brought rain as well as news Kitty wouldn't be able to get back from her trip until the following Tuesday afternoon. However, barring any changes in schedule, there was a good chance she would be able to stay over until Sunday evening. During their conversation, they discussed at great length the stepped-up occurrences and his numerous visits with the old woman. Other than the apparitions appearing more frequently, the patterns of behavior remained the same.

While standing at the counter fixing breakfast, Matt noticed Jason and Heather bringing supplies aboard their boat. Shouting out of the port hole, he asked if they would care to join him for the impromptu meal. Declining the offer, the two promised getting together later that evening. The phone ringing ended the brief conversation.

"Hello."

"Matt. Pete, here."

"Hey, Pete. How've you been? Long time no see."

"Yeah. Things have kept me jumping. Wondered if you'd like to make a few bucks next week? We've got a back load of small boats needing bottom paint and other repairs."

"Sounds great. Could use the money, for sure."

"How's Saturday morning to start?"

"Aw, man. I'm going to have company through next Sunday, but I could start the following day and go as long as you need me."

"That's fine. No problem. I'll see you then."

"Thanks a million," Matt said, hanging up the phone. Delighted at the opportunity to increase the bank account, getting a break from his current routine was equally welcomed. Maybe the day hadn't started off so bad after all, he thought.

Due to the added influx of recent distractions, the boat showed telltale signs of neglect. As an extreme to his normal behavior, clothes were strewn throughout and dirty dishes piled in the sink. Taking advantage of the miserable weather, and his elated attitude, he delved into the large project of getting things back in shipshape order. Between trips to the Laundromat, squeezing in grocery shopping and spurts of cleaning here and there, he made progressive headway.

Vacuuming adding the final touch, Matt proudly viewed his finished effort. It was early afternoon before taking a break. After fixing a Scotch and water and lighting his pipe, he relaxed in his favorite chair listening to a tape of soft semi-classical music.

The melodic strains floated through the room sedating his consciousness. A vision of clouds swirled in rhythmical movement obscuring faint images captured in its mass. The dissipating vapor began to form the figure of a young girl gliding across the floor in a graceful waltz. The youth's long auburn hair flowed in the breeze as she twirled and spun like a ballerina in an endless motion while humming a haunting tune and emitting a captivating smile across her lovely face.

Her movements slowly altered to seductive gestures luring him to join her in dance. Reluctantly reaching for her extended hand, a loud noise shattered the reverie. Regaining a sense of reasoning, Matt doubted he had been asleep. Was it a daydream, or another apparition? he wondered.

Nevertheless, the racket persisted. Gaining the bridge, the CB was on full blast and static thundered through its speakers. Before being able to turn the switch, the unbearable racket was replaced by the murmurs and whimpers of a girl. Matt turned it off.

Compelled to leave the boat, he got his coat and headed directly for the house, regardless of the downpour. He arrived at the backdoor, finding it locked. "Damn, you," he shouted. "What in the hell do you want from me?" He slammed his fist against the door. The padlock came undone.

Upon entering the back room, the old woman sat in her rocker as times before. She replaced her sewing in the box and walked to the table to rearrange her flowers. "Oh, aren't they so lovely?" she said. He didn't attempt to respond. She turned, holding a single flower against her breast. "You're soaking wet. Let me fix you a cup of tea. And take off your coat, Richard, you'll catch your death in a cold."

Matt's knees nearly buckled under the impact of her words.

"Come. You can warm yourself by the stove while I boil the water." She moved into the kitchen and he followed close behind.

Although stunned by the events, he managed to stable himself to accept what was happening.

The old woman placed a kettle on the wood stove and busied herself straightening one of the shelves. Everything was clean and neatly in place and an array of polished copper pots hung from one of the walls.

"I know you like lemon in your tea. I've always liked mine that way." She retrieved two small cups from a cupboard and poured the steaming liquid.

Gaining courage, Matt asked, "Are you here alone?"

"I really love Jonquils. They're my favorite of all flowers. You know, they are one of the first signs of spring. Oh, how I do love the spring. It's the fall that makes me sad. I really don't like seeing the leaves on the trees wither and die. It really makes me sad."

"Do you like the summer?" he asked, trying to get a direct response.

"I really love Jonquils. They're my favorite of all flowers."

Matt realized she didn't identify with anything he said.

"You haven't touched your tea. Don't you like it?" She suddenly moved to return to the entrance room. Matt saw her disappear in the doorway.

The outer room was again barren and in its current day state. Staggered with confusion, he returned to the now messy kitchen and found a full cup of a steaming dark liquid sitting on the corner of the stove. Based on the aroma, it was unquestionably tea.

Carrying it cautiously back to the boat, he emptied what was left of the contents of the cup into a small jar, noticing a sediment in the bottom, most likely to be tea leaves. Maybe there was some significance to them. Maybe they might be analyzed to determine their origin. In his state of mind, he wasn't sure about anything.

"Damn," he said. "What a time not to be able to get in touch with Kitty." He wanted desperately to talk to her and share the breakthrough; even more, the most recent manifestation of the teacup. Forced to contain his exuberance, he decided to treat himself to dinner at the local restaurant.

"Hey, Matt," he heard Pete's boy, Sonny, call as he entered the bar area.

"Yo. How you doing?"

"All right. Want a beer?"

"Naw. But thanks. I'll take a rain check."

"Dad says you're gonna give a hand next week."

"Yeah. I'm looking forward to it."

"Sure you don't want a beer?"

Matt shook his head in a negative reply. "I stopped in for food. Want to join me?"

"I got my dinner right here." Sonny laughed, hoisting his bottle of Bud.

"Catch you later," Matt said, walking into the restaurant, spotting Jason and Heather sitting at a corner table. "Mind if I join you?"

"If you catch the bill," Jason teased, breaking out in laughter.

"Don't pay any attention to him," Heather said, giving Jason a scolding glare.

"Aw, come on. Matt knows I was only joking."

"No, I don't." Matt goaded Jason further, stifling his chuckle.

"I'll pay the check," Carol said, interrupting the debate.

"Thank God," Heather laughed. "I thought I'd get stuck with it."

Carol giggled. "Want a drink first?"

Jason ordered a Coors, Heather a white wine, and Matt requested coffee.

"Is Kitty coming down?" Heather asked.

"Not until Tuesday. She's in Chicago lecturing."

"So, what have you been up to?" Jason asked.

"Making sure your boat doesn't sink." Matt smiled.

Jason chuckled.

"How's school coming, Heather?"

"Okay. I can't wait to get through this semester."

"I never did ask what your major was."

"Computer sciences and minoring in psychology. It's been a hard."

Carol interrupted her in mid-sentence. "Well, here you are." She sat the drinks in their proper places. "Ready to order?" The three itemized their choices and she spun on her heels heading for the kitchen.

"You were saying," Matt said to Heather.

"It's not easy," she smiled. "But, not to change the subject, let Kitty know I've got all of the material she wanted, if you hear from her first."

"What's that?" Jason asked.

"Nothing really," Matt said. "Just some stuff having to do with one of her side interests."

"Oh. You mean that hocus-pocus stuff," Jason said.

Heather gave Matt a give-it-up look.

"Are you going to haul your boat this spring?" Matt asked Jason.

"Yeah. Got to do the bottom."

"Let me know. I'll give you a hand."

"That'll be great." Jason smiled. "I just hope there aren't any blisters."

"We'll tackle that if we have to."

Carol returned with their dinners. "Matt. Don't get away until I get the chance to talk to you." She immediately retreated.

The meal was good, as usual, and the company superb. Matt had truly come to identify with the young couple as part of his family. Oddly, in recent days, he shared more time with them than he did his own.

Carol arrived with the check. "Sure you don't want anything else?"

"That'll be fine," Jason said, wrestling the check from Matt's grasp.

"I need friends like that." Carol winked and smiled at the same time. "Matt. I just wanted to let you know I thought of something else that might be of some help. I don't have time to go into it now, but stop by tomorrow morning around eleven."

111

"I will," Matt assured.

The bill covered, the threesome left the restaurant and drove back to the marina. "How about a nightcap?" Matt suggested.

Jason looked at Heather. "Sure. Why not?"

Walking toward his boat, Matt paused to stare at the old house. "Heather. Do you see a light on over there?" he asked.

Heather moved to get a better view. "No. I really don't. Except for the lights reflecting from across the way."

Jason confirmed her finding.

"I don't mean to be rude, but I'll only be a few minutes. Go on aboard and fix us some drinks. I'll be right there." Matt left them standing and walked toward the old dwelling. Jason started to follow his suggestion and Heather detained him by the arm. They watched Matt enter the backdoor of the house.

Matt stood inside the outer room as the old woman made an entrance from the kitchen. She moved to her chair and began sewing. "What are you making?" he asked.

She didn't respond to his question and started humming the strange tune. A few moments later she replaced her materials and needles in the box and walked to the table. She turned the knob on the kerosene lamp making it glow brighter. "There, now. That's much better," she said. "It's stopped raining outside. I hope you didn't catch cold."

"I'm fine," Matt answered. "The hot tea helped a lot."

"Yes, it is good for a chill. I'm glad you enjoyed it," she returned.

"My, God." Matt tried to choke back his outcry as soon as it was uttered.

"Are you all right?" she asked.

"Yes."

"I love Jonquils. They're so lovely. You know, they're an early sign of spring. It's the fall I don't like."

Matt interrupted. "Why don't you like the fall?"

"It just makes me sad. The leaves die in the fall. Everything dies in the fall." She began to weep softly, but the sounds were much like a child.

"I didn't mean to upset you," he said tenderly.

The knob on the lamp turned by itself and the room began to darken. Suddenly the old woman was gone and the only available light filtered through the open doorway he thought to have been closed.

He shut the door behind him. Jason and Heather waited at the edge of the backyard.

"If you're going to go inside, I'll get a flashlight from my boat," Jason said.

"I've already . . ." Matt stopped his reply. "Never mind," he said. "Let's go get that drink."

* * *

Still feeling tired, but unable to get back to sleep, Matt got up and stumbled into the head. He splashed cold water in his face, then brushed his teeth and plopped on the commode. He reached into the shower, fingered the faucet knob settling on a moderately warm temperature, shortly standing in the middle of the pummeling force of the water's spray. Matt dried, dressed and, feeling more alert than before, got the old body to full attention with a steaming cup of java and a couple of pieces of light toast.

After getting a notepad from a cabinet drawer and searching for something with which to write, he settled into a seat at the table. He began with a food list for later shopping, then paused to sip from his cup and ponder about whatever it might be he had forgot to include. As he toyed with the pencil, a force began to take control of his hand moving it across the paper in a writing motion. Unwillingly, words formed neither generated in his brain or penned in his own handwriting.

Matt couldn't focus on their meaning nor cease the action. Although his mind seemed functional, for moments he became unable to concentrate or rationalize. The writing ceased. He sat quietly for a moment, feeling a tingling sensation of something passing through or leaving his body. He looked down at the pad and read its barely intelligible scribbling: 'Richard. I love you.'

Surprised at having remained so calm, he pushed the note aside and moved to the sink. Washing his hands seemed to rid himself of having been violated -- the spiritual intrusions always leaving an eerie feeling of uncleanliness. The phone rang as he dried himself with paper towels.

"Hello."

"Hi, hon." Kitty sounded cheerful.

"Damn, I'm glad you called. You're not going to believe

113

what's been happening."

Matt reiterated his visits with the old lady and everything else recently happening. Kitty was amazed in learning about the manifestation of the cup of tea; however, most impressive was the conversations between Matt and the spirit. Before hanging up, she asked Matt to give the jar of tea to Heather without explaining why.

The conversation ended -- the phone rang again.

"Yeah."

Ozzie responded, "Mornin'."

"Hey. What's happening?"

"Just wanted to make sure you were gonna be around. I got a new boat and thought I'd put it in this afternoon and wondered if you could give me a hand."

"Sure. No problem."

"Should be down around noon. Lunch is on me."

"Sounds fine. Got no other plans for the day. Meet you at the Harbor."

"See ya, then." Ozzie hung up.

Before replacing the receiver, Matt dialed his daughter's number getting a busy signal. Smiling, his thoughts compared Ellen to her mother and their addiction to telephone gab. He fixed another cup of coffee, then went on deck for a breath of fresh air. A slight mist lingered in the rapidly clearing sky as he stood under the cover of the bridge -- the aroma of budding wildlife stimulating his senses.

It was almost impossible to believe the official season opening lay only a few weeks away. As every year, with the warming of spring, bay side towns all over the Chesapeake stirred from virtual hibernation in preparation for the oncoming summer.

A frenzy ensued as winter storage yards quickly emptied and marina slips began to fill. Arriving from every direction, trailers hauling practically every type of craft imaginable invaded the sea shore. Inland waterways churned with activity -- sanders hummed, saws buzzed, and paint brushes flew, while boat dealer's hearts pumped with anticipation, and boat shoppers shopped.

He was no different. Boating fever and the love of the sea clearly encompassed his existence.

Matt felt a sudden chill and instinctively looked in the direction of the old house, glimpsing what he thought to be a young girl walking inside the back door. Startled at the observation, he left the boat and proceeded directly to the eerie property. The door rested slightly ajar and he immediately entered. The old woman sat in the rocker and hummed her usual lilt. Matt spoke to her, but there was no response. She rose and went through the door leading to the stairs.

Matt stood silently watching her disappear into the steps. At that instant, at the top of the staircase, a young and very lovely girl took shape and drifted down the staircase, past him, and into the room. He recognized her as the girl in his dream. There was no sign to indicate she was aware of his presence and she began to glide around the room as if waltzing to a silent tune.

He watched from near the outer doorway and did not speak. However, as her dancing movement passed closely in front of him, he dared to reach out and attempt to grasp her arm. Suddenly, his body went icily cold as the apparition passed though his hand and temporarily fused with his inner being. He gasped in fear with the shock of the experience and stared into space as the vision disappeared and the room returned to its normal state. His hand and forearm ashen in color.

Still stunned, it was moments before he was able to stir and eventually stagger from the house. Lying on the doorstep was a freshly cut Jonquil. Matt stooped to pick it up. Immediately, the ashen discoloration disappeared.

At the boat he placed it in a tall glass of water. He desperately needed to shower.

CHAPTER XIV

Before heading for the Harbor to meet Ozzie, Matt dropped off the jar of tea to Heather. He decided to walk to the restaurant and still arrived before his friend.

"You look like you've seen a ghost," Carol said as she laughed and placed a menu near his elbow. "I don't know why I do that. You've got to know it by heart."

Matt gave a combination of a shrug and a nod, and said, "You've got that right," his response hiding its double meaning.

"By the way," Carol said. "About last night, I just learned one of the older neighbors of the Colison family is still alive. If anybody around here other than my mother being of some help, she would most likely be it."

"That's good." He greeted the news with half-hearted enthusiasm.

"You sure you're okay? Carol noticed an uneasiness, brushed it off, and then continued. "I found out she's in a nursing home over in Edgewater. My daughter does charitable work there and talks about her a good bit. It took a good while before I put it together, but the woman's name is Dorothy Hands."

Matt got the rest of the details just as Ozzie arrived.

"Hey, pardner. How ya doing? Hello, Carol," he said in the same breath.

"Hi, Ozzie. Need a menu?"

"Naw. Anything good on the specials?" he asked.

Carol ran through a short list and scurried into the kitchen.

"Meatloaf sounds great to me. What do you think?"

Matt wasn't in the mood for food, but agreed. "You brought the boat down?" he stupidly asked, fumbling for conversation.

Ozzie looked at Matt slightly concerned. "Yeah. I rented a

slip at your marina."

Matt squirmed in his chair.

"Something's bothering you. You don't look so good," Ozzie said.

"I'm all right. Rough night. Been flirting with a cold."

Ozzie accepted Matt's response and motioned Carol to the table, gave the order for both of them, and suggested they check the boat out while waiting for the food.

As they walked across the street to the parking lot, Matt espied the craft -- a twenty-five-foot Classic, featuring a center console allowing scads of room to move about. A large 150 hp Mercury outboard hung attached to its stern.

"That's a helluva outfit," Matt said, as he neared the trailer and boat hooked to the back of Ozzie's pick-up. "That thing's perfect for fishing."

"She still needs some stuff installed," Ozzie meekly stated. "I was wondering if you'd mind giving me a hand. I bought a CB, ship-to-shore, horn and a depth-finder."

Giving a hand meant doing it for him. Ozzie meant well, but was all thumbs when it came to things of an electronic nature. Matt wasn't in the frame of mind to be tinkering with his gadgets and suggested he'd do it in the next few days.

It was nearly three o'clock by the time lunch was over and the boat put into the water. Ozzie's boat being at Matt's marina meant working on it wouldn't be that inconvenient. Before leaving, he gave Matt an extra key with the offer he could use the boat whenever he desired.

Matt felt unusually exhausted. He found welcome refuge on his boat by visiting the Advil bottle and resting in his recliner. His earlier physical confrontation with the younger spirit had been more unsettling than he had allowed himself to accept. *God,* he thought. *Why in the hell me? I've never done anything to deserve what's happening.* He suddenly sensed being uncontrollably drawn away from his thoughts as his mind became increasingly confused and incapable of rationalization. Although struggling to fight the urge, he succumbed to an overcoming unconsciousness that was far from being an escape.

The black void of sleep began to be interrupted with brief flashes of a slowly growing brilliance and intensity. As dark was the dark, the light became almost unbearable to visually confront. He was compelled to stare into it, unable to resist. About the moment Matt felt like screaming, the blinding illusion softened. From its center evolved a swirling shape blending itself into that of a young girl. It was Sarah. She spun across the huge floor with the grace of a beautiful swan skimming the water. Clad in a long flower print dress buttoned to her neck, a lengthy shroud of fine net draped from her shoulders and waist flowed in harmony with her movement. A haunting melody emanated from nowhere complimenting her motion, but somehow strangely discordant at the same time. Matt found himself seated in a simple wooden chair, totally immobilized by an unseen force. There was fear, but not fright -- calm, but not peace.

Sarah danced closer until she glided in a circle surrounding his position. Arriving in front of him, she paused and looked directly into his eyes while producing a pleased smile from between strands of hair streaming down the sides of her face. Leaning forward she touched his hand. The shivering chill he had earlier experienced surged through his arm with a burning force. At the same instant he felt her lips brush his cheeks with an unexpected warmth stimulating even more discomfort.

An ungodly noise rushed Matt to consciousness. It was moments before he realized the sound had been his own distressful cry. Cold perspiration beaded over his entire body. He ached as if suffering from the burning sensation of frostbite.

Matt scanned the boat's salon, realizing it was dark outside and had no idea how long he had slept. The message light flashing on his answering machine denoted several calls received during his hallucinatory absence. Not once had he heard the phone ring. Shaking his head from side-to-side did little to clear it and only exaggerated the ache pounding within.

Matt finally raised himself forward to sit on the edge of the reclining chair, placing his elbows on his knees, his head cupped in his hands. Following the long pause, he looked across at the microwave squinting his eyes to read the time. It was close to ten o'clock. He had been asleep for over six hours.

Matt's clothes were saturated with sweat. The dampness heightened the inner chill and he stumbled on weakened legs to the head. Undressing as quickly as possible he spun the faucets and bore the waters force pounding his body from top to bottom. He lathered himself with soap over and over again, but couldn't seem to rid himself of the uncleanliness he felt.

It suddenly occurred to him the event was repeating itself. It was the identical sensations he had first experienced after waking from the dream in the Pennsylvania motel. Matt stayed in the shower so long he spent all of the available hot water and began to shudder from the cold.

Stepping from the shower's basin, he quickly toweled his upper body and donned a terry cloth robe. After drying his lower extremities, Matt used the towel to wipe the head's wall mirror clear of the clinging heavy moisture while opening the door to dissipate the lingering steamy air.

He popped the top from a bottle of Advil, gathered four capsules in his palm and tossed them into his mouth, chasing it with a large gulp of water from the sink's tap.

Standing upright, while reaching for a hair brush, he gazed at his reflection. A portion of his left cheek appeared ashen, and then he noticed his left hand. It, too, was pale and absent of the pinkish tone shared over the rest of his body. He pulled up the robes sleeve. The void of coloration extended to his shoulder from the tips of his fingers.

A ringing sound interrupted his stupor. The answering machine picked up before he could get to the device and he heard Kitty's voice beginning an imploring message.

He answered the phone. "God, I'm glad it's you."

"Matt. I've been worried sick. What's wrong?"

He avoided the recliner and slumped on the couch with an exasperated sigh. "God, Kitty. I don't believe what's happening. I feel like I've been through hell."

Kitty's voice trembled. "I've tried to reach you since late afternoon. I left three other messages on your machine."

Matt calmed her immediate concern and started relating the events of the day in as much detail as possible.

Kitty, as usual, waited patiently to comment, well aware of his agony and current instability of thought and reason. "God, what you've been through," she began. "It's hard to find the right words. But, I did warn you about deeper involvements becoming more intense. You've got to build a stronger will . . . not against

120

the power, but to cope with it, and the unexpected."

"What in the hell could I have done?" Matt blurted in response. "The damn thing took total control of me."

Kitty displayed no offense at his slight show of anger. "Nothing under the circumstances," she replied. "But, you'll learn to gain control as time passes."

"Damn," he said. "I just want it to be over." Matt's mood was rapidly changing and he became aware of it. "I'm sorry, Doc. I'm taking it out on you. Please, I'm sor . . ."

"Remember what Celeste said, "never say you're sorry." Kitty paused briefly. "And there's nothing to forgive. You've been through a terrible ordeal."

Matt chuckled, remembering the fact she was a psychologist. He was regaining perspective, and she was much of the reason for it. "That's right. You're the Doc."

"It's good to see you still have a sense of humor," she said.

Matt could actually see her smiling in his mind.

"Oh, babe," she continued. "I wish I could be there to hold you."

"Me, too, to you, too, Doc."

The phone conversation lasted for over an hour. After some heavy goodbyes, Matt fixed another drink, equally strong as the first. He paced back and forth, then reached for the remote and switched on the TV. It spurted to life right in the middle of Freddie Kruger doing one of his things. Matt reeled in disgust and switched the channel. A more serene wrestling match popped into view.

He sat down on the couch and crossed his legs. It was then he noticed the Jonquil found earlier. The flower had wilted in the vase.

Matt was mad. He was getting more irate by the minute. "Son of a bitch," he blurted. "I've had about enough of this shit."

Without further delay he began dressing, shortly finishing the chore by tying his shoes. He left the boat in haste, pulling on his jacket, not hesitating to rush directly for the house even though he had promised Kitty he would evade contact for a while. The fact the house was dark made little difference. Arriving at the back door, he immediately entered.

The room danced alive with light emanating from a pair of

candles and the kerosene lamp. The old lady rocked slowly in her chair, resting quietly with her hands folded in her lap.

"Where's the young girl?" Matt demanded. "What do you want? What are you trying to do with me?"

The elderly spirit offered no reply or even recognition of his presence.

"Talk to me," he shouted, and then immediately mellowed his tone. "Please, talk to me."

The old lady's eyes opened as tears streamed down her face. She began to slowly disappear as did the light inside. Matt felt a surge of cold air rush through the back door as it flew open. He stepped outside.

CHAPTER XV

Matt did 'almost' keep his promise. Other than Friday night's late visit to Sarah's house following the phone call with Kitty, he avoided further contact. Even though a lot of activity in the garden took place -- the old lady working her butt off -- he ignored the presence and went about other matters.

By later afternoon, spiritual activities were all but nonexistent and a developing misty rain confined him to the TV watching a professional golf tournament. He ended the evening having a late phone conversation with Kitty, followed by a good and uninterrupted night's sleep.

Having experienced a peaceful weekend, he awoke Monday morning feeling rejuvenated.

While swabbing down the aft deck he noticed Kitty's car pull into the marina. Upon meeting her in the parking lot, it led to an overwhelming embrace before she had time to shut the lid to her trunk. Hand-in-hand they headed to the boat -- he carrying a valise and she her attaché case.

"Time's really unfair," Kitty said. "It seems to pass slower and slower every time we're apart."

"I know," Matt replied, as he squeezed her hand, then released it and headed to the aft cabin placing her bag on the bed. "By comparison, the few hours we spend together go too damn fast."

Kitty moved to put her arms around his waist. Matt responded. They remained for quite sometime without a single word -- the only communication: the surge of inner-warmth and love passing from one to the other through their physical contact. Finally, Kitty eased away lightly touching her lips to his and slipped off her coat.

"Something to drink?" Matt asked.

"You know, I think I'd like some hot tea."

Matt agreed with a nod and reached for a small canister on a shelf and spun off the top.

"You sit down," she said, as if a demand. "I'll fix it."

She filled a small pot half-full of water and placed it on a range burner, turning the knob to high. Without inquiring, she retrieved his cup, rinsed it clean, and poured him a fresh cup of coffee.

"Thanks," Matt said, taking the steaming liquid from her and carefully touching it to his lips so as not to burn them. "You could spoil me real easily." He laughed. "I could adapt pretty quick."

"Don't let it go to your head," Kitty said, joking in return, with an impish smile. "I get breakfast in bed as compensation. Pay backs are hell, aren't they?"

"Uh, . . . you are staying tonight, aren't you?"
"Better than that. How about two nights. Think you can put up with me?"

"Oh, God, Doc. Can I? You bet your pretty buns I can." He reached up and grabbed her arm pulling her to his lap. She landed with a thud and a big giggle, and then kissed the tip of his nose before bouncing back up to her feet. "Where you going so fast?" he asked with a pout.

"Water's boiling."

Matt enjoyed opportunities to simply sit and gaze at her. She stood against the sink counter dunking a tea bag up and down, clad in designer jeans accentuating the trim of her legs. A loose fitting double-knit pale blue sweater exposed the lower half of her tight buttocks. Wearing her hair bunched in the back of her head, gathered by a ribbon comb on each side, added a softness to her lovely neck.

Dressed as she was, or clad in a business suit, she could easily pass as a model. Too slim for many men, she was perfect to Matt.

Kitty noticed his stare. "A penny for your thoughts."

"I was just marveling at your body and how you turn me on." He projected a broad smile.

"Well, now," she retorted as she carried her tea to sit beside him. "I'd say that's at least worth a dollar." She laughed.

He leaned and gave her a light bite on her neck. "It's a good thing I'm not a vampire."

"Sometimes I wish you were." Kitty moved closer, laying her head on his shoulder as he placed his arm around her. "I've never been so worried as I was the other night," she whispered, rubbing her left hand along the inside of his leg.

Matt gently squeezed his arm around her.

"I had to take a couple of days off to be with you." She nuzzled her head closer against his neck.

"I'm really glad you're here," he whispered. "You do realize I had to spend St. Patrick's Day all by myself, don't you? I didn't want to be alone to face all those weird things that supposedly happen."

Kitty snickered. "That's Halloween, silly."

"Oh. My mistake." He chuckled. "Anyway, I always feel better when you're around."

Raising her head, she kissed him on the cheek and got up. "I'm a little hungry, how about you?"

"Famished. What do you feel like? Breakfast or lunch?"

"I really don't care," Kitty answered. "Why don't you let me take you out to eat? Treat's on me."

"Hummmm." Matt expressed favored interest. "Maybe I'll have lobster."

"Don't you wish?" Kitty threw a wet dish towel at him. "Hey. Where did you get that pretty flower? Is it for me?"

Matt moaned. "Aw, geeze. Not again. I forgot to tell you about it."

The jonquil stood tall in the glass, rejuvenated back to full blooming life -- Matt having intended to save it in its wilted state.

"You're not going to believe this." He shook his head. "Or, more likely, you will. I found the flower on the doorstep as I left the house the other morning. It looked like it had just been cut."

Matt got up and moved to the counter. Taking a short glass from the dish tray, he filled it half-full with brandy and offered Kitty a sip.

She refused.

"I brought it back and put it in the glass." He swallowed a large quantity of the drink and wiped his lips with the back of his hand. "After the dream episode with the young girl, that evening it had died. It was hanging over the edge of the glass all wilted and discolored."

"God. And now its back to life."

Kitty took the jonquil's stem between her fingers. No sooner had she grasped it and uttered the statement, the flower quickly withered in her hand. As if stung by a bee, she dropped it at her feet. They both stood in a stupor staring at the crumpled object on the floor.

"Maybe we better stay here and talk," Matt mumbled as he bent down and gathered pieces of the flower into his palm.

Kitty retrieved an envelope from a drawer.

Matt dumped what remained inside and sealed the flap shut, placing the packet among the other items of evidence.

"I agree," Kitty confirmed. "We do have to talk." She reached and squeezed his hand.

Matt began putting the dishes away after their simple repast, more out of nervous reaction than necessity. "There's something I really don't understand," he said, breaking the silence. "I'm being confronted by the mother and the daughter, both. How's that possible?"

"That's a good one," Kitty said. "Look's like they're teaming up on you." She laughed, as if hoping to ease Matt's nerves.

Matt didn't seem to appreciate her humor.

"I'm sorry, hon. I know it's really serious, but, again, you've got to try and ease up. Fight it."

"Yeah, you're right." Matt dried his hands. "Well, what I think is, there isn't two of them. I've got the feeling both are the same person, spirit, whatever you want to call them. I really don't know why. It's mostly a feeling, except for the time the old lady disappeared into the stairs and the young Sarah appeared. At least to me, it makes sense. I've never seen them actually together at the same time."

"You could very well be right. It seems to be the first event combining the two spiritual images near, but not at the same time." Kitty sounded excited. "If that's the case, I would think it's more likely Sarah is assuming the role of the mother, more than the mother assuming the role of the child. That's remarkable. You're remarkable." Kitty rushed to him and gave

126

him a big hug and kiss.

"How about a trip to the aft cabin?" Matt groaned his passion.

"Nope. Not now. Later." She pulled from his grasp. "Come on. We've got to get down to serious business."

"But, that is serious business," he said, faking a plea.

Kitty laughed. "Oh, shut up and sit down." Kitty got her case and sat it on the table. Opening it, she removed material and then placed it on the floor next to where she sat. "I thought we'd wait and get into this tomorrow, but maybe it's better not to put it off any longer. I've collected a good deal of information. Let's get that out of the way before diving into more recent events."

Matt's silence confirmed agreement. He had put together a plate of various cheeses and crackers and placed them on the table, shoving them to the far end out of the way. On following trips he brought two glasses, a bottle of chilled ginger ale, and two store-bought premixed dips. Matt sat down across from Kitty. "All right, Doc. Let 'er rip."

"Well, I really don't have anything earth shattering, but every little bit helps. While I was away, I pulled in a favor due and had the agricultural research department at the University of Maryland do some analysis for us. The tea leaves from the cup were identified as being a domestic blend. The longer leaf and tiny fibers found from its container indicate it was the loose variety and not from a tea bag."

"Were they able to read them?" Matt made a bad joke.

Kitty smiled. "That's not too far from getting a positive answer. It's amazing what modern technology can do. More telltale was the water used to make it. The chemical make-up of the water found in the tea leaves indicated it came from a well not meeting current health standards. It was very heavy on sulphur and contained a high-bacterial content conducive to conditions existing years ago. There was also minute evidence of lead particles that would have come from a very old plumbing system."

"Wouldn't that have made them ill?" Matt asked argumentatively.

"Yes and no. Life threatening, . . . doubtful. Dysentery and minor ails, . . . possibly. More than likely their bodies adjusted to

127

it to a degree and their largest use of the water probably came after boiling or in cooking." Kitty paused to test the impromptu hors d'oeuvres. "Ummmmm, they're good," she said. "Thanks, honey." She tried a second and sipped her drink.

"Where's that leave us?" Matt asked, joining her in the snacks.

"So far, not very far. We're just beginning. Jeff . . . I'm sorry, my friend at the university's lab, suggested we take a sample from the house so he can make a comparison. "And, I've already sent copies of the report to several tea manufacturers for verification. If we can definitely connect the water to the house and pinpoint the period the tea leaves were produced, it would positively help corroborate paranormal intervention."

Matt was confused. "We know it came from the house. It wasn't there and then it was. I saw her make the tea."

"I know, hon. But, that's not good enough. If a second sample should show a difference it could enforce our position. In other words, it would be a step showing the water used came from the past. We don't even know if the water system is still working. You haven't tried it, have you?"

"Now that you mention it, no."

Kitty fought to choose her words. "Please don't misunderstand. Your involvement and welfare in the middle of all this is my greatest concern. But, babe, it's an awfully lot bigger than just us. Whatever's been happening is so unique, it stretches even paranormal logic. There's little, if any, documented proof of psychic phenomena as complex or as extensive as in this case. God, you've had audio, visual, and direct oral contact with a spiritual being." Kitty sipped from her glass to quench the dryness building in her throat. "Not to mention the objects that have appeared," she said. It's terribly important for us to record what's occurring. We need proof to firmly establish all of the factors that are most surely setting precedents in the psychic world. The more we can positively ascertain and confirm, the greater the impact there will be in parapsychology."

"I forget sometimes it's your business," Matt said in a sullen tone without thinking.

"It's not my business, Matt. I'm only a psychologist. It's

only an interest."

He clearly noticed an immediate hurt in Kitty's face. "Doc, I didn't mean that like it sounded. It's just all of this is getting to me. Maybe I'm selfish, but all I can think about is me, right now. I'm sor . . ." He caught himself in the middle of the apology. "Damn it. I am sorry. So friggin' sorry I could cut my tongue out."

"Still hung up over what Celeste said?" Kitty smiled. "I do understand, though. But, we need all of the help we can get if you're going to face this thing. Believe me. Physics are a heckuva lot more skeptical most of the time than your typical doubters and disbelievers. In our situation, proof will buy a lot more assistance than money. Jung, Freud, there's been numerous creditable giants in psychology that have sought to tie the knot with parapsychology and theosophical beliefs. To those who do believe, they go hand in hand . . . one not without the other."

"What I said just showed my ignorance, Doc. I'm so far in over my head I have difficulty telling it from my ass most of the time."

Kitty laughed as Matt produced a sheepish grin.

"They're not going to come in here, set up tents, and sell tickets, are they?"

She laughed even harder. "You're a nut, sometimes," she said, as the laughing subsided. "But, I love you." She was suddenly aware of what she had said.

Matt showed no reaction other than to gaze deeply into her eyes. "I love you, too," he responded softly as he leaned across the table. Cupping her face in his hands, their mouths met in a long and gentle embrace.

As they ended their contact, Kitty sat back in her chair -- a tear noticeably in the corner of her eye.

"I love you very much," he repeated.

Kitty smiled as the tear began to move down her cheek.

Matt reached and caught it with his fingers, then touched it to his lips.

"I never knew I could feel like this." Kitty started to tear again. "It's wonderful." She laughed and choked at the same time and reached for her empty glass.

Matt gave her his. "You're so beautiful," he said. "Not just physically, but all the way through. It's no wonder you mean so much to me."

Kitty sniffed as she dried her eyes with a napkin. "You're not so bad yourself, you know. It's really hard not to be with you all of the time. You're constantly on my mind. It's a miracle I get anything done at all."

"You can move in anytime you want," he said with a smile. "Lock, stock, and barrel."

"Better be careful. You might be biting off more than you can chew." She laughed. "I've really thought about being here over spring-break and spending the summer after the semester. I've already told them not to count on me for any summer sessions."

Matt's smile beamed from ear-to-ear. "God, you have no idea how happy that makes me. I was going to ask you if you would, but couldn't get up the nerve. Even had dreams of us boating off somewhere together."

"I'm sure a deserted isle away from all this would be a great escape." Kitty got up and moved around the table to sit in his lap. She placed her arms around his neck and their embrace held more meaning than ever. Their lips parted and she kissed his forehead. "Enough of that," she said, rising to return to her seat. "We've got more work to do."

"Awwww. Are you going to leave me hanging in my present state?"

"I don't know what you mean," she said, in a teasing manner. "Take a cold shower. We can converse through the curtain." She laughed devilishly. "That makes us even for that earlier cruel remark."

"That's not fair," he said, laughing back and making a fake lunge for her. She leaned backward in her seat.

The levity over, Kitty's professional side again surfaced. "Seriously, hon. It's pretty evident the spirit has no intention of letting you go. Don't think I haven't thought of suggesting getting out of this area, and maybe move in with me, but it seems to follow you no matter where you are. The New York incident . . . a perfect example of its connection to you and its power." Kitty stopped to pour more soda.

Matt held his hand over his glass.

"That's not to say a more permanent move might not cause the spirit to eventually lose interest. Then again, it could even heighten its determination. I really think . . ."

"There's something I haven't told you," Matt interrupted. "I didn't make the connection until after Friday afternoon." Matt toyed with the rim of his empty glass. "I had a similar episode to the other day's dream while I was in Lancaster. I dozed off in the middle of a movie and around midnight woke up in a chilling cold sweat. The room was temperate and comfortable without covers. At the time, I thought I was catching something, and had an insatiable need to bathe myself again and again. I couldn't get rid of the appalling feeling. It was as if sin was oozing from my pores. I don't remember what happened in my sleep that night, but the reaction after the last one was identical. Could I have dreamed the same dream both times and not remembered the first?"

Kitty didn't respond for several moments. It was evident she was impacted by the disclosure and weighing his story in her mind. "Maybe. I think so. I can't be sure. I really need some time to digest it. . . . Well, whatever. But, we still don't know positively for sure if we have two spirits to deal with instead of one."

Matt realized Kitty was struggling in attempting to analyze the situation. "Why don't we get out of here for a while? Let's go for a ride," he suggested. "We'll drive down to Chesapeake Beach."

"I'd like that."

CHAPTER XVI

Little conversation occurred during the short jaunt to their destination. Kitty peered out of the window taking in the passing scenery. Occasionally she would make a comment or ask a question about the area -- other than that, nothing mentioned regarding current spiritual matters.

Kitty was amazed at learning the domicile area observed once teemed with weekend vacationers and nightly entertainment as Matt related the history of Uncle Billy's pier and the onshore/offshore slot machine gambling. The few buildings still standing evidenced its dying past, boasting boarded windows and padlocked doors. Nothing remained of the jutting pier nor anything left indicating it ever existed.

"It's kind of sad," Kitty said. "I can almost sense the lively activity that must have abounded at one time."

Matt smiled. "My parents brought me here a lot when I was a kid. Used to be a small amusement park over there." He pointed across the street. "And an indoor skating rink next to it."

"Did you like to skate?"

"I loved it."

Kitty's eyes lit up. "That's wonderful. We'll have to do it sometime soon. It was one of my favorite things when I was young."

"You bet we will," Matt said, but his tone began to sullen. "It does bring back some sad memories." He paused for several moments.

Kitty sat quietly waiting for him to continue.

"When I was in my teens, I had a best buddy. Our birthdays were only two days apart, he being the eldest. Did virtually everything together. Playing every sport imaginable to vying over the same girls, trying to outdo one another for attention. It was a game we played," Matt innocently added. "Came here practically every weekend during the summer season and got stupid drunk on just a few beers like crazy kids do. Paul went out on the end of Uncle Billy's pier and dove into the water trying to show-off. Even at high tide the water's barely more than three feet deep. He snapped his neck and been a paraplegic ever since."

Kitty moaned. "Oh, God. That's horrible. What a terrible tragedy. She moved to put her arms around his neck and kiss his cheek. "We shouldn't have come here."

"It's all right. I resigned myself to the fact it was an act of fate. Paul was always the daredevil type. Sooner or later something was bound to happen. He constantly lived on the edge. Haven't seen him in years. It's something I should really do, but lost track of where he is. His mother remarried a couple of times. I don't have any idea of what name she's using. Maybe . . ." He didn't attempt to finish the sentence.

Kitty rested her head on his shoulder for several moments before Matt responded.

He kissed the top of her head and raised her chin to make brief lip contact. "I love you with all of my heart," he whispered.

* * *

Weather in the mid-Atlantic region could change in the blink of an eye. As unseasonably warm as recent days were, Mother Nature struck a devastating blow to the area. She was well on her way in delivering fourteen inches of unexpected white precipitation east of the Blue Ridge Mountains -- a great deal of the accumulation occurring overnight.

Matt stood on the bridge in the early morning straining to see through the plastic windows of the canvas cover trying to determine the extent of the coverage outside. There was no way Kitty would be able to get into work and he inwardly applauded the fact.

Discontent with his ability to view the surrounding area, he unzipped the entrance and snow tumbled inside. It was nice something was happening in his favor for a change.

The grey sky continued to spew huge flakes adding to the depth already accumulated on the ground and all in its path.

Never being a skier, or attracted to the sport, he had always detested the inconveniences snow created. For some reason, now, it didn't seem to matter. He stood with his head protruding through the opening marveling at the beauty of tree limbs being transformed into patterns of lacelike magnificence.

Matt closed the canvas cover and returned to the salon. After checking on Kitty, he decided to work a while on his dollhouse rather than disturb her. After spending about an hour on his efforts, he checked on her again before returning to the deck, deciding to clear some of the snow.

"Hi, honey." Kitty sleepily yawned, walking up the steps to join him on the bridge. She stood clad in Matt's bathrobe. "What'cha doing?" She noticed the snow nearly covering his feet. "Oh, my lord. Did it snow?"

Matt stood just outside of the opened tent cover. "A little bit." He laughed and turned to face her. "Come here, Doc. You're not going to believe this."

She moved to a position next to him as he met her, placing his arm around her waist. Kitty peered through the opening and gasped with delight. "It's gorgeous," she said, expressing much elation at what she beheld. "Oh, look at the trees. Aren't they wonderful?" She placed her left arm around Matt and gave a big squeeze. "Let's make a snowman later. Can we find somewhere to go sleigh riding?"

Matt was stirred by her enthusiasm. "You bet," he said, laughing with the response. "I'm not sure what we can do about sledding without a sled, or hills for that matter."

"I didn't say sledding, I said sleigh riding. There's a big difference, you know." She poked him in the ribs with her finger emphasizing the point.

"Ouch." He reacted as if deeply impaled. "Where in the world are we going to find a sleigh around here?"

"I trust you. If anyone can do it, you can." She smiled devilishly.

Matt simply shrugged his shoulders and shook his head in disbelief as he spun her around to go below. "You don't seem too concerned about not being able to get into work," he said, as they reached the salon area.

"Nope." Kitty went directly to the refrigerator and began

selecting things for breakfast. "Bacon or sausage?" she asked.

"Whatever."

She shook her head and grinned. Determined not to get into one of their typical bantering sessions, she fixed some of both. "Classes will be canceled, anyway. The way it looks now, the same could be true for tomorrow."

Matt approached the counter and poured two fresh cups of coffee. Doctoring them both the way they should be, he took his cup and sat back in the recliner. He turned the TV on with the remote and fingered the buttons until reaching the a local network channel where the morning news appeared on-screen. The weather, as expected, dominated the programming as listings of school and special event closures scrolled from top to bottom. "You were right. All classes canceled at GMU."

"Told you so. Are you sure you can put up with me for another day or two?"

"Well, now that you mention it." He laughed. "You've got to be kidding. If I had my way I'd lock you in the aft cabin, tie you to the bed with your legs spread apart, and never let you leave."

"Hummmm. That might not be such a bad idea." She took a sip of coffee and returned to dicing fresh potatoes for hash browns.

"Glad you like the idea. So, what do you say?"

"You realize, you'd have to bring me breakfast, lunch, and dinner in bed," she countered.

"I knew there was a catch in it," he said, laughing. "Anyway, I'm tickled to death you're stuck here."

Kitty continued busily preparing the meal. Matt's offer to assist, flatly denied. He ran through several of the channels, all having reports similar to each other. He pressed the power button to its off position.

"While you're doing that, I'm going to try and get rid of some of the snow in case we have to leave the boat."

Kitty nodded her head in agreement.

Matt donned a heavy coat and skull cap and grabbed a broom from a closet before heading to the bridge. The snow had accumulated to such a degree, the broom was an ineffective tool until he was able to use his feet to remove much of its depth. Pushing large chunks over the side and into the water took a great deal of effort. Finally, he reached a level where the broom became useful and swept the aft deck clear.

Warmth from inside the boat kept the snow from sticking to the surface allowing easier removal. However, attempts at clearing the dock was another matter. Cold winds gushing under the piers had created a thick impenetrable frozen layer beneath the new fallen snow.

Matt paused from his backbreaking task, standing upright and rubbing his brow with the back of his hand. No one could be seen in any direction. The old house appeared somehow even more eerie under its blanket of white. What tale did it hold? he pondered. Whatever it was, there was one thing for sure. Each time he went inside he sensed pain and anguish being present -- more so whenever the spirit manifested itself.

A sudden thought entered his mind. He reeled and boarded the boat. Stopping long enough to re-fasten the cover, Matt's attention was drawn to the property. His mouth agape, he stood gazing in disbelief. As large flakes continued to fall, the house was barren of snow and sat within an oasis of early spring. The back door opened and Sarah appeared, moving to the side of the house to tend to the garden.

Matt quickly turned and called for Kitty. "Doc. Come here. Quick." When he spun around to again observe the house, it had returned to the way it should be -- covered with snow.

"Yeah, what's up," Kitty said as she started up the stairs.

"Forget it, Doc. It's all gone." Matt moved to the steps as Kitty retreated back to the salon.

"What's all gone?"

"Another apparition," he said, fumbling in removing his coat. "Just as I was coming back aboard, the old house reverted into a world of its own. It, and everything near it, appeared as if it were springtime. The spirit did her usual garden bit . . . and when I called you and looked again, it was gone." Matt rubbed his hands over the heater gingerly as he continued. "I had a thought outside and was coming in to tell you about it and I forgot what in the hell it was. Anyway, this time the spirit at the garden wasn't the old lady, it was Sarah."

"Oh, my God. That's even more of an indication they're probably one and the same," she said. Kitty had everything prepared and sat the meal on the table. "I think I'll call Celeste after we eat." They both sat down across from each other and began filling their plates. "Don't feel bad about my not getting there in time. I seriously doubt the manifestation could be seen by anyone other than you."

Matt took a bite of his potatoes. "Uummm. These are great. What did you do to them?"

"I sautéed the onions and peppers in a bit of vinegar and lemon juice. Glad you like them."

He returned to the original subject. "I'm curious about something. Do you think if someone like Celeste had been here they might have seen what I did?"

"I guess it's possible. I'll ask Celeste's opinion when I talk to her. Now, eat."

Finished with the meal, Matt did the cleanup. Kitty made her call. He could only hear the one side of the conversation, but able to determine she was getting a great deal of information in response to her questions. Having completed his chores, and Kitty still on the phone, Matt went to the aft cabin to make the bed.

"I would have done that," Kitty said, as he smoothed out the last wrinkle.

"No problem. "What did she have to say?"

"Quite a bit, as you can probably guess. She loves to talk. Come on up and I'll give you the details." They returned to the salon posthaste. "All right. Now, where to start?" she asked as they sat down.

"How about the apparitions?" Matt suggested.

"Good idea." Kitty got up and went to the galley to fix two coffees. "Celeste feels a medium could possibly be cognizant of what you've observed, but there's no guarantee. More than likely, they would be able to make contact in some form or another. Whether they could actually be tuned into a manifestation appearing to you is questionable at best. Personally, based on all of the events that have occurred, I doubt anyone would be able to coordinately experience the phenomena. Simply from circumstances and what I've observed I'm convinced they're intended only for you."

Kitty returned with the coffee and handed Matt his cup. She

sat down beside him and continued. "On the other matter of the old woman and girl being the same spirit, Celeste feels it's more than likely as she's said in the past. She said a spirit has the ability to alter its form to fit its purpose. This lends support to the concept the spirit of the youthful dead could imitate the aging process, or appear in the form of someone he or she loved. The same process is reversibly true for the older spirit."

"We keep getting a lot of possibilities, but no sure conclusions." Matt tried miserably to hide his frustration.

Kitty easily sensed his dismay. "I know it's hard to accept, but if you stop to think about the time that's passed since the beginning of physical manifestation, it really hasn't been very long." She got up to get her cigarettes. "I realize the point is little consolation, but it's really important. Time means nothing in the next plane. At least, it's not determined on a basis like ours. The spirit seems to be trying so hard to communicate. I think there'll be a major breakthrough soon. Celeste agrees," she added, taking a cigarette from her pack and lighting it. "I came up with an idea of you being equipped with a tape recorder during your visits to the house. I have one at home that's pocket size and sound activated. The more I think about it, the more I feel you should have it nearby, even when you're sleeping. There's no telling what we might luckily get." Kitty paused for a long drag, and slowly released the smoke as she gathered thoughts. "Celeste said something I found rather disconcerting. While we were discussing both spirits being the same, she insisted she felt a distinct, but weak, presence of another entity."

"I thought you said she agreed the woman and girl could be just one."

"She did," Kitty confirmed. "That doesn't mean another separate spirit might not be present or involved." Kitty lit a second cigarette.

"Maybe it could be the spirit of her boyfriend, Richard, if he's dead, or maybe even her father. That would certainly help to tie-in a lot of loose ends," Matt said.

"We have to assume Birdie is right and Richard is still alive. You know we haven't confirmed that situation, and really should." She paused to relight her cigarette. "Of course, here again, we're on the verge of jumping to easy conclusions, and

Celeste couldn't be absolutely positive about there being yet another spirit present. We have to avoid doing that and capitalizing on things seeming to be simple solutions. I do admit it appears exceptionally logical under the circumstances, but I'll bet a dollar to a donut we're way off base."

"Damn." Matt was more confused than ever. "Just when you think you've got something covered, there it goes." Matt reached for Kitty's pack of cigarettes.

She didn't say anything, but gave him a dirty look.

He placed the filtered tip between his lips as Kitty struck a match to light the other end. Matt blew out the flame, replacing the unlit cigarette back into the near empty pack. "When will you have to get back?" he asked, totally ignoring what had just happened.

"As soon as the road conditions permit, I guess." Kitty was well aware of the jittery state Matt was experiencing. "Have you heard any more on the weather?"

"Nope. But I can get a better report on the marine radio. They're a lot more accurate than the TV stations." He sprung to his feet and tuned into the weather channel. The storm was wider spread than anticipated, stretching over an area from Richmond northward along the Atlantic coast states into New England. The local forecast called for the precipitation to change to rain or sleet late in the evening with freezing temperatures until near dawn when another warmer front was due to arrive. Emergency snow regulations remained in effect and gale warnings still posted for the entire bay and lower Potomac River. It was evident rush hour traffic would be a bitch.

"That settles that," Kitty said with a smile.

Matt returned to the set to end the transmission. Before tuning the knob, the taped report was interrupted by the wailing sobs he had so frequently heard. He paused briefly and snapped the switch to its off position. Turning to confront Kitty, he was shocked at the expression on her face.

"I heard it," she mumbled. "Matt. I heard it," she repeated with increased excitement in her voice. "God, Matt. I really heard it."

"Thank you, Jesus," he exclaimed, rushing to take her in his arms. "What did you hear?"

"I . . . I heard the crying. It . . . it was just like you described. I couldn't tell for sure, but it did sound more like a younger girl."

Matt hugged her tightly in his arms. "Why do you suppose you were allowed to hear it? Do you think it's beginning to recognize you as being a helpful friend?"

"I don't know." She hesitated. "But I'm really glad I experienced the phenomena. It was breathtaking. And exciting."

He pushed her away to arms length. "Well, Doc. You were right. You predicted a major breakthrough being on the horizon. Maybe this is it."

Kitty turned and moved to the galley, taking a buck glass and filling it with Grand Marnier. She took a healthy gulp and then handed it to Matt. "I've finally realized the impact these occurrences have. I'm not sure how I might react under the physical contact you've experienced. I could easily become alcoholic, I think." She forced a smile.

"What do you think about calling Celeste and letting her know?"

"I'd rather wait for a while. Maybe something even more profound might happen. Anyway, we might as well save the long-distance call until we can really make it worthwhile."

Matt took a sip from Kitty's drink and returned the glass to her.

She finished its contents and sat the empty container on the counter. "Is it still snowing?"

Pulling the curtain aside and peeking through a port side window, Matt gave an affirmative reply.

"Let's go build a snowman."

There was no way he could deny her plea. Dressing as warm as possible, Matt insisted Kitty wear a pair of his long-johns. The rest she was prepared to provide for herself. Bundled up like Eskimos, they departed the craft and struggled their way to the shore. It was foolhardy and broached stupidity to risk falling into the icily cold water from the difficult to travel dock.

Making it to firmer ground, Kitty scooped snow and packed it with both hands into a huge ball, flinging it at Matt and hitting him square in the rear end.

"Oh. You want to be like that," he shouted, gathering a weapon of his own. He received a second volley before getting off his first. "No fair. No fair," he complained, and dove forward to catch her by the ankle.

She toppled backwards into the snow, laughing hysterically. Before he could react, she regained her composure and leaped on top of him, rubbing his face deeper into the snow by pushing on the back of his head. He came up with his beard full of white flakes and ice.

Kitty rolled over and laid beside him panting from the strenuous action. Matt covered her face with his, rubbing his cheeks all over hers. She continued laughing and making unsuccessful attempts to avoid his attack. Their lips made contact and their tongues met in a deep embrace -- no more laughter, only deep-felt emotion.

Matt got to his feet and pulled Kitty up in the process. They stood under the snow laced tree gazing into each other's eyes. Their smiles of contentment leaving no need for words.

CHAPTER XVII

The new morning once again brought the smell of sizzling bacon filtering into the aft cabin. Matt rolled to his back, stretching his arms above his head. If this wasn't heaven, he thought, what could ever be better?

Kitty had eventually fallen asleep on top of him as he gently caressed her back. He, too, had visited dreamland almost as quickly as she. God, how much he really did care for her. He hadn't tried to make himself feel as he did, nor could he avoid it. His love for her was as compelling and haunting as the spiritual manifestations experienced.

Matt swung his legs over the side of the bed. He sat several moments before realizing he was nude. Kitty appeared in the doorway wearing one of his long-sleeve shirts buttoned near the bottom. The blood quickly sizzled in his veins.

She could see the look in his eye. "Down boy, down," she insisted. "We've got a big day ahead of us. Get your butt in the shower. I've got breakfast almost ready."

"I thought I was supposed to make you breakfast in bed."

Kitty laughed. "This doesn't mean you're off the hook. Now, get going." She disappeared up the stairs.

"What time is it?" he called after her.

"Seven o'clock."

"Geeze," he said. "She means business."

Ten minutes later, Matt was seated at the table. Kitty sat a plate in front of him laden with food -- shortly joining him with one of her own. "Boy, good sex sure builds the appetite," she said, purposely avoiding eye contact. "Then, again, maybe it'll even get better." She burst out laughing.

"Aren't we happy this morning?" Matt said, goading her in

return. "Bet you're not as happy as I am."

"That's a bet you'd lose." Kitty jumped up. "Forgot the orange juice. Want some?"

"Sounds great. Squeeze it yourself?"

"Funny, . . . funny."

"I love you today," he said in a change of mood.

"As much as you did last night?"

"More. A whole lot more." Matt easily sensed the delight felt by Kitty. Her smile expressed a glow brighter and more lovely than the new day sun.

With breakfast completed, he cleared the table, washed the dishes and straighten the salon while Kitty showered and dressed. After fixing more coffee, Matt took his cup and went to the bridge to officially welcome the morn. The air still held a slight chill, but it was apparent temperatures were on the rise again and, as predicted, headed for another warm spell. He unzipped the back section and opened it wide to expose the aft deck and newly accumulated snow covering it.

Noticing a fellow mariner, Matt waved and received one in return. Soon there would be a lot more activity in the marina. And if the weather report was accurate, the white blanket on the ground would quickly dissipate over the next few days.

Kitty joined him on deck. Standing by his side she surveyed the area and took a deep breath followed by a sip from her cup. "What a beautiful morning. I've never felt so glad to be alive."

Matt put his arm around her waist. "I know the feeling."

They remained as they were for several moments before Matt suggested getting to work.

Below deck the two prepped the table with papers and writing equipment. Kitty's earlier suggestion to expand their notes into a more chronological and detailed order seemed logical. Matt fingered through his papers specifically looking for dates associated with various events. Kitty was shuffling though her own material and excused herself to access the computer still set up in the small stateroom. She was gone for almost an hour and returned as Matt was completing his task.

"Got it all together?" Kitty asked.

"Yeah. How about you?"

"Just about. I'm still waiting for a transmission. The

computer's set up to receive it whenever the host is ready."

"Damn. Those things are amazing. You're going to have to show me how to use them."

Kitty smiled. "First things, first."

"Where do we start?"

"Where we left off," she said. "You asked me about the dream sequence. I've given it some thought and although it's not a conclusion, it's a logical concept." Kitty was still toying with some papers. "As is usually the case in paranormal events, they gradually build in intensity rather than enter with a big bang.

The crying over the radio was the initial contact. At first, only you could hear it, even though someone else was listening at the same time. That, in itself, indicates a linking of physic waves being in tune. In short, you and the spirit are on the same almost identical wavelength. No differently are the visual emanations. Only you are able to see and talk to the spirit, at least up to now. I've given it even more serious thought about bringing in a medium to investigate, but we'll get into that later," she said, as an aside. "Anyway, everything indicates a pattern of intensification in a slow, but deliberate manner. You had a number of sightings at a distance before anything immediately present. There were many meetings before verbal communication occurred, and so on, and so on." Kitty got up to go to the counter. "I'm going to have juice. Want some?"

"No thanks," Matt said. "But think you've got a couple of things wrong. . . . Not your fault, though. Haven't mentioned it before. The crying wasn't the first contact. The deeper we get into this, I'm sure I was in the house as a child."

Matt continues relating the hurricane episode and now what he believes to have been a spiritual contact causing his collapse at the height of the storm. And, his being drawn to the house on his first arrival in Deale some forty-years later.

Kitty gasped. "Oh, my God, Matt. Could she have had an influence over you for all those years?

"Seems so. . . . I've only began to put a lot of this together. That's why it wouldn't surprise me if she had something to do with our being introduced."

Kitty just shook her head in disbelief.

"Well, didn't mean to interrupt, but thought it important."

"You have no idea," she muttered.

"Getting back to the rest you were talking about, so, what your implying is the spirit's initial dream contact was insufficient to manifest itself into a full-blown subconscious mental image. The second time it broke through a barrier."

"That's a fair analogy." Kitty returned with her glass and sat down. "Spirits frequently use dreams to make contact. There's a great deal of documented information regarding dream visits by loved ones after a physical death has taken place. Sometimes shortly thereafter. Sometimes years later." Kitty sipped her juice.

"I'm sure you've heard of out-of-body experiences, when people being near death, or even having been clinically dead, return to life for unexplained reasons. There's an accepted theory that those having spiritual contact during dreams actually have these same experiences. Their own spiritual plane leaves their body to make better contact with those of the other world. If you stop to consider, it's a lot easier for we of the human plane to alter our existence to their world than they to ours. Then, again, they know what's on the other side of death. We don't."

"Damn. It makes me shudder." Matt got up to refill her glass. "I don't mean entirely in an eerie sense. Always considered myself a God fearing and loving man. Never realized until now how little serious thought I've really given death or the hereafter. Even losing someone close, you listen to the minister and everyone else says they've gone to a better place, but, hell, how many really have a concept of what it means. I guess the not knowing is etched in the back of our minds. When you stop to think about it, if God created us, the earth, and everything we know, who in hell are we to think or say he stopped there."

"Now you're talking like a parapsychologist." Kitty smiled. "What you've said is very true. You should realize it more than ever having had the contacts with the other side."

"But, what is it? Is there a heaven and a hell?"

"There's no positive answer. However, psychic belief differs from the usual Christian heaven versus hell concepts. As I've said before, the belief is there are those on the next plane that are happy, some confused, and others burdened with their own misgivings, . . . and there is always reincarnation. For example, a person suffering from self-persecution and committing suicide in this life to escape, finds no escape at all. Instead, they carry with them everything negative and each delusional fact that caused them to do what they did. As they were in this world, they continue to be totally alone with their self-indulgence in the next. To the extreme, those passing on from this world who have led lives of greed, corruption and done harm to their fellow man, will flounder forever in a lost dimension of the first plane one might think of as being in limbo. However, many of the advanced or 'higher' spirits try to help those having difficulties and willing to accept their efforts. But there are those so troubled, they turn their back, so to speak, and refuse or deny what is the reality of their world. This could very well be the case in our situation."

"Wow. That's heavy," Matt said. "But it does make some sense."

"Unfortunately, on the next plane, for the most part, spirits unable to shed their 'egos' are no different than here in our world. There's a learning process to accept their stage in the spiritual ladder and advance."

"That doesn't sound like being much better than what we've got in this life."

"As I've explained before, what I refer to as the next plane is just the first of several planes one can attain . . . the ultimate being, the presence of God. By the time one reaches that pinnacle, it is totally ethereal. It's impossible to imagine the euphoric state it represents." Kitty pulled an open pack of cigarettes from her case sitting on the floor. "Sorry," she smiled. "I need a fix."

Matt got the ash tray next to his recliner and his pipe at the same time. He provided a light for them both.

"Not everyone gets past even the first level. Probably the most controversial concept is reincarnation. There is little known about it except certain of us, after death, are allowed additional chances to correct mistakes and misgivings in previous earth lives. Sometimes a soul will experience numerous reincarnations. Simply put, a soul from the next plane is reborn and embodied into a new human form. On the other hand, some go from one plane to another. It all takes a very long time by our standards. Time is irrelevant there."

"So, that brings us back to Sarah. You feel she falls in the 'confused' category."

"Very likely." Kitty thought for a moment while taking a drag from her cigarette. "You've seen the movie Poltergeist, I'm sure. Well, the release between the dimensions is the light. In virtually every documented case of near death experiences, the subject has always seen the light in one form or another. Having not gone into it, or having been refused to enter it, has returned them to this life." Kitty took another puff. "The spirit we're dealing with is probably totally befuddled and possibly unaware as to where she actually is. She may not even know she is dead . . . by earthly standards, of course. If that's the case, something traumatic has probably kept her in a state of mental confusion. She may not even be sure of what she's looking for or trying to overcome. The bottom line . . . we've got to find the answer if you want to be rid of her. It's that plain and simple."

"Aren't you tired of the whole damn bit?" Matt asked.

"Honey. In the beginning, especially after personally experiencing the appearance of the doll, my interest was mostly stimulated by work and a desire to make a significant contribution to my field. That part hasn't changed, it's even intensified. Since that time, my need to be involved goes way beyond that aspect. I love you and want to help you more than anything else. I can't stand to see you hurt or tormented. I want you to be rid of her so we can make a life for ourselves. Besides, there's only room for one woman in your life. . . . Me."

Matt smiled. "Well, that settles that. What's up next, Doc?"

"I really never finished filling you in the other day. I guess it's as good a place to start as any." Kitty lit another cigarette and searched among her papers. "Here it is." She brandished a second report. "Without you knowing it, I also had a small piece of the doll's dress analyzed. They concluded it was made from material used in making feed bags back in their time, just like I surmised."

"Yeah, I remember my mother telling me about all of the clothes my grandmother made for her out of the same type bags. She said they came in all kinds of patterns and prints."

Kitty agreed. "I got many of the same stories. It's a strong tie to the past and definitely rules out having been made recently."

"Did you consider finding out what it might be stuffed with?"

"No. But that's a great idea," Kitty smiled. "We'll include it on our 'what to do' list."

Matt looked at his watch and it was almost eleven. "You know. I think I've been coping with most of this pretty well. The only part really flipping me is the sensation of making physical contact. It's a bitch to say the least."

"I would guess so," Kitty sympathized. "That's what I'm trying to get information on at the moment. There's a lot of areas I'm not up on," she admitted. "Physical spiritual contact is one of them."

The phone rang once.

"That should be the transmission I'm expecting."

"How do you know?"

"The computer answered the signal. I heard a beep, so it should be receiving the message right now," Kitty said. "It'll take a little while for the file to be transmitted."

Matt shook his head in amazement. "What's this world coming to?" He excused himself and went to the head. Hovering over the commode, the boat suddenly rocked causing him to lose his balance. Urine went onto the floor and down the leg of his pants. He cursed, looking out of the porthole to spot the culprit. "Damn these assholes flying through here." There was no evidence of a wake left by a passing boat. "What in the hell?"

Taking the bath towel used earlier he wiped up the mess. The chore accomplished, Matt filled the basin with water and stuffed the towel in to soak. As he left the head, he saw Kitty disappear into the computer room. "Everything all set?" he called.

"Be there in a second."

Still perplexed by the unusual bounce of the boat, Matt went to the galley and washed his hands. He could find no reason for what happened. "Maybe it was a whale nudging the boat," he joked.

"God." Matt heard Kitty gasp. "Matt. Come here."

Matt spun on his heels and turned the corner in a flash. "What's wrong?" he shouted, rounding the doorway where Kitty sat gazing at the computer.

"You've got to see this," Kitty said, expressing disbelief combined with a hint of distress. She punched a couple of keys on the keyboard as Matt leaned over her shoulder observing the screen. "This is the beginning of the transmission," she explained. "As you can see, it's originating from Duke University in North Carolina." Kitty held the down cursor button to slowly scroll through the document. "There's several pages to go through, but everything's coming through fine." She punched a different key and the screen jumped a page at a time until stopping at a determined spot. "Look at this code." She pointed to an EOT designation preceded and followed by a series of asterisks. "That indicates the end of the normal transmission. It's a signal by the host computer to terminate the call and return our computer and telephone to normal function. All of these symbols appearing after the cutoff shouldn't be here."

Matt saw, but still didn't understand what she was talking about. The figures she referred to ran off the bottom of the screen.

"The actual material received is a little over six pages in length. The transmission itself runs for ten more pages of these garbled characters."

"I really don't understand. What does it mean?" he asked, truly expressing his confusion.

Kitty pushed yet another button and the screen jumped to the sixteenth and last page of the transmission. At its end, four clearly discernable words appeared: 'Richard, I love you.'

Matt reeled on his heels as if being struck by a physical blow. "My, God. How could this happen?" He shuddered. The initial shock slowly ebbed as he continued to stare at the computer.

Kitty stood and put her arms around him. Detecting perspiration beading on his forehead, she took him by the hand and lead him up the stairs to the couch. Before sitting down beside him, she left long enough to get a wet wash cloth and placed it across his brow as he leaned his head on the back of the sofa.

"Could you get me some brandy?" he asked in almost a whisper.

In a jiffy, Kitty returned with a glass filled with an orange-brown liquid. "There wasn't any Napoleon left. It's Grand Marnier instead." She sipped from its contents before placing it in his left hand resting on the couch's arm.

"I never mentioned it because I didn't think it mattered," he said without moving. "Until now, at least. And, maybe it isn't anything, anyway. I don't know."

"What are you talking about?" Kitty asked, attempting to make sense of his rambling.

"My middle name is Richard," he stated.

"Holy mother of God." It was Kitty's turn to be stunned. She sat down on the edge of the couch and reached for his glass. "I need this as much as you do," she said with a weird chuckle. She tipped the glass to her lips, took a long swallow, and then another, before returning it to his hand.

Matt sat up -- the wash rag falling into his lap. "Yeah, it's Matthew Richard, all right. No one knows that." With second thought he said, "Only my kids." He paused, scratching his head. "How in the hell does a so-called entity, from somewhere on the other side of nowhere, know my middle name? Richard was my father's first name . . . he was a third . . . my older brother, the fourth." He took a large gulp from his glass. "How in the hell does she know?"

"We're only assuming she knows," Kitty cautioned. "Of course, your middle name being the same as her boy friend is sure one fantastic coincidence. There's no question it could be a major factor in why you were contacted. Then, again, it may not have any bearing in the matter at all."

"That doesn't tell me what you really think."

"I don't know what to think. I've never heard of anything like this with such involved and persistent paranormal activities existing. That's not true. Yes it is. Oh, damn. What I mean is the part about practically everything being unprecedented is true. The other is . . . I do think something." Kitty paused, then started laughing. "I sound frustrated as hell, don't I?"

"A little bit . . . to say the least," he said, and laughed. "It's really crazy. Most people would think we're both crazy. Sometimes I think I am."

They both stood at the same time and he took her into his arms. She laid her head on his shoulder, placing her arms around his waist. "This is a lot better," he whispered.

"Yes it is," she said, with a sigh. "Don't ever let me go." She held him even tighter and continued in a soft subdued tone. "I'm so afraid of losing you."

"I cared for my husband, but never with the same feelings I have for you. I know if he had lived we would still be together." She pressed her lips between the neck opening of his shirt. "That scares me. I would never have met you."

Matt raised his hand from her back and stroked her hair.

"I know the same would be true about you and Catherine. I can never take her place. I'd never try." Tears trickled down her cheeks. "I just love you so much."

Matt gently turned her head upwards with his hand. "We'll get through all of it fine." Their lips parted and met in a brief embrace. "I can't imagine ever being without you. I love you more than you'll ever know."

Kitty wiped her eyes with her finger tips, moving to the galley for a paper towel. Wetting it under the cold faucet, she then dabbed it against her cheeks and eyes. "Tears and mascara don't mix." She laughed.

Matt smiled back.

"It's really weird to be sad when you're so happy." She sniffled and quickly changed the subject. "It's lunch time. Seems like we're always eating, but never get fat."

"I could use a bite," he responded. "Why don't we fix something and have a picnic up on shore?"

"In all of this snow?" Kitty queried, and quickly amended her judgment. "What the heck. It'll be fun. What do we have?"

"Nothing I can think of." He laughed. "Tell you what. Let's zip over to the store and get some chicken and whatever else suits your fancy."

"Great."

CHAPTER XVIII

The grocery represented a short trip and the roads were in very good shape after being plowed and salted. While Kitty was preoccupied with making selections, Matt slipped next door to the florist and bought a dozen long-stemmed red roses. After explaining what he was doing, the sales girl expedited the transaction and he was able to hide them in the trunk of Kitty's car and get back to her before she realized he was missing.

"Oh, good," she said. "I wanted to ask you something. Do you like your potato salad with eggs or without?"

He answered with a question. "How about you?"

"I don't care. Either is okay with me," she said, her eyes wishful for his decision.

Shrugging his shoulders, they stood looking at each other and then burst out laughing. Kitty turned to the clerk and said, "I'll take a pint of cole slaw, thank you."

Matt laughed. "A pint of egg potato salad, too."

"Good. That's my favorite," she said, with a devilish grin.

On the way back to the marina, they made a stop at the liquor store and browsed through the wine section. Matt opted on several selections, and figured it was as good a time as any to refill the cabinet. The box of booze took up the remainder of the back seat. It took several trips to the boat before getting everything unloaded, even though dropping a lot of it off in the picnic area on the way.

Matt got a broom from the marina shed and cleaned all of the snow from one of the tables and its benches while Kitty busied herself unpacking and putting items not intended for lunch into the refrigerator. Sneaking a vase off of the boat, he filled it with water from the dock. After retrieving the flowers from the car, he placed them on the bench where he intended Kitty to sit and hid the vase beneath it -- just in the nick of time. Kitty strode down the pier with her hands full of eating accessories and a pack of napkins stuck under her arm.

"Let me give you a hand," Matt said, rushing to meet her.

Kitty moved to the far side of the table facing the water and spotted the long green box tied with a large red ribbon. Her face reflected her surprise and elation as she looked at Matt. She picked up the flowers and laid the carton across her lap as she took a seat sideways on the bench. Without uttering a word Kitty opened the lid and gasped. Drops of moisture on the roses glistened in the sunlight as if they were tiny diamonds matching the tears welling in the corner of her eyes. She gazed intently at the large red buds, lightly caressing them with her finger tips. Taking the small card tucked inside the tissue she read its message: 'Doc. For all the things you have been and will be to me. Me, too, to you, too. Matt.'

As the tears trickled down her cheeks, Matt moved around the table and knelt by where she sat. He smiled. "Come on now. You've got to stop doing that. I didn't want to make you cry. I wanted to make you happy."

"I am, silly. No one's ever given me roses." She softly laughed between sniffles and smiled, gazing into his face. "They're so beautiful."

"Not as beautiful as you." He winked. "Dry those lovely eyes and let's eat." Matt lifted her chin with his finger and touched his lips to hers. "I love you."

"As you would say; Me, too, to you, too." She beamed a broad smile.

Matt took a seat beside her as Kitty started to rise. "Where you going?" he asked.

"I'll be right back. These should be in water."

He caught her arm. "Wait a minute," he said, leaning down and grabbing the hidden vase. "Presto. Just what the Doc ordered."

* * *

Other than finishing a list of things to do regarding the spiritual phenomena, the remainder of the previous day was spent relaxing. Leftovers from lunch were enjoyed later in the evening

154

while catching a movie on TV. By the time they were ready for bed, Kitty had a bit of a glow from a slight over consumption of wine and slept like a baby. The morning began as most other days whenever she was aboard, but something Matt would never take for granted. Beating her to the punch, he was up at the crack of dawn and repaid his breakfast debt.

"First the roses, and now this," Kitty said, wiping the corner of her lips with a napkin as she sat in the middle of the bed. "Who's spoiling who?"

Matt sat on the floor with his plate balanced on crossed legs. Having a mouth full of food, he was unable to comment.

Kitty said, "I feel terrible. You look uncomfortable sitting there."

Matt swallowed. "I'm fine. And we're even." He laughed.

She faked a pout. "Not if you love me."

"Ho, ho. Going to be like that, is it?"

"You know better," she said, tweaking her nose. Kitty sat the tray aside and doubled her knees to her chin, wrapping her arms around her legs. "You never mention Catherine. Does it bother you to talk about her?"

"No. Not really. . . . Why?"

"I don't know." She paused, rubbing her chin against her knees as she gathered thoughts. "I guess it's a facet about you I know so little about. I realize you must have really loved her. But it's strange. I don't feel threatened by that at all."

"You shouldn't," he said, placing his plate on the floor and leaning back on his hands.

"My husband's name was Gregory," she said, as if letting her thoughts roll from her tongue. "We met in college and became good friends. A lot of our compatibility came from both of us majoring in psychology. He wanted to become a psychiatrist and my interests were in teaching. Greg was a year ahead of me and we didn't take all of our classes together. Even though we both had full scholarships, we eventually agreed it would be cheaper to live together than separately. I got my masters and he went on for a doctorate. It was a matter of helping each other along the way." Kitty raised her head to make a point. "I don't mean to make it sound so callous. We did care for each other. A great deal as a matter of fact," she added, as she repositioned her chin against her knees. "I always felt I was in love. Now I realize it's difficult, if not impossible, to measure the depth of love and desire until there's something to compare. I guess if I hadn't been so immersed in my career I might have taken a more in-depth look into my own relationship." She laughed. "That's great. A psychologist unable to recognize her own problems, isn't it?"

Matt responded with a smile and a nod of his head. He realized she was unwinding and needed to get it all out in the open.

"Well. It goes to show you how complex we really are. It's so much easier to be critical and see the problems of others than to see inside ourselves." Kitty stretched out her legs and scooted to the edge of bed. "We were good to each other. Not always attentive, but good." She slid off the bed onto the floor and took a position sitting in front of Matt. "Greg was not a romanticist. He never gave me flowers and we rarely exchanged gifts. Our social life was more or less limited to professional functions. I don't ever remember sitting down and watching a TV movie together." Kitty squirmed in her sitting pose. "I never had a sexual climax during my marriage."

Matt reflected surprise at her remark, but showed no emotion. He reached to touch her.

She wrapped her fingers around his and stared at their hands as they rested on her leg. "Gregory was a large part of my life for many years. He was a good and generous man in his own way. And, I was content with what we had, although I knew there was a great deal missing between us." She looked up and gazed into Matt's eyes. "You have no idea what a change you've made in my life. I've never felt so needed and desired. Sometimes you make me feel like I'm on a pedestal and I get scared I might fall and disappoint you. When you touch me, I tremble. When you make love to me, there's no words to describe my satisfaction. For the first time, I know what it's like to feel erotic."

"That you are," Matt said, in a soft tone, squeezing her hand. "I've never been aroused so easily by anyone as you. All I have to do is look at you. To touch you is to want you even more. But it's more than sexual arousal, it's a feeling inside stirring all of my emotions." Matt scooted across the floor to sit beside her with his back against the bed.

She adjusted her position and laid her head in his lap.

"Our pasts are alike in some ways. Neither one of us evidently dated much when we were younger. Catherine and I graduated from high school together and got married a year later. The oddest part is we didn't pay much attention to each other until toward the end of our senior year. We did have the sense to wait for children until I got my architectural degree from night college. It wasn't easy. We both worked and she helped a great deal in getting us through it." He gently fingered strands of her hair spread across his legs. "Catherine and I did have a lot in common. Among other things, we were both athletic and enjoyed participating and spectator sports. She loved the water. And to fish," he added. "You were right about one thing, for sure." He paused for a moment, tinkering with her hair.

Kitty turned her position to look up at him.

"The part about comparisons. I was a virgin when we married. So was she." He looked for a reaction, but saw none. "I guess our sex life could best be described as wholesome. Most of the youth oriented passion mellowed early in our relationship as the love and respect we felt for each other grew. Like you said about you and Gregory. We were the best of friends and lovers second."

Matt felt his chest tightening from deeply embedded emotions he had previously been able to keep hidden.

Kitty sensed the building melancholia and softly rubbed his leg in an understanding and comforting fashion.

He cleared his throat. "It took me a long time to wean myself away from her and admit she was gone. I was like a flounder out of water and could have probably salvaged my business, but didn't care." He paused, and then continued. "I've thought about both of our circumstances. Your loss, being so sudden, had to be even more difficult than mine." Matt let out a low sob he could no longer subdue. Tears streamed down his face and he whimpered softly, straining to control his emotions.

Kitty moved quickly and sat on her heels taking him in her arms. She pulled his head to her breasts and caressed his hair and neck. "Let it go, honey. Let it go." Matt's tears were wet against her chest. She held him even closer.

"I never cried for her."

"That's why it's so important to release your feelings. It only does harm to keep things pent inside," she whispered, pressing her lips to the top of his head until he had calmed.

Matt drew away and laid his head back over the edge of the bed. He took a deep breath, blowing the exhale toward the ceiling with a sigh. "Wow. I feel like a baby," he said, as he sat upright, slapping his hands against his thighs.

"There's an old adage, . . . 'A man's not a man until he cries.'"

Matt smiled. "Is that the Doc talking, or you?"

"Both." She poked him in the ribs. "You were way overdue to let that out. I can't believe you kept it in as long as you have."

"I do feel better," he admitted. "It's hard to explain, but somehow I feel like I've let Catherine go. I don't mean from my mind. When you were holding me to your breast, I felt something was being drawn from by body. It's like I've been keeping her from going on beyond me and she was finally being released. I began to feel a glowing sensation and no longer sad. It was almost like saying goodbye."

"You were," Kitty confirmed. "Catherine had remained part of your ego . . . your inner-self. But I sincerely doubt you were actually hindering her from normal transitional death between the planes. More important, you've experienced the release, and I'm sure she's aware. She'll always remember the love you shared and it will always remain a part of her.

"It's a beautiful thought. I want to believe it." Matt got to his knees, then stood. He staggered, having to catch himself against the dresser. "Getting old. Bones ain't what they used to be."

Kitty laughed and also rose. "Here. Let me help the old man up the stairs." She grabbed him around the waist and they headed for the salon. Matt went directly to the galley area and began filling the sink. "Don't bother with those. I'll do them."

"Nope," Matt said, emphatically. "Tarzan cooked . . . Tarzan clean."

Giggling and shaking her head, Kitty went below to gather the dishes cluttering the aft cabin and returned with a full tray.

"You sure you don't mind," Kitty persisted.

"Get outta here and get to work." He swatted at her with the

158

dish towel.

Kitty headed directly for the computer room still clad in his robe.

Matt did the dishes by instinct, not concentration -- his mind totally distracted by thought. It was true. He felt as if a tremendous weight had been lifted. There was an inner peace never there since Catherine's death. Any guilt complicating a relationship with Kitty was gone -- realizing it hadn't been done alone.

"Don't forget," Kitty called from below. "You've got a lot of calls to make."

"Nag, nag, nag," he said loud enough to be clearly heard. He pulled the stopper and cleaned the counter and range before completing his task. He decided to take care of personal matters before getting into the business at hand. He talked to his daughter and then his son, both forcing a promise he would make an early visit. After hanging up, he wondered when he would muster the nerve to mention Kitty. She was considerably younger than their mother, plus there was the questionable acceptance of her heritage. He shook it from his mind and pored into his notes searching for phone numbers. Not having heard from Rebecca Fletcher, Matt dialed her home in Pennsylvania and again got her aunt. After an abundance of apologies for having failed to give her the message, she provided Rebecca's work number.

"Good morning. CID Corporation," the voice announced, following several rings. "May I help you?"

"Ms. Fletcher, please."

"One moment, sir." There was a brief pause. "Ms. Fletcher is in a seminar this morning and isn't expected at her desk until later this afternoon. May I take a message?"

"Yes. Please. I'm calling long-distance. Would you have her contact Matthew Bodine as soon as possible? It's very important and I'd like her to call me collect." He provided his number before ending the conversation.

"Well, let's see. What's next?" he asked himself, as he found the note about Dorothy Hands. He dialed the nursing home to get information on the former Colison neighbor and learned of the liberal visiting hours. The Amish Hospitality Center in Lancaster was next on his list. He spoke with Peter, the center's director met earlier, requesting information on the possibility of a tie to other Colisons who may have been associated with Jeremiah. The elder agreed to check into the matter. Matt further related his lack of progress in following up the Fletcher lead.

"How's it going?" Matt hadn't noticed Kitty standing at the counter freshening her coffee. "Want some?"

"Yeah, please. And not so good. So far I'm batting zero." Matt gave her a brief rundown. "How about you?"

"I've been studying the material we received yesterday and accessed a couple of libraries on the computer. Still at it." She shrugged her shoulders as she took Matt's cup and refilled it before heading back to the impromptu office.

"Uh, Doc," Matt called, as she got to the bottom of the steps. "I'm going to run up to the nursing home. Wanna come?"

"No, hon. I better stay with this. I want to take the disk with me so I can fax quite a few things at work. You go ahead. But do me a favor while you're out. Pick up some cigarettes. I'm almost out. Love ya."

"Love you, too. Be back before long." Matt grabbed his jacket and was on his way.

CHAPTER XIX

It felt good to get out -- the drive a much needed break. Traveling the back roads provided a tour through wooded landscape and farmlands ready for the early growing season; a slight green haze among the tree tops denoting a more definite sign of the oncoming spring. While passing a small open area to the right of the highway, Matt noticed a large patch of jonquils growing near a small pond. It was an unwelcome reminder of things he wished forgotten.

His destination: Edgewater, a small town bordering Annapolis on the southern side of the South River. The trip to the nursing home required a little more than a half-hour. He pulled into the visitor's parking lot and had his choice of spaces.

"Damn, it," he growled, hitting his knee on the window handle while getting out of the car. He proceeded with a slight limp, heading for the front door.

Once inside, Matt confronted a long hallway leading to a main desk strategically placed in the center of the single-story sprawling building. A trio of ladies dressed in white uniforms with light blue collars and cuffs on their long-sleeved blouses worked busily behind a chest-high counter.

"May I help you?"

Matt stopped in his tracks and spun on his heels, coming to face a middle-aged lady sitting behind a desk in a corner he had failed to notice upon entering the area. "Uh, . . . yeah. . . . Yes, thank you," he corrected, amending his demeanor as he walked closer to her location. "I'd like to see Dorothy Hands, if I may."

Thumbing through an index file, the information lady reached the 'H' section and pulled a card upwards to scan its contents. "Dorothy should be in ceramics at the moment. If you'd like, you can visit her there or we can have her meet you in the lobby."

"No. No, that's fine. I don't want to take her from what she's doing."

"The crafts room is at the end of the north wing." She pointed toward the proper direction. "It's the last door on the left," she added.

Matt turned to walk away, but paused to express his belated thanks. He arrived in an open doorway, observing a handful of elderly women and a single gentleman engrossed in various stages of pottery making. He opted the younger lady present to be the crafts instructor, slowly approaching while carefully attempting to avoid distracting others at work. "Excuse me," he said softly, but loud enough to attract her attention. She looked up expressing some surprise at his presence. "I'd like to speak with Dorothy Hands."

She smiled. "Forgive me. I didn't see you come in."

"That's okay." Matt returned the smile. "I apologize for disturbing you and the class."

As she rose from her seat, she offered her hand with a greeting. "I'm Shelley," she said. "And, you're not interrupting anything. In fact," she added, "it's all too infrequent our residents get to have visitors. Are you family?"

"No. I . . ." Matt hesitated, wondering if it would make a difference. "We haven't met before. A mutual friend suggested she might be able to help me locate a family she once knew. They were neighbors."

"Good luck." Shelley gave a little giggle while reaching to touch Matt's forearm. "Forgive me," she said. "Before I introduce you I think I should let you know Dorothy can be a bit of a 'bird' sometimes. Although she's usually lucid, she has her bad days like most of the other elderly. I should warn you there are instances when she drifts away into fantasy." Shelley gave a slight tug on his arm and removed her hand. She turned, walking toward a lady sitting in a wheelchair at a table near the windows. Matt followed. "Dorothy. There's someone here to see you."

Dorothy's response was curt and carried a raspy tone in her voice. "What make's you think I want to see them?" She ignored their presence and continued cleaning a small green-ware figurine.

Matt nodded to Shelley indicating he would handle the situation, drawing a nearby chair to a position near Dorothy.

Shelley smiled and returned to her own project.

Matt sat down and patiently watched Dorothy adeptly manipulate the piece of ceramics between her long slender fingers.

Her steel-grey hair pulled back into a tight small bun added in exaggerating a high brow. She wore a dark blue dress speckled with small pink and light-blue flowers. An apron hung loosely from her neck, tied at the waist and covering her lap. She appeared articulate in her mannerisms, but her movement certainly slowed by the many years. When it came to judging the age of an older person, Matt was at a loss.

Entranced in wandering thought, Dorothy unexpectedly interrupted his stupor. "Not bad for an old broad, huh?" she asked, turning the object in her hands in adoration of her efforts.

Matt suppressed a laugh. "It's really nice," he said. "Are you ready to paint it, now?"

"Of course not, silly. It has to be fired first." Dorothy looked at Matt for the first time. "Don't you know anything about ceramics?"

"Uh, . . . no, I really don't. Not very much," he corrected.

"Don't surprise me much. You never did pay no like to pretty things after you growed up."

Matt's aspiration of gaining valid information began to slowly fade.

"Why haven't you come to me see, Richard? You don't care."

Matt was stunned. His gut wrenched with sudden discomfort as adrenalin rushed through his veins. God, he thought, she thinks I'm Richard.

"I never knew why you couldn't be more like your brother. He was always kind to me. He was always good to his mother, too."

Further shock staggered his already befuddled mind. Moments sped past before he could muster a response. "I . . . I've never forgotten you," he found himself saying, sensing it best to placate her belief. He continued. "I'm here, now."

Dorothy stared into his face -- her glare slowly ebbing into a

163

weak and passive smile. She looked away, focusing her gaze through the windows. "I can remember when you brought me jonquils in the spring. I was your favorite aunt. I always knew you took them from the neighbor's flower garden."

Matt seized his moment of opportunity. "I can't remember their last name."

"Carlton," she quickly responded.

"Oh, that's right, Colison," he corrected, without making it seem so.

"Yes, Colison. That's what I said. Colison." She twisted in her chair and began brushing ceramic dust from her lap.

"I haven't seen Sarah in a long time," Matt tactfully commented.

"She died," she said, in a somewhat subdued tone. "They all died, . . . except me and Birdie."

"I'm still alive. I'm here with you." Matt wondered if he was going too far.

Surprisingly, Dorothy spun the wheels of her chair to face him. "Who are you? You're not Richard." She looked at him in a puzzled manner. "My name is Dorothy. Who are you?"

"Matthew," he said, softly. "You're right. I'm not Richard. I have a friend who thought you might be able to help me."

"Help you, what?"

"Please. I don't want to upset you. I'm just interested in buying the old house the Colisons lived in, and I don't know how to get in touch with the owner." Matt had no idea how much she was able to comprehend. "Anything you could tell me might help."

"Hummmpp," she muttered. "A likely story." She started to turn her chair away and stopped. "Mary Margaret . . . we was friends. Didn't have much use for her husband. He was a mean one." She paused, as if collecting her memory. "Richard liked Sarah a whole lot. I liked her, too." Dorothy again started wiping her lap with the back of her hands. "She died. Sarah died. They all died."

"Did Sarah's father die?" Matt reluctantly asked, afraid he might break her talkative spell.

"Of course not. Only the good ones die." Dorothy hesitated, evidently aware of what she had said. "I don't know," she continued, altering her opinion. "He moved away. Sarah died and he moved away."

"How did Sarah die? Was she sick?"

Dorothy's eyes reflected a sudden emptiness -- her hands moving more rapidly against the folds in her apron. "She drown. Sarah died." She started to whimper and tears began to trickle down her cheeks. Her words became a whisper. "Richard. My poor Richard."

Matt moved to kneel beside the wheelchair, enveloping his arms around her shoulders. Holding her head to his chest, Dorothy wept.

CHAPTER XX

Waking without Kitty nearby seemed strange. She reluctantly left shortly after Matt's return from the nursing home. Her unexpected elongated stay due to the snow storm spoiled them both. Although heartened by the turn of events, neither easily accepted the concept of being apart.

Matt laid in bed daydreaming, typical to his usual routine before arising. Dorothy Hands would never realize the wealth of cooperating information she provided. Following the visit, he had met with the home's supervisor learning the son and daughter were responsible for having made original arrangements for Dorothy's committal to the facility and occasionally visited their mother. Unfortunately, policy made it impossible to divulge personal information regarding the family, but Matt was assured they would contact Dorothy's children informing them of his interest. There was little more he could do than simply wait. Matt smiled with his thoughts and said, "Damn," as he sat up swinging his legs over the side of the bed. Richard was Dorothy's nephew. "Damn," he said, again. It was another break-through they desperately needed. If only the relatives would call. His mind swirled with possibilities.

After gaining his feet, Matt stretched his arms and legs letting them know it was time to go to work. One thing was for sure, after forty, the limbs weren't what they used to be, especially the knees -- after fifty, even worse. He climbed the short stairway to the salon, turning to the galley area and smiled in noticing the new automatic coffee maker Kitty had bought -- its freshly brewed aroma filling the cabin. After dousing a nearly full mug of the steaming liquid with sugar and milk, he took a careful sip and headed for the shower. As usual, it proved to be the final touch bringing all of his body parts to life. He pulled the shower curtain aside and stepped from the basin. The phone rang. Matt grabbed a towel and rushed to beat the answering machine.

"Hello."

"Mr. Bodine?" the voice on the other end queried.

"Yes. Could I help you?"

"I'm David Hands. Sorry to call so early, but Saturday is one of my busier workdays."

Matt found it difficult to contain his exuberance.

"Mrs. Marsh at the nursing home said you were interested in speaking with me regarding my mother."

"Yeah, . . . I . . . as you're aware, I met with Dorothy the other day. She was very helpful, but I was hoping you could shed further light on the matter."

"I don't follow you," David said.

Matt finally realized the son was totally in the dark regarding his interest. "I apologize. I took it for granted Mrs. Marsh had mentioned the reasons for contacting your mother." Matt was beginning to shiver from not having dried. "Could you excuse me for just a moment?" David agreed, and Matt returned in a matter of seconds pulling on his robe. "I was just getting out of the shower when you called. It's good we weren't on those television phone contraptions." David politely chuckled as Matt continued. "I learned from a friend that your family and the Colisons were neighbors. I understand their old house is still owned by the father and I've been unsuccessful in locating him. You see, I really want to buy the property. Anything you could provide would be deeply appreciated."

There was a slight pause. Matt could tell he was taking a long drag on a cigarette.

"I'm not sure I can be of much help," David finally said. "They were a strange family and kept to themselves for the most part. Mother and the Colison woman were friendly when the old man wasn't around. Of course, Richard was chummy with the daughter . . . Sarah. Yeah, Sarah. That was her name." He paused for another drag of smoke. Anything I know came from my Mother. She said the Mrs. Colison died and Sarah had an accident about a year later. It was about the same time Richard had his accident. Other than that," he said, "a short time later the

168

house was deserted and I have no idea whatever happened to Mr. Colison. I can't remember his first name," he added as an afterthought.

"Jeremiah," Matt offered. David didn't respond. "Do you think your wife or Richard might know something more?"

"Don't think so, but Beth, my sister, might," he said. "Richard? I really doubt he would be of any help."

"Then, Richard's alive?" Matt hopefully asked.

"Yeah," David answered. "Oh, I see. I mentioned his accident and you assumed it was fatal." Before Matt could respond, David continued. "Richard fell and suffered a head injury the same night Sarah drown. He's never been right upstairs since. It left him with a mental disability."

"That's tragic," Matt managed to say.

"I don't mean to be rude," David interjected, "but I'm running a little late. Let me give you Beth's phone number. You should be able to reach her at home later today. Mother lived with her for several years before going into the home. I'm sure she probably knows more than I do."

Matt graciously thanked David before ending the conversation. He pulled off his robe, using it to towel the rest of his body dry while heading for the aft cabin to get dressed. Mission completed, he paused long enough to freshen his coffee, then plopped on the couch and dialed Kitty's number.

Although disappointed in getting her answering machine, he fully realized how busy her schedule was in making up for many absences. After leaving a witty message, Matt was disturbingly reminded they wouldn't be seeing each other until the following weekend.

"Damn," he said. "I miss you, Doc."

Still holding the cordless in his hand, it rang, startling him.

"Hello."

"I have a collect call from Rebecca Fletcher. Will you accept the charges?"

"Yes, I will," Matt said, expressing a tinge of excitement he couldn't control.

"Mr. Bodine. I tried to return your call earlier, but wasn't able to catch you."

"I apologize. I've been on the go. But, thank you for being

persistent." Matt began relating his Lancaster experiences, including all of the events leading to his eventual contact with her. "So, you see," he finalized, "it's very important I find Jeremiah."

There was only silence on the other end of the phone. He heard Rebecca sigh before she spoke.

"I'm trying to digest all of this," she said, almost apologetically. "I don't think I can be of much help. Anything I might know has came from overhearing family talk."

"I understand," Matt said. "But even the least little bit of information might lead to locating Mr. Colison. Would you mind telling me about your family background? I realize a lot of years have passed, but something as simple as learning where various relatives may have moved or settled could be an important key."

"I'll try," she offered. "I'm not sure where to start."

"As far back as you can. Everything you know or remember hearing."

"Well, Joseph Colison, my great-great-grandfather, had four sons and three daughters. My great-grandmother, Rebecca, was the eldest. I was named after her. One of her brothers married another Mennonite and had a number of children. One of them, John, who is my great-grandfather, married and fathered Jacob, and he fathered my mother. She, in turn, married my father who wasn't of Amish faith. Grandpa passed away at an early age, and I never knew him, nor remember much about his brothers . . . . My aunt and I are the last of the Fletcher family to remain in the Lancaster area. From what I understand, all of my great-uncles and their families moved away because of the depression. I remember Mother talking about some kind of government work program, I believe."

"Yeah," Matt confirmed. "It was most likely the WPA."

"Anyway," she continued, "other than the Fletcher side, I've barely had contact with any Colison relatives. I know there are distant relations nearby, Amish of course, and you're evidently aware of the others' disassociation. As far as I know, any real Colison connection ended with my parent's marriage."

"Are your parents still alive?" Matt queried.

"Yes. They're retired and living in Florida."

Before he could ask, Rebecca offered their help.

"Mother should know a great deal more than I do. I'll give you her number if you'd like."

"That would be wonderful," Matt said, and quickly jotted down the information.

Rebecca wished him good luck. The conversation ended.

"Wow. What a day," he shouted, placing the phone into its receptacle. "Two down and two to go." He was ecstatic.

As luck would have it, he spent the rest of the afternoon trying to reach his remaining contacts, neither being at home. Later in the evening Kitty returned his call. She was thrilled with all of the good news, but equally disappointed at being home alone. Even though it was after midnight when the conversation ended, Matt decided to make notes on everything he had learned. Trying to get the Colison/Fletcher family tree in order was somewhat complicated. Shortly after three a.m., pleased, but very weary, it was apparent sleep was needed and he fumbled his way to the aft cabin. Just before climbing into bed, he snuck a peak out of an aft cabin port hole. The old house appeared dark with only the distant shore lights reflecting in its windows.

The morning brought the first of several days of balmy weather. Matt spent most of Sunday cleaning the boats exterior, except for a few hours in the afternoon watching an Orioles exhibition game on TV. Jason and Heather had paid a short visit in the evening prior to a quick nightie-night call to Kitty. The rest of the week was occupied with helping Pete and his son paint boat bottoms and make various repairs mostly due to winter damage.

By Friday evening, he was glad the work was complete. Every bone in his body reminded him he wasn't as young as he used to be. After a long and enjoyable shower, he fixed a Scotch and water and relaxed in front of the TV catching up on the news. Discontent with the broadcast's endless report focusing on street violence and drug busts, he changed channels just as the phone rang. In his haste to answer the call, he knocked over his drink and uttered a few choice words.

"Hello," he said, mustering a forced control of temper.

"Mr. Bodine?" the voice asked.

"Yes."

"I'm Dorothy Hands daughter, Beth."

Matt responded. "Oh. . . . Yes."

"I hope I'm not calling at a bad time," she said, and continued without hesitation. "David told me about your interests. I assume you've been trying to reach me and I'm sorry I haven't been able to speak with you before now."

Matt didn't have time to respond.

"Mother suffered a stroke shortly after you spoke with my brother last Saturday. She passed away that evening."

"Oh, my God," Matt said.

"It was only a question of time. Mother's heart was much weaker than her spirit."

Matt was confused by her seemingly lack of remorse.

"We've been involved with her funeral and this has been my first opportunity to contact you."

"Thank you for calling. And, I'm truly sad to hear of her passing," he said.

"Thank you," she said, with a noticeable change in her disposition.

"I guess I had pretty bad timing."

"Not at all," Ann said. "Life must go on." She reverted to her complacent attitude. "David said you're interested in buying the old Colison place."

"Yes. I am. You're aware I've had no luck in locating Mr. Colison. I assume he's still alive," he added. "I've checked and the property has never changed names."

"I have no idea," she said. "I remember very little about their family. Most of what I know about them, came from things Mother would talk about over the years."

"Yes," Matt said. "David mentioned you cared for her for quite some time before she entered the nursing home."

"I did. Mother was quite lucid for a good while and then Alzheimer's took its toll."

"Dorothy talked a great deal about Mary Margaret and Sarah during my visit with her. She said little about Mr. Colison," Matt said. "I feel the more I can learn about the family, the better the chance I might be able to locate him."

"She didn't like him very much. Evidently, Mary Margaret's husband, . . . Jeremiah, I believe that was his name," she said, thoughtfully questioning her recall in the middle of her statement.

"Anyway, he wasn't very friendly. Mother confirmed what I could remember about the family. They were from an Amish background and kept to themselves. Mary Margaret was much more down to earth, but the typical obedient wife. From what Mother said, Sarah was a little slow mentally. Not really retarded, but a dreamer of sorts, and slow in learning. She was harshly restricted by her father, especially after Mary Margaret died."

"Do you remember anything about Richard and Sarah being friendly?"

"Richard and I were very close when we were children. There's only a year separating us; I, being the eldest. He was infatuated with her and would take every opportunity to see her whenever possible. Sarah didn't go to school. Richard would skip just to be with her. I can recall being jealous of his being brave enough to risk being caught." She laughed softly for a moment and then her mood became sullen. "The night Sarah died, Richard fell and hit his head. He's never been the same since."

"Could you elaborate more about the circumstances?" Matt found himself almost pleading.

"All I really know is they both had accidents. Sarah drown and Richard hit his head. We've never been able to determine what actually happened, but Richard was found lying on the ground not far from the jetty in Deale the morning after Sarah died. Her father supposedly pulled her from the water and wasn't able to revive her."

"Doesn't that seem strange? Do you think the accidents were related?" Matt's mind was going a mile-a-minute.

"Would you excuse me for a moment? Someone's at the door."

She left the phone before he could answer. Matt could hear some background noise and muffled conversation in her absence. He took the opportunity to quickly freshen his drink.

"I'm sorry," he eventually heard her say on her return. "It was the next-door neighbor delivering a package she had received for me." Beth hesitated for a moment. "Where were we? Oh, yes," she continued before Matt could refresh her memory. "Yes, to your question. I've always thought both accidents had something

173

to do with each other. You have to remember; however, back in that time law enforcement wasn't as thorough as it is today. The fact their misfortunes seem to have occurred within a short distance of each other is odd, to say the least. We eventually concluded Richard injured himself trying to save Sarah."

"I see," Matt said. "Sarah may have been on the jetty and fell in the water?"

"Again, it's only conjecture. She may have drown anywhere along the creek, or even from her own backyard, for matter. The water was much deeper, then, than it is now."

Matt changed his direction. "Is it possible Richard might know what happened to Mr. Colison?"

"Not likely," Beth said, slightly chuckling. "He's in a world all of his own."

"Do you see Richard often?" Matt's persistence was becoming more apparent.

"To your question, no. But, there's something that's beginning to bother me," she said, showing concern. "I understand your desire to find Mr. Colison, but I'm somewhat confused by your questionable interest in details about Sarah and Richard. I certainly don't see how that can help you in anyway."

"I . . . Matt stopped, collecting his thoughts, afraid to confront Ann with the truth behind his concerns. Using the excuse of having an incoming call, he put the phone on hold to muster courage. Finishing the contents of his glass, he got a quick refill and decided he had to take a chance on possibly blowing her mind. He reactivated the conversation. "Please forgive me. I can't tell you how much I appreciate the time you've allowed in helping me." He hesitated. There was no response on the other end of the phone except for hearing her breathing, denoting her presence. "Please bear with me briefly. I promise to explain more in a moment. But first, how long did you live in your home after the accidents and Mr. Colison deserted his property?"

Moments passed before she responded. "I was seventeen when Sarah died, and twenty-six when I married and left home. Mother kept the property for several years after Dad died in 1969. He didn't leave her with much more than the house and a meager social security income." She again paused. "I still don't see what

. . ."

Matt interrupted. "Did you ever notice anything strange regarding the Colison home after everything happened?"

"What are you inferring?" Beth definitely sounded perturbed.

"This is very awkward," Matt confessed. "I've been inside of the house and experienced some rather strange feelings. It's as if there's a presence of something unusual, . . . maybe weird." Silence over the line was almost deafening. Matt waited to hear the receiver on the other end close the conversation. Instead, Ann's increased breathing became clearly audible. "Are you still there?" Matt finally asked.

"Yes." Her response was short and without expression. She offered nothing further.

Matt was at a loss. He didn't know what else to say. The following moments seemed like endless hours. Finally, the quietude was over.

"This comes as a shock," Beth began. "I haven't thought about it for years."

Again, there was a pause. Matt didn't interrupt.

"I thought I was crazy. A long time ago, I mean. I still don't know if they were dreams or simply imagination. I was a young adult at the time. I remember thinking I saw an old woman working outside of the house on different occasions. One time I would look; the next minute she would be gone."

Matt suffered another pause.

"Mother talked a lot about the same things happening. But, that was only in her later years," she added. "She talked about Mary Margaret gathering jonquils long after her death. They were the flowers Richard brought to Mother before his accident." Beth began sobbing.

"Please forgive me. I had no idea my questioning would cause distress." Matt could clearly detect her blowing her nose. He assumed she was also wiping away tears.

"No. Forgive me," she corrected. "It's ridiculous to allow these things to be upsetting. Mother and I both felt the occurrences were a result of Richard's misfortune and the impact his accident caused. There was something special about Richard and his loving nature. It really hurt me when Mother turned against him in her later years. I felt it unfair she blamed him for the alienation his retarded condition created."

"I realize how much Dorothy loved Richard. It was evident during the conversation we had. For a brief period of time, she thought I was Richard."

Beth quickly responded. "I didn't know that. What did she say?"

"Well," Matt started, "she sort of chastised me by comparing me, that is, Richard, to David. It was as if she was very hurt by Richard's lack of commitment to her."

"That's consistent with her latent feelings," Beth agreed. "Mother felt he had deserted her. As she grew older, her fantasies increased. Mother talked more and more of things happening at the Colison's house. I've always felt her infatuation with all of it as being delusional. Now, at this moment, I'm beginning to wonder."

Matt started to respond, but was again too late.

"What have you seen? What have you experienced?" she asked.

"I'm not sure," he lied. "It's just a feeling, I guess." Matt wanted desperately to be more truthful, but found it impossible. "You've been more than helpful," he said, trying to escape the issue. "I really regret upsetting you and hearing about your mother."

Beth virtually ignored his apology. "I've heard stories that would make you laugh from disbelief. Richard never spoke of Sarah after his accident, but my father swore he experienced some of the same apparitions as my mother. I sense you're being reluctant to be open about something."

"Believe me. It's not important. However, I'm not sure I'd take anything mysterious about the old house for granted. It definitely has a character of its own." Matt waited for a response, but received none. "Do you feel it would do any good for me to meet with Richard?" he asked, changing the subject.

"I doubt it." She sounded relatively sure, but not positive. "I see no harm in your contacting him, if you'd like. He lives and works in Solomon's Island, but doesn't have a phone. It's rare we get to see or hear from him. I can give you his address and where he works."

Matt thanked her profusely and welcomed the information

regarding Richard's whereabouts. After promising to call Beth following his visit with her younger brother, the conversation ended.

"Another day, another lead," he said, as he replaced the receiver. "That was enlightening, to say the least." However, Matt was aware his best chance of locating Jeremiah leaned even more heavily on his ability to contact Rebecca's mother.

CHAPTER XXI

Appearances of the elderly spirit became more frequent. Matt had enjoyed the earlier lull, but questioned the reason for it. Ghosts were more than unpredictable, he thought, while sorting through dirty laundry. His mind quickly turned to more pleasant matters -- Kitty was on her way to spend a long weekend. Hustling through various chores, including a trip to the market, Matt pulled into the marina parking lot as Kitty got out of her car.

"Hi, babe," she called, motioning for him to come to her. Matt honored her request and received a bouquet of flowers in return. "These are for you," she said, kissing him on the cheek. "I've missed you so much."

Matt's blush was well apparent, even through his beard. "God, Doc. I've never gotten flowers, before. They're really pretty." Tastefully, the spring arrangement was void of jonquils. "Lord knows I've been lost without you." He wrapped his arms around her and they lingered in a long embrace.

"Hey. I saw that," Jason shouted from the other end of the lot.

Kitty giggled.

Matt responded with a middle-finger salute.

"Up yours, too," Jason called back, laughing.

"Where's Heather?" Matt shouted, giving Kitty a final squeeze.

"She's coming down later. I got away from the office early."

"Why don't we have them over for dinner?"

"Good idea." Matt smiled his approval as Jason neared.

Following the invitation, and exchanging further amenities, they parted ways and went to their respective boats. The timing for the evening repast having been arranged, Jason insisted on bringing the steaks.

Matt's cheerful mood was well apparent due to Kitty's presence. They breezed through putting groceries away and completed the arrival routine with Matt sitting on the bed watching Kitty unpack her valise and place items in drawers set aside for her use.

With several hours to spare, and having little left to do before their company was to arrive, the two mutually decided on a long walk to enjoy the warming afternoon. However, getting away from the marina proved easier said than done. Numerous encounters with fellow boaters not seen through the winter months necessitated general chitchat and introducing his new companion.

Strolls through the community without sidewalks represented a common and enjoyable source of exercise for locals and weekenders alike. Across from the marina, a path, probably existing for decades, snaked through a patch of woods and along the edge of the marsh for several hundreds of yards leading to the long rock barrier protecting the channel inlet into Rockhold and Tracy's Creeks. Unfortunately, Drum Point's jetty, for all the benefits it provided, was unlit and occasionally took its toll on careless boaters or those unfamiliar with the area.

Matt's mention of the jetty brought Kitty's gleeful plea for them to go to it before ending their tour.

Circling back through Deale Beach, they approached from a different direction and stood atop the row of rocks where they began high on the shore.

"Let's go out to the end," Kitty delightfully squealed, as if imagining it a special opportunity to more closely embrace the swelling sea.

A strong breeze suddenly arose sending intermediate waves slapping against the large stones, making the rocks slippery due to the spray. "I don't think it's such a good idea," Matt said, grabbing her by the arm.

"But . . ."

"Believe me, Doc. It's not worth it," he interrupted, insisting she heed his word of advice.

Instead of responding, Kitty stood gazing out to the end of the jetty.

Putting his arm around her shoulders, he asked, "Are you all right?"

"Uh, . . . yeah. I guess," she sluggishly answered, then turned her head and smiled before planting a brief kiss on his cheek. "Come on. It's time we got back, anyway."

Dinner was excellent and the evening full of fun. A large part of it telling jokes and playing a limited version of charades, there was much laughter and frivolity -- a perfect dose of distraction away from the seriousness of recent weeks.

Not wanting it to end, it was three-thirty before hitting the sack and almost noon by the time they crawled out of bed -- both suffering from slight hangovers. Jason and Heather having returned to their own boat allowed the freedom to roam about scantily dressed. Clad in boxer shorts, Matt fixed a pot of coffee as Kitty sat in the recliner wearing one of Matt's long sleeved shirts, with its tail tucked between her thighs.

"Do you feel as bad as I do?" she moaned.

"I reckon," he softly mumbled, and laughed. "Don't talk so loud."

Kitty forced a smile he didn't see. "I'm sorry about last night. I really wanted to make love, but I think I was asleep before my head hit the pillow."

"I think I beat you to it. Otherwise, I would have heard you snoring."

"I don't snore." She tried to sound indignant. "Do I?" she immediately asked, in a manner wishfully expecting a negative response.

"Just joking." He poured two mugs full of the rich steaming liquid and started to doctor them, but stopped. "Hope you agree. I think black is a better color for you right now," he said, handing her one of the vessels.

"Is there an ethnic inference in that suggestion?" Kitty started laughing.

"Go to hell, . . . and careful. It's really hot."

She accepted his offer and sat it on a small table next to her chair.

Matt plopped on the couch across from her. "Last night was almost worth the pain."

"Uuhhhh," she groaned, sitting up to sample her coffee.

"Isn't it grand to be so energetic after having so much fun?"

"When you're ready to do some pushups, let me know." Even the thought of exercising made him feel exhausted.

They both sat silently for quite some time trying to sip their woes away. The phone rang startling them from their stupor.

Kitty was closest. She answered. "Hello." Following a pause she handed the phone to Matt. "It's a her," she commented, sticking out her tongue.

Matt cleared his throat and took a sip of coffee before speaking. "Hello," he said into the receiver. Another pause. "That's great," he commented, a brightened smile reflecting across his face. "Good. I'll do that right away. And, thanks a million." Again, another, but shorter pause. "I definitely will. I promise," he assured. "Bye."

Kitty had popped to full alert by Matt's enthusiastic reactions during the conversation. "Good news, huh?"

"Super," Matt said. "That was Rebecca Fletcher. I haven't been able to reach her mother in Florida because she and her husband have been in the Bahamas. . . . They're back. She said I could reach them tomorrow."

"Oh. Heck. I thought it might have been Sarah," she groaned, trying to be funny, but quickly wishing she hadn't made such a distasteful remark. She breathed a sigh of relief when, for whatever reason, Matt ignored having heard her.

"Damn, Doc. I really feel this is the important link to locating old man Colison. God, I hope so," he added. Matt put the cordless back in its cradle, leaned and kissed Kitty on her cheek, and excused himself while he retired to the head.

The phone rang, again. Kitty answered, but there was no response from the other end. "Hello," she repeated, for a second, third, and fourth time.

Matt returned as she hung up the phone. "Who was that?"

"Nobody there. Wrong number, I guess."

"Want some more coffee?" he asked, moving to the sink to rinse his cup.

"Lord, no. Not black, anyway." Kitty got to her feet and joined him in the galley. "There wouldn't be any tomato juice by any chance?" she asked, opening the refrigerator door.

"As a matter of fact, yep, but not in there. It's in the

computer cabin closet. I've started using it as a pantry. I'll get it in a minute."

"Don't be silly. I'll get it." Kitty disappeared around the corner and shortly returned sporting a six-pack of V8 juice and a quart of vodka in her other hand.

"Need a little hair of the dog, huh?" he said, laughing. "Make me one, too."

"Stop making fun of me, and I will," she said, whimpering.

Matt chuckled and sat two glasses taken from the cupboard in front of her on the counter. As she started to open the bottle, he moved to stand behind her and slowly ran his hands upwards under her shirt until they cupped her naked breasts.

Kitty pressed backwards against his body, leaning her head against his shoulder while feeling the strength and security of his arms encircle her torso. Slowly she turned to face him, his hands lowering to tenderly grasp her buttocks. A look of heightened passion welled in her face and eyes. Kitty placed her hands inside the waist band of his shorts and slipped them downwards until they fell to his ankles.

As if by telepathy, they both slid to the floor simultaneously, never losing contact with each others lips. The deep shag carpeting lent the sensation of fur against their bodies. Matt's lips caressed her skin, pausing briefly at each nipple, and proceeded their exploration until his tongue manipulated the softness nestled between her slightly opened legs.

Matt's touch became too enjoyable to bear. Kitty raised slightly from her prone position and begged him to hold her. As they turned to lie on their sides, Kitty's left leg rested across his hip. She moaned as his penetration caused an eruption of erotic spasms originating deep within her abdomen to speed throughout her body and to the very tips of her fingers and toes. Her nails dug deeply into Matt's back. He groaned in ecstasy and thrust himself even deeper. Kitty pressed her hips downward and toward his groin in total acceptance of his need. With renewed exalted tremors, she climaxed for a second and, then, a third time.

Matt rolled Kitty to her back without causing withdrawal. Her legs cradled his lower body as he showered kisses across her face and neck. Kitty swooned momentarily from the experience. He could feel her body tremble with a final throe of unprecedented rapture. And then came silence. There was no movement for what seemed to be an endless period of time, save the swells of their chests breathing contentment.

"Is it necessary to tell you how much I love you?" Matt whispered.

Kitty touched her lips to his neck. "Never more," she softly answered. "But I'd like to be reminded like this more often."

Matt smiled and gently rolled to his side.

Kitty turned to face him.

He ran the tip of his index finger from the nape of her neck slowly downwards between her breasts and across her stomach until he stopped and began lightly stroking her pubic hair.

"Was Catherine a brunette, like me?"

"No. She was blond."

"Is it true blonds have more fun?"

Matt sensed her devilish-side surfacing. "What do you think?" he answered with a question.

"No way, Jose." She pulled away and sprang to her feet and bent over offering her hands in assistance for him to follow suit.

"Hell. You think I can't do what you just did, don't you?" He popped to his knees and made it no further, plopping to his other side. "Aw, geeze," he said moaning. "I'm not good for anything, any more."

"You'll never get me to agree with that." She laughed, and again offered her help. "Come on, Grandpa. Join me up here in my world."

Matt took her hands and slowly gained his stance. "I thought sleeping on the floor was supposed to be good for the back."

"We weren't sleeping. Or, didn't you notice?" she said.

"Smart-ass. You know better than that." He tried to pinch her butt, but she dodged his effort.

They heard Jason shout from the bridge door entrance. "Anybody home?"

"Oh, God." Kitty gasped and made a beeline for the aft cabin.

Matt grabbed for the white Afghan draped across the back of the couch. He barely had time to swirl himself into it before their intruder reached the salon.

"I like your gown." Jason winked with his witty comment.

Matt could do nothing but laugh. To keep from falling down,

he sat on the front edge of the recliner due to the cover becoming tangled in his feet.

"If you're having a toga party, I'm really hurt we weren't invited. Got any coffee? We're out."

"You're crazy. I thought I was nuts, but you take the cake." Matt continued his hysterics and shaking his head.

"All right. 'Fess up. You and Kitty have been asked to make an appearance on 'Let's make a Deal.'" Jason laughed and carried his cup of java to take a seat on the couch.

"When you get a little older I'll tell you all about it." Matt choked his final words, attempting to stifle his laughing gig.

"Oh, wow. I didn't almost . . . . Did I?" Jason's face altered to an embarrassed frown.

Matt lost it again and got up to struggle to the sink and douse his face with water.

"I did. I know I did. Geeze, I'm sorry, Matt. I shouldn't have barged in the way I did."

"Forget it," Matt managed to say, wiping his face against his wooly garment. "We were just testing out a new parlor game on the floor. Take my word. It's great," he said in a devious tone, and then added, "but rough on the backside."

"Aw, Matt. I really apol . . ."

"Damn it, Jason. It's okay," he assured. "Hell. If anything, you popping up added a startling conclusion to an already hellava climatic end."

Jason laughed. "Okay. But I'm sorry, anyway. You want I should leave?"

"No. Hell, no. Make yourself comfortable while I get cleaned up and dressed. If you haven't had breakfast, go get Heather and we can cook over here."

Matt fumbled his way below and met Kitty entering the head. Seeing him in his attire initiated a sinister giggle and a shove into the shower.

* * *

The following morning brought rain and telltale scars of yesterday's rememberable moments. Kitty wore a quite noticeable bruise at the base of her neck and Matt's back bore evidence of animalistic claw like marks. However, they were easily accepted as wonderful painless reminders of something more beautiful than either had ever experienced.

Kitty awoke early, with dawn's light just beginning to illuminate the cabin. Matt rested on his side with his back to her. Carefully, so as not to awake him, she moved to bring her naked body in contact with his and placed her right arm around his waist. He stirred slightly and enveloped her forearm with his, drawing it to his chest. "Love you," he said.

"Sorry. I didn't mean to wake you," Kitty whispered.

"Uuummmm," he moaned, in a low tone. "It's okay. I like you to hold me."

She placed her lips against his back for several moments. "Matt."

"Yeah."

"Yesterday when we were at the jetty" She paused to kiss his back, "I had a strange feeling."

"What?"

"I don't know what it was, but when you restrained me, I wanted to pull away."

Matt turned in his spot to face her.

"It was like I didn't feel the wind or see that the rocks were wet and dangerous." Kitty paused to collect her thoughts. "I just felt a great need to be closer to the water."

CHAPTER XXII

After Kitty left early Sunday afternoon, Ellen called her dad to ask if he might be available to take care of Terry for a couple of days. She was ill with chicken pox and neither she nor Jack could afford missing work. Matt packed enough to tide him over and called Kitty before he left, leaving a message and number where he could be reached on her answering machine.

Terry survived; Ellen tremendously pleased, and Matt exhausted after spending four days keeping up with his eight-year-old granddaughter. He could have never imagined how much he would ever look forward to the solitude offered by getting back to the boat.

After arriving at the marina around noon, the first thing he did was pour a double Scotch and water and settle into his favorite of all-time chair. He reached for the remote, pushed the power button and punched a series of keys, but could get nothing other than static on all of the channels.

"Damn," he said. "Friggin' cable's out again."

Turning it off, he sipped his drink and settled back in thought. Only seconds later, he sat upright, then got to his feet while reaching for his wallet. Pulling a slip of paper from inside, he opened it, reached for the phone, and placed a call to Florida.

The phone rang numerous times. On the verge of hanging up, someone answered.

"Hello."

"Mrs. Fletcher?"

"Yes."

"This is Matt Bodine. I've been in touch with your daughter, Rebecca, and she suggested I speak with you."

"Oh, yes, Mr. Bodine. Rebecca said to expect your call."

Matt considered letting her know how difficult it had been to reach her, but thought better of it.

Before he could respond, she continued. "We've been so much on the go, I apologize if you've had difficulty in reaching me. My husband and I have gotten spoiled with retirement and don't know when to stay home."

Matt laughed politely. "I envy you," he said, in a complimentary manner.

"Rebecca told me of your interest. How may I help you?"

"Well, your daughter was able to provide some family history, but somewhat unsure of certain details. I assume you're aware of my intent. That's to purchase Jeremiah's property, which is still titled in his name, at least." Matt paused briefly, but received no response. "I'm semi-retired. My wife passed away a few years ago and I'm living on a boat quite near his old house. The old place is badly deteriorated, but, having been a builder, I've become intrigued with restoring it. My problem is locating Jeremiah."

"Oh, my lord. You ask for miracles," she said, laughing. "I haven't seen him in so many years I can't even remember. I didn't even know he was alive."

"If you could please give me any information about what took place back in the thirties it might be very helpful. From what I've been able to find out, Jeremiah deserted his place not long after his daughter died."

"Yes. I do remember Sarah having had an accident, but I really wasn't aware of what happened to Jeremiah following the incident."

"Rebecca said you had four uncles, but she couldn't recall their names."

"They were long gone before she was even born. It's regrettable, but our family, the Colison side I mean, seemed to fall apart over the years. Of course, I feel the depression had a great deal to do with it."

"Could you give me your uncles names? Rebecca wasn't sure."

"Certainly. I should have already."

Matt asked her to wait for a second while he got a pen and then she continued. "James, Matthew, Peter, and of course,

188

Jeremiah. James was my favorite. He was the youngest, and closest to my mother, too."

Matt noted every name on the cover of a boating magazine.

"If it hadn't been for James, we would have known nothing at all. He wrote to Mother for quite some time, even after they moved to Virginia."

A tinge of excitement surged through Matt. "Do you think they might still be in Virginia? And when you say they, I assume you mean all of your uncles except Jeremiah."

"They may well be. And that's correct. When Grandpa Jacob

died, he left a small legacy to each of his children, including my mother. From what I understand, Jeremiah was only fifteen when Sarah was born out of wedlock." She coughed and cleared her throat. "Please, excuse me. I caught a bit of a cold on our cruise. I don't believe I ever knew Sarah's mother's name, but she was even younger than Jeremiah. Such a shame," she added. "It's hard to imagine those things can happen, even back then."

Matt wanted to say it was disgusting, but didn't.

"Jeremiah took her and the baby off and got married. Again, if it hadn't been for James, we would never have known anything about it. He must have used his inheritance to buy the property, I guess."

"I take it he was also close to James."

"A bit more than the other two, but they all got along pretty well according to Mother. She was the one they ignored for the most part." She coughed again and excused herself. "The Amish have some strange ways.

When great-grandfather Joseph was disowned, it didn't change many things. A great deal of the culture lingers on as if it's part of you, not just in your heart or mind. In my lineage, I was the only one to make a decided deviation from the Amish traditions. The rest clung to Mennonite tradition, for the most part, or in Jeremiah's case I'm not sure."

"Did the other three move from Lancaster directly there?"

"Oh, no. They lived somewhere near Washington, D.C. for a while. I don't know for how long, but Mother talked about them working for the government. Now that I think about it, between the three of them, they were probably able to invest into a sizable piece of land. I'm sure that's what they must have had in mind when they left. Being in your area gave them a good opportunity to locate something of value."

"You don't have any idea as to where in Virginia they might have gone?"

"Not really. Even then, there's no guarantee Jeremiah ever joined them, although it is a strong possibility."

Matt's mind whirled in attempting to digest everything.

"I do have some pictures I found among Mother's things after she died. I don't see how they could help, but, I'll send them to you if you promise they're returned. They really have little meaning to me, but they are keepsakes."

Matt was taken aback by her offer. "That's almost too generous," he managed to say. "But, I certainly accept. I'll see that you get them back right away. In fact, if you have no objections, I'll make copies of any I feel important. But, I'm curious about something. I really know very little about the Mennonite culture, but isn't it unusual to allow photos to be taken of themselves."

Mrs. Fletcher laughed. "Yes, that's very true, but those boys were always independent in their actions. While they followed the old lifestyles to a great extent, they rarely denied themselves of modern conveniences," she said. "I sincerely wish you luck in your search."

Matt provided his address before the conversation ended.

Things were looking up, he thought. His enthusiasm was difficult to control, but he reluctantly gave up the notion to call Kitty at work, deciding it best to wait until she arrived home. To his delight, she called shortly after four p.m. having taken off a bit early. Kitty's news was as welcomed as his own in learning of her plan to have a series of guest lecturers for Friday classes, freeing her for long weekends.

Three days later, the photos arrived via UPS. There were eight pictures in total -- three being group shots of the brothers, minus Jeremiah. The remainder were candid copies of their children and other relatives; the date and names of most of those included in the snapshots appeared on the back. Initially, Matt felt great disappointment with what he observed. Trying to find them by their family name was like looking for the old proverbial needle in a haystack.

God, he thought. It's only supposition they're still in Virginia. They could be anywhere, by now. "That's stupid," he said, and then returned to his thoughts. What are the chances of the entire family all moving at the same time? They did it before, he argued in his mind. But, that's when there were fewer roots, he countered.

Matt rose from the sofa, placed the pictures on the table, and moved to the cabinet to retrieve a magnifying glass. Before returning, he took time to grab a glass and poured a coke over a couple of ice cubes. Taking a seat at the table, he carefully spread the pictures neatly into two rows of four each and began examining them more intently.

This time, he focused on the surroundings instead of the subjects. Two held some promise. In one of the photos, Jeremiah's brothers were standing in front of what seemed to be a shop of some kind or another. In the other, several children were playing in a yard and in the distance there appeared to be a large farming structure. Straining to see more detail, Matt decided to go above deck for better lighting. He found some improvement, ascertaining there was definitely letters embedded across the top of the door jamb leading into the building behind the three brothers. Even then, the age of the photo and a shadow from the porch roof made it impossible to read. To further complicate matters, an old horseshoe hung in the center of the wording.

In the second picture, what had appeared to be a line of bushes in the background behind the children now could be discerned as a large herd of cattle. A wooded area beyond them obstructed a clear view of the building, except for its rooftop, but one of the three silos brandished lettering, again, too blurred to read.

"Hey, Dude. A penny for your thoughts," Jason said. Matt was too preoccupied to notice his arrival.

"Uh, yeah," he answered. "Sorry, . . . off in another world."

"Got a problem?" Jason asked.

"No, and yeah. I'm trying to locate some people and these are all I really have to go on." Matt extended the snapshots and the enlarging glass to Jason as he arrived on the aft deck. "Supposedly, they were taken somewhere in Virginia. You can see on the back how many years ago that was. Looks to me like there's lettering above the door in the one shot, and also on one of the silos in the other."

Jason spent several moments scrutinizing each of the photos. "You're right on both counts," he finally agreed, and eventually added. "But, I can't make any of it out."

"There's some more below," Matt said. "Want a drink?" Matt started down the stairs before getting a reply.

"Take a beer."

After spending about an hour going over the pictures and shooting the bull, Jason excused himself due to several pressing matters he wanted to confront. His assessment that photo-enhancement might prove beneficial was a possibility, especially after explaining there were new technologies involving computer-assisted methods that might foster excellent results.

Matt's experience with computers was limited to what little Kitty had taught him. However, basing his reasoning that law-enforcement undoubtedly used such techniques, and sure he had seen such a thing in a movie, he concluded it a concept to investigate. One of his golf buddies happened to be an inspector with the Prince Georges Police Department and represented the perfect place to start.

Luckily catching his friend at the station, Matt learned a great deal about the feasibility of his project and even got the name of a company occasionally contracting various analysis projects for his friend's department.

Matt immediately made a phone call and the outfit's representative suggested he submit the photos for review at his convenience. Reluctant to trust the mail, it was agreed he could hand-deliver the photos.

Matt stuffed some cold cuts between two slices of bread, poured a glass of milk, and devoured both, posthaste.

After a quick shower he tried contacting Kitty without success. He left a message at her office, and a few additional details on her machine at home. He placed the snapshots in a small envelope and put them in the inside breast pocket of his sports jacket.

It was two p.m. when he slid behind the wheel of his sports car; the drive requiring the better part of an hour. As anxious as he was to get going, he never made it out of the parking space. The engine coughed a few times and refused to restart.

"Damn it," he bellowed, in complete disgust.

Two seconds later he felt remorse for cursing the small automobile that had always been so faithful. He got out of the car, pulled the hood latch, all the while knowing the action was useless. Carburetors he could handle -- fuel-injection drew a complete blank.

Jason was on his way to the store and noticed the hood sticking up in the air and sought to be of help. It was soon a foregone conclusion Matt was stuck until he got bonafide mechanical assistance.

Jason eventually made his departure and Matt disappointedly headed back to the boat with the intention of trying to contact Kitty again and call a tow truck.

As Matt approached the pier, he found himself straining with each forward step. His legs rebelled against their intended purpose and his breathing became increasingly labored. He came to a halt and bent over placing his hands on his knees and hanging his head trying desperately to gain air into his lungs.

A low ringing in his ears rose in pitch then slowly subsided into a haunting murmur of a young girl's voice beckoning him to come to her. "Richard, I love you. I need you." The words echoed time and again as a siren might do to lure its prey. Matt's attempts at trying to resist were futile. And then, no longer was there the ability to rationalize, although somewhere deep inside remained a confused sense of awareness. More important, he couldn't control what was happening to him or whatever he was about to do.

Matt straightened his stance and gazed toward the house. He began to walk slowly approaching it; his movements freed from previous restraint.

The world seemed to be standing still. He was oblivious to all else save the mesmerizing voice filling his brain and Sarah motioning him to come to her from the doorway of the old wooden home.

As he reached the entrance, her shape faded into nothingness, but the power drawing him onward did not ease. He stepped inside and again witnessed the awe of entering another dimension; the house being as it must have been over sixty-years past. The air was saturated with the scent of fresh flowers. The faint sounds of the old lady humming her tune seemed to originate from everywhere, but nowhere at the same time.

With unexplainable intent, Matt moved through the hallway and stood at the bottom of the staircase. At the top, Sarah's shape formed, extending her left hand beseeching him to continue. Matt's steps upward slowed slightly. A small ray of strength struggled deep within to pull away from the spirits dominance, but failed in the effort.

"Richard, I've missed you so," the misty image said, extending each syllable and word into a drone-like slur, her lips moving as if in slow motion.

Matt reached out to grasp her hand, finding nothing. The ghostly mirage had dissipated and now appeared just inside the small bedroom where he had found the diary. Entering the room, the spirit hovered at the end of the bed -- now tastefully made and covered with a patchwork quilt.

As if knowing her next desire, Matt moved to the bed, turning to sit on its edge. He laid back, altering his position so as to lie on his back with his head resting on the pillow. Sarah begin chanting her melody which, for the first time, Matt realized was the same tune the old lady constantly hummed.

Sarah began swirling in dance covering all of the available floor, back and forth, and again and again. Her image slowly began to ascend until her movements carried her to a point as if she would continue on through the ceiling, but the ceiling was no longer there. In its place was a dark void -- an endless nothingness eking despair.

Matt was frightened. He was afraid and he realized it. His emotions were starting to surface; his muddled mind beginning to find limited focus. Hovering above him, Sarah began drifting downward -- a chilling aura preceding her not unlike a cold winter wind. Her hand touched and pressed against his chest until she came to lay upon him, then permeated his body and very soul.

Matt wanted to scream. He tried. He couldn't. Nothing but muffled sounds escaped his throat. He wanted to cry from the pain of the hideous cold surging throughout his body. Yet, he couldn't move. He laid in disgust listening to the moans and throes of the perpetrator's unearthly orgasm.

Then there was darkness; no sound; no movement.

* * *

"Oh, dear God," Kitty screamed, as she rushed into the aft cabin seeing Matt lying on the bed swaddled in blankets.

Jason was right behind her.

"Matt. Please, Matt. Speak to me."

There was no response of any type, only labored breathing.

Kitty checked his pulse and pulled the covers down to examine him more thoroughly. He was still clad in his clothes. His neck, hands and arms, like his face, were all lacking color and ashen in appearance -- his skin unnaturally cold to the touch. There was little doubt in her mind Matt had experienced a full-fledged physical contact with the spirit in some form or another. She had been warned of these possible consequences by Celeste.

Jason left the cabin briefly to grab a bottle of brandy and a glass, filling it half-full. On his return he offered it to Kitty. She started to accept and suddenly began to weep hysterically.

Jason sat the drink next to the bed and pulled her into his arms to calm her.

"Tell me. Tell . . . tell me again what happened," she stammered, between sobs.

"I found him . . .

"No. From the very beginning. Everything. Everything earlier."

Jason paused for a moment to gather his thoughts. "Well, Matt was having trouble getting his car started and I tried to give him a hand. We didn't have any success, so I left to take care of a few chores. As far as I knew, Matt was headed back to the boat. I wasn't gone more than a half-hour and noticed Matt standing in the doorway of the old house. I called to him, but he didn't answer. Then, I saw him tumble forward onto the ground. It was a sure thing something was really wrong and I got to him as quick as I could. He was unconscious and I needed help getting him onto the boat and into bed. The first thing I did after that was call you." Jason squeezed his arms as if to reassure her. "Are you sure you don't want to call an ambulance?"

"He's suffering from shock. You did the best thing by

keeping him warm." Kitty caught herself choking back a sob as she pulled away from Jason. "If he doesn't show any improvement in the next couple of hours, we'll do that."

Matt moaned. His head writhed slowly from side-to-side. "No," he said. "Naaaa . . . No," he screamed, and became still once more -- his breathing slightly improved.

"Matt, it's Kitty," she implored. "Please speak to me."

"Cold," he muttered. "So cold."

"Jason, help me. Raise his head a little." Kitty reached for the glass of brandy and placed it against his lips. Matt choked a little, but managed to swallow a few small sips, most of it running down his chin and cheeks. He was out again. "Come on," Kitty said, motioning with her hand, "let's go to the salon. He needs a lot of rest."

Jason went immediately to the refrigerator and got a beer. "What in the hell's going on?" he asked, his voice showing a great deal of frustration. "He looks like he's been to hell and back."

Kitty meekly grinned and, exhausted, plopped on the couch. "You're not too far from the truth." She leaned back, placing both hands over her eyes and forehead. "It's a very long story, Jason, but in short, Matt has just went through a paranormal experience of monumental impact. He's made physical contact with a spirit from the other side."

"You're kidding m . . . no you're not," he corrected in mid-sentence. "You're serious, aren't you?"

"Never more so in my life," Kitty said, sitting forward. "What happened a little while ago was just another step in a progression of events that's been taking place since before I met Matt. The old house is haunted . . . for the choice of a better word, and its spirit has identified itself with Matt. We've done a lot of research and investigation into whatever's occurring, but haven't yet been able to determine why."

"Holy, shit," Jason said, shaking his head as if to jumble everything absorbed into place. "This is what Heather's been helping you with?"

"Yes. But she has no concept of the complexity or details of it all. I thought it best to keep it that way." Kitty stood and went to check on Matt and returned after several moments. "He seems to be doing okay, but could you give me a hand. I want you to help me get him out of his clothes. He'll be more comfortable."

Jason followed Kitty to the aft cabin and raised Matt by his shoulders as she slipped Matt's arms from the sleeves of his sports coat. Unbuttoning his shirt, she noticed a slightly rectangular area on the left side of his chest which appeared to be a bruise. After a brief examination, they completed removing everything except his shorts and managed to get him between the sheets and under several additional blankets. He remained unconscious the entire time.

Kitty gathered his clothes and carried them to the salon. As she handled the sports coat, the envelope Matt had placed inside fell to the floor. Picking it up, she fingered the flap open and found the two pictures.

Jason moved to look over her shoulder. "They're the photos Matt had earlier. Two of them had some lettering we couldn't make out and I suggested he have them enhanced." Jason literally snatched one of them from her grasp. "Jesus, God," he gasped. "I don't believe it."

"What is it?" Kitty implored.

"This picture. This is one of them. It had the words we couldn't read," Jason blurted.

Kitty strained to see the small inscription which now was distinct. Above the doorway was the name of the store: 'Magrueder's.' The horseshoe, once hanging in the center, was no longer there.

CHAPTER XXIII

Kitty awoke with a start, quickly sitting upright on the couch as the blanket covering her slipped to the floor. The sun shone brightly through the starboard portholes denoting it to be early afternoon. Looking at her watch confirmed the fact it was twenty past one. She was exhausted. The past three days had been harrowing and the previous night Matt was extremely restless. Kitty had sat on the floor beside his bed until the wee hours of the morning. It had been almost daylight before he settled down and she was able to rest. She slowly got up and moved to the galley, pouring a cup of yesterday's brew into a mug. She placed it in the microwave, setting the timer for two minutes and patiently waited. The beep finally sounded. Taking the cup in one hand and her cigarettes and lighter in the other, she made her way to the bridge and took a seat in a deck chair, immediately lighting one of the filter-tips.

A smattering of people milled around the marina doing one thing or another. Other than that, activity on the creek was at a minimum. Kitty gazed at the old house as she sipped her coffee. Her mind became full of fantasies about what Matt may have experienced during his last visit.

Celeste wasn't surprised when Kitty called and related the occurrence. However, other than knowing it to be of traumatic proportion, she knew nothing of the details. She advised things had gone well beyond the point of no return. Matt had no choice other than to see the matter to its end. The spirit had established a portal between the dimensions and would never relinquish its hold until its needs were satisfied.

A tear trickled down Kitty's cheek. She wiped it away with the tips of her fingers, taking a final drag from the almost spent cigarette. Stubbing the butt in an ashtray, she heard the phone ring and rushed below to answer it.

"Yes."

"Kitty. It's me."

"Oh, Jason. Hi."

"I've got the results of the enhancement enlargements of the two photos. It's amazing. I've got a little more to do at the office but I'll be down right afterwards. See ya. Bye."

Kitty replaced the receiver and unexpectedly heard the sound of rushing water coming from the stern.

Matt was taking a shower.

She rushed to the head throwing open the door. "Are you all right?" she asked with great exuberance.

"Doc, is that you? What are you doing here? Pulling the shower curtain aside he stuck his head out and kissed her on the cheek. "Love you," he said, closing the transparent curtain while continuing to lather his body with soap.

"How do you feel?" Kitty asked, lowering the toilet cover and taking a seat.

"Okay, I guess. I didn't sleep well last night. I kept having dreams, but I can't remember what they were about." Matt caught a mouth-full of water from the sprinkler head, gargled, and spit it out. He continued to lather himself, rinse, and do it all over again.

Kitty sat still, hesitant to say anything.

"You never answered me. I thought you weren't going to be able to make it down. I sure am glad to see you, though." Matt pulled the curtain aside. "Hand me a towel, hon." He began drying himself.

Kitty got a second towel and began to dry his back.

"That feels good," he said, "rub harder." Matt's back was already dry, as well as the rest of his body, but he continued to scrub his skin with the towel until it began to appear raw.

Kitty placed her arms around his waist and gently kissed him between the shoulder blades.

"Don't do that," he shouted, wrenching himself from her grasp. He immediately stepped back into the shower, turning the faucets on full blast.

Kitty was stunned. She couldn't fathom the notion her touch

could be repulsive to Matt. Trying to cover the hurt, she left the head to return to the salon. "Calm down," she said. "Calm down." There's got to be reason for his actions, she rationalized, and sat on the couch in deep thought.

Matt eventually came into the salon and went directly to the refrigerator, getting a coke. "What's wrong with me?" He turned his back to the fridge and slid down until resting against it and sitting on the floor. His knees drawn against his chest, his face buried in his hands -- he began to cry.

Kitty rushed to kneel before him, reluctant to touch him in anyway. "It'll be all right, sweetheart. It'll be fine."
Matt looked up. Tears streaming down his cheeks. "Hold me. God, please hold me. I feel so lost."

Kitty scooted to his side, placing her arms around him. They sat for a long time until he gained control.

Matt finally attempted to rise and struggled to get to his feet. He moved to the sink, washing his face with cold water.
Kitty pulled off some paper towels and handed them to him.
"Thanks, hon." He dabbed his face dry while Kitty opened his drink and poured it into a glass of ice.

"Feel a little better?"

Matt drank generously. "I guess. Just feel really tired." He moved to sit on the couch. She followed. "When did you get down here?"

"Five days ago."

Matt looked confused. "What? . . . What day is today?"

"Saturday. You've been out of it since Monday," she said.

"Come on now, you're kidding me," he said. His smile faded seeing Kitty's serious expression. "What was wrong with me?"

"You were in shock for quite some time." Kitty patted him on his hand. "Are you sure you're up to talking about this?"

"Shock? From what?" Matt was getting edgy. "Yeah, I'm okay. What happened?"

"I don't know any of the details, but you had some kind of a trying experience at the old house last Monday. Can you remember anything at all?"

Matt stood up and went to the bar, pouring himself some brandy. "Want some?"

"Yes, please." Kitty moved to sit at the table. She opened a pack of cigarettes and lit one as Matt placed her glass in front of her. He sat down on the opposite side.

"I don't know. I remember I was going to take the pictures to a company in Beltsville and the car wouldn't start. Jason tried to help me with it and then left to go to the store. I got a little irritated and headed back to the boat to call a tow truck. I don't think I ever did." Matt sipped his drink.

"We're not sure what exactly happened, but Jason saw you come out of Sarah's house and fall to the ground. He got help and they carried you here and put you in bed. Jason called me and I came immediately. You were suffering from shock, at first, and then delirium later."

Matt just shook his head.

"From your appearance there was little doubt in my mind you'd had physical contact again with the spirit, but this time to a much greater extent."

"I just can't remember."

"That's fine, hon. Please, don't let it worry you. The mind has a way of blocking out things too difficult to handle sometimes. In time, it may come back to you." Kitty smiled and changed the subject. "You've got to be starving. It's been a while since you've eaten."

"Now that you mention it," Matt said, "I am sort of hungry. Have you eaten?"

"No, not yet. What would you like?"

"To be honest, my stomach feels a little jittery."

"How about some homemade chicken soup? I made some yesterday."

"That sounds good." Matt got up and sat his glass on the galley counter. "Think I might feel better if I put some clothes on." Matt disappeared down the steps, heading for the aft cabin, while Kitty prepared the food. Several moments later, as she was setting the table, she heard Matt cry out, "Oh, my God."

Terrified, Kitty ran to the stern and found Matt staring into the mirror. "What's wrong?" she screamed.

"The little bitch violated me. The fuckin' little bitch raped me."

"Oh, good God." Kitty gasped. "Matt. Are you all right?"

"No. I'm fuckin' mad." Matt turned to face Kitty as he

pulled on his pants. "She thinks I'm Richard. The little shit thinks I'm her boyfriend."

"You need to get out of here for a while. I think fresh air would do you some good."

"I need to do something for sure. To get out of here before I decide to burn that damn house down."

"Matt. Listen to yourself. You've got to calm down. Let's take a walk. No, . . . let's go fishing."

"Hell . . .

"Now! Before you do something you'll be sorry about."

Matt showed slight evidence of calming. He noticed Kitty trembling and took her into his arms. "Aw, Doc. I'm sorry."

Kitty gained her composure. "There's nothing to forgive. You haven't done anything wrong."

"I've upset the hell out of you."

"You couldn't help it. I'm just happy you're going to be all right." She sniffled.

Matt released his embrace and finished zipping up his pants. "Let me finish getting dressed and we'll go out for a while. We'll use Ozzie's boat."

"I've never been before. I don't know how to fish. Wiggly worms. Ugh."

* * *

Matt steered Ozzie's boat into the channel leading into the bay, passing the jetty on the way out.

"So that's the infamous Drum Point jetty," Kitty said.

Matt didn't respond, the recall of his experience and anger not completely gone.

"When we get back, I want you to take me there again."

They arrived at a buoy just off Holland Point. Matt dropped anchor and began rigging two fishing poles -- the sea unusually calm.

"I was totally helpless. I can't remember anything from the time Sarah violated me until I woke up and took the shower." Matt baited the hooks with raw shrimp and nicked his thumb. "Shit. . . . This isn't the best bait, but it'll work."

Kitty watched him warily.

Matt dropped a line over the side and handed the pole to her.

"What am I supposed to do if a fish gets on this thing?"

Matt's mood shifted -- his anger giving way to a chuckle.

Kitty made a funny face back at him. "I'm more than convinced now your apparitions far exceed simply being attempts to make closer contact."

"Closer contact? She was on top of me, Kitty."

"I know. I'm sorry. She's trying hard to tell us something."

"Yeah, that she thinks I'm her damn boyfriend and she's horny as hell."

"What I mean is that her believing you're Richard is an attempt to cry for help, more than any sexual purpose.

"What about Richard?" Matt asked. "We've got to find him."

"I agree. Especially with what's happened. I'm not sure how this all fits, but we can't ignore him or his connection. All we have is Birdie's word on it, as to how badly he was injured."

Kitty's pole jerked and bent sharply as a fish made its strike. She shrieked loudly.

Matt shook his head and grabbed the net.

* * *

They had great success, boating almost twenty good-sized Norfolk Spot. Having a great deal of fun cleaning the fish back at the marina, Matt taught Kitty the art of scaling and filleting their catch. Kitty was amazed at Matt's skill, and his technique of accomplishing the task without having to gut the fish. Moreover, Matt explained the remains would certainly not go to waste. He would freeze them and have excellent bait for his crab pots, assuring any number of excellent meals.

"By the way, what happened to the pictures?" Matt asked.

"Oh, I didn't think to tell you. Jason took them and he called earlier before you got up to let us know there were good results in the enhancements. "He's supposed to be by a little later."

"Was he able to make out the lettering?"

"You're not going to believe this, but your encounter with Sarah did more than you know. When I first saw you, you had a rectangular bruise on the left side of your chest. Right about the spot where you carried the pictures in your sports coat. As we were removing your clothes, they fell on the floor. I'd never seen them before, but Jason vowed they had already been altered for the better."

Matt started laughing sardonically. "Christ. She just won't

give up, will she?"

* * *

Jason's arrival with the pictures brought a semblance of relief. Not only did the one picture clearly show the name of the store, the other snapshot displayed letters of what seemed to be the beginning of a name and, beneath it, the first four letters of a word on one of the silos as being 'STRA.' Matt especially marveled at the fact the horseshoe hanging over the store door was gone. However, the four letters were their biggest clue, raising hopes it might indicate the area of location.

Even with Kitty's computer capabilities, the process of searching for answers wasn't easy. They had narrowed the town down to being Strasburg, Virginia, but still couldn't be completely sure. It was possible the pictures could have been taken in another state.

Checking phone numbers for Colison in that area proved negative. The name Magrueder was also a dead end. They concluded their best opportunity was to gain it through local and first-hand knowledge.

Jason and Heather were eager to volunteer to do the leg work. The two took Friday off and traveled to Strasburg, combining their search with a pleasure trip to the not too far away caverns. At the local postal office, they found there was a Colison family in the area. Calling Matt and Kitty, on their return, brought much elation.

"Damn, Doc. I can't believe all that's happened. At last, maybe we're getting somewhere."

"I hope so," Kitty said, not being as enthused as Matt. "Of all things, I don't want to deflate your hopes, but there are endless things unanswered. We can't be sure Sarah's father is the answer to everything. He might not know anything about what's going on, or the reason for it." Kitty got up from her seat and started pacing the floor. "Maybe Richard's the key to it all. We never checked out that possibility. Maybe we should have."

"Sit down, hon." Matt's voice carried an unintended demanding tone. "You're right about Richard. But, I disagree with you about Sarah's old man. I think he knows most, if not all, that's happened. But, I doubt he would admit anything unless he was confronted with irrepressible proof. Have you ever

205

considered that?" Matt got up and started pacing while Kitty was seated in his recliner.

"Yes, I have. Quite a bit as a matter of fact. But we do have the doll and tea cup which I'm sure he would recognize. I've got a feeling he wouldn't have approved of the diary and probably never ever saw it," Kitty said.

Matt's frown turned to a smile, then a chuckle. "That just shows how dumb I can be. I hadn't even considered it." Matt sat down again. "You know, sometimes I think the things happening have more meaning to them than we realize. Suppose the spirit, or spirits, have been leaving these things as clues. What if certain events were something more than just attempts to get through to me?"

Kitty rose from the recliner and moved to sit on the couch with Matt, offering him a cigarette.

He refused.

"I think there's a pretty good chance of that being the case," she said. "I haven't mentioned anything, but I've been trying to interpret the phenomena all along."

Matt smiled. "Why didn't I know that?" He chuckled.

Kitty coughed slightly from the smoke and smiled. "The problem is I haven't been able to come up with anything conclusive." Kitty paused to take another drag as Matt got up to fix a fresh pot of coffee. "It goes without saying, the diary speaks for itself. As far as the doll's concerned, I've come to believe it was meant to tell you it was Sarah, and not her mother. I decided that after your recent experience, and the diary mentioning her doll as being 'baby Sarah.' As far as the tea goes, I'm at a loss. The same is true about the jonquil."

"What about the old lady?" Matt asked.

"Her, I've got mixed feelings about. There's always the possibility it is Sarah's mother. She could be trying to help her daughter through her ordeal. I kind of doubt that, though." Kitty put her cigarette out. "I have a stronger feeling Sarah is using the second form to show the better side of her id. In other words, the young Sarah is troubled, vengeful, and determined to right a wrong. The older lady is also Sarah's spirit, but presenting the positive side of her ego, by emulating her mother in someway. If that's true, it would explain a lot of things. The good Lord knows, the power of this spirit is so strong, I doubt there's little, if anything, it can't achieve."

Matt fixed a cup of coffee for Kitty without asking. "That really makes sense, Doc." Matt handed her a cup and sat back down, sipping from his own.

"Your experiences with Sarah have been erotic and of a somewhat subversive nature. As the old woman, she's been sweet, kind and caring. The young spirit recognizes you as Richard and her lover. But remember, the elderly spirit has also referred to you as Richard, too. Kitty sipped her coffee and sat the cup on the end table, lighting up another cigarette. "I'm really glad we finally talked about all of this. Believe it or not, it's made a lot of fuzzy areas a lot more clear to me."

"Do you think we should pursue meeting with Richard?"

"Yes, I do," Kitty firmly asserted. "Even though he's latent, I think every little bit helps."

"Can I ask a dumb question?" Matt asked. "What happens when a retarded person is placed under hypnosis?"

"How much do you know about hypnotism?" Kitty asked in return.

"Not a lot. I've seen it performed on stage and over the television. Of course, a few movies have tapped on the subject. Like Bridie Murphy, you know."

Kitty grinned at his response. "Well, therapeutic hypnosis is a little bit different from that," she said. "But, getting back to your question, to my knowledge there's never been any specific research on latent subjects. Basically, any individual having the ability to focus their attention should be able to be hypnotized. Of course, the subject has to be willing, as well."

"I think we should see Richard."

CHAPTER XXIV

Solomon's Island was actually a small land mass at the tip of a southern Maryland peninsula bordered by the Chesapeake Bay and the Patuxent River. Kitty and Matt waited until the following day to make their fifty-some mile trip to see Richard.

The morning proved to be beautiful -- a perfect day to get out and away from the marina. They decided to stop in Prince Frederick, having brunch before continuing on their way.

After arriving at the boatyard where Richard worked, he was pointed out as being the man polishing teak on a sail boat nearby. He appeared trim and muscular with slightly graying hair. Matt started to approach Richard, but Kitty stopped him, grasping his arm. "Let's wait a minute. I'd like to observe him working," she said. The two watched Richard as he displayed an intensive effort in doing his chore.

"Come on," Kitty said. "Let's go meet him."

"Mr. Johnson? Could we speak with you for a moment?"

Richard remained with his back toward them, continuing to work.

"Richard?" Kitty said.

Richard turned to face them, saying nothing.

"Richard. I'm Matt and this is Kitty. We'd like to talk to you if it's all right."

"Hi. I'm Richard. I have to do my work."

"Is it okay if we talk to you while you work?" Kitty asked.

"That will be okay."

It was more than apparent Richard did have an amplified latency problem.

"Did you learn that kind of work when you were a boy?" Kitty asked.

"I don't know." Richard moved to another section of teak. "I like to do this, it makes it pretty."

"You're doing a fine job," Matt said. "Do you remember Sarah?"

"Sarah? I don't know Sarah," he said.

Kitty decided to try another direction. "Do you have a doctor you go to when you're sick?"

"Oh, yes." He answered with a first time smile. "I like Dr. Perry a whole lot. She's really nice to me. She has a candy dish on her desk."

"Do you really like candy?" Matt asked.

"Oh, yes. I like the root beer ones best."

Kitty patted Matt on his arm. "We better go."

Matt agreed with a nod of his head.

"Well, Richard. We have to leave, now, but we may visit with you another time if you'd like."

"That would be fine."

Kitty and Matt walked away and stopped on the other side of the boatyard. They stood watching Richard from the distance for a short time. He remained totally dedicated to his work.

Before leaving the boatyard, Kitty visited the office asking if she could use their phone directory while Matt got the car. Finding a Charlotte Perry listed as a physician in Solomon's, Kitty wrote her phone number and address on the back of a business card.

"Richard's sister was sure right," Matt said, as he steered his car out of the parking lot. "Aw, well. It's a nice drive down here and it sure is good getting out."

"It wasn't as non-productive as you might think. While you were getting the car, I found Richard's doctor listed in the phone book."

"What good will that do?"

"When we were discussing hypnotism, and the possibility of using it on Richard, my main problem was how to deal with responsibility. Richard certainly isn't mentally astute enough to make a decision about being hypnotized on his own and I would hesitate at legal ramifications. Since he seems to really like his doctor, I may be able to gain her assistance."

"If she'll go along with us, when do you think we might be

able to do it?" Matt asked.

"It could take a week or two to get it set up. Monday morning I'll get in touch with a psychiatrist I know who is also a hypnotist. I want to talk to her first before I do anything else."

* * *

Monday morning, Kitty was still with Matt on the boat. Not having a class until the afternoon, there was no need to hurry. Waiting until after nine o'clock, she dialed the psychiatrist's number.

A receptionist answered the phone. "Dr. Placid's office."

"Good morning. This is Dr. Smallwood calling, is Dr. Placid available."

"One moment, please."

Several seconds passed. "Kitty," Dr. Placid said. "It's good to hear from you. How've you been?"

"Fine, Beth. And, you?"

"Chugging along. What may I do for you?"

"I need to talk to you about a situation involving possibly hypnotizing a retarded gentleman."

"That sound's intriguing. Why don't we have lunch one day this week?" Beth asked.

"I don't think that's possible. My schedule is unbelievable." Kitty paused for a moment. "Do you still have Saturday hours?"

"No. Thank the good Lord I put an end to them about a year ago."

"How would you like to spend a leisurely day on a beautiful boat belonging to my friend?" Kitty asked. "I can assure you it would be enjoyable and my friend is part of the matter I wish to discuss with you."

"That sounds wonderful. I do love the water."

Kitty gave her directions before ending their conversation.

* * *

Kitty waited until Saturday morning to make the trip to the boat, arriving shortly before Beth. After her introduction to Matt, the three lounged on the aft deck having coffee and sweet rolls.

"Your boat is beautiful, Matt," Beth complimented.

"Thank you," Matt said. "I'm really glad you were able to make it."

They spent about an hour dabbling in varied conversation.

211

"Beth," Kitty said. "If you don't mind, I'd like to go ahead and get the business out of the way so we can relax and enjoy the rest of the day."

"That sound's fine to me," Beth said.

"Without going into the reasons why," Kitty began, "I'd like to have a subject placed under hypnosis for the purpose of recalling information from the past. "As I mentioned earlier, the gentleman, Richard, is retarded as a result of an accident many years ago. I feel he's focused enough to be hypnotized. My concern is in getting a legitimate approval to perform the procedure."

"Does he have living family?" Beth asked.

"Yes he does," Matt said. "A cousin. But, according to her, they haven't seen him in years. I got the impression from her their family never was very closely knit."

"I'd prefer to speak with his doctor and solicit her help," Kitty said. "Richard seems to be closely attached to her. But, besides that -- first things first. What's your feelings about his being able to be hypnotized? And, do you think using age regression could bring any positive results."

"You're right, Kitty. First things first." She turned to Matt. "Would you think too badly of me if I asked for a Bloody-Mary?"

Matt laughed. "Of course not. How about you, Doc?" He got up to go below.

"Please. That sound's good."

Matt disappeared as the conversation changed to another unrelated topic. Returning a short time later, he distributed the drinks and retook his seat. Matt lifted his Scotch and water upwards. "Cheers."

Kitty and Beth followed suit.

Beth brought the original conversation back to focus. "Regarding Richard being receptive to hypnotism, from what you've told me, I think it's a viable possibility. Knowing whether age regression will work or not is more difficult to consider. It's possible his brain injury didn't wipe out his long-term potentiation entirely, and a partial loss of his past was caused by emotional distress. If this were the case, yes, I believe there could be at least some positive results."

"Good," Kitty said emphatically. "That settles it. I'll contact

Richard's Doctor on Monday. If I'm successful in convincing her, would you be available to assist me next Saturday? It would have to take place in Solomon's Island."

"Definitely. I'm looking forward to it. But, you promised to tell me what's behind all of this."

* * *

Kitty hit it off quite well with Richard's doctor. Besides being an M.D., she also held a degree in psychology. Although hesitant at first, Dr. Perry finally agreed she would see Richard to prepare him for such a situation. If he approved, the first date she could be available was the Saturday after next -- two weeks away.

Matt and Kitty agreed they would use the coming weekend to go to Strasburg and try to locate Jeremiah Colison.

Arriving in Strasburg about midday on Saturday, they first checked into a motel, and then followed Jason and Heather's directions to the Colison's farm. Located about five miles out of town, the property rested at the base of a mountain a short way from the main highway.

"Well, it looks like were here," Matt said, breaking the silence.

"I thought the Amish didn't believe in using modern conveniences," Kitty remarked, referring to a large flatbed truck, and a small pickup parked near the barn.

Matt smiled while pulling into the driveway, then coming to a halt next to the house. He and Kitty got out of the car and walked to the porch as a younger man dressed in Amish attire, black work pants and a white long sleeve shirt, appeared at the front door.

"Good morning," the Amish lad said, as he closed the screen door behind him.

"Good morning," Matt said. "I'm Matthew Bodine and this is Kitty Smallwood."

"And, I am Luke."

"We apologize for not being able to announce our coming like this, but we're trying to locate Jeremiah Colison."

"I see," Luke said. "May I ask your purpose?"

Matt picked up on the boy's response as a positive sign the old man was still alive. "We're from Deale, Maryland. We understand Jeremiah still owns a piece of property there. We're interested in finding out more about it."

Luke moved to the far end of the porch where there were several wooden chairs. "Please. You may sit if you like," he said.

Kitty and Matt took seats next to each other as Luke moved a chair to sit opposite them.

"Jeremiah is my great-uncle. He is not here at this time. He has gone to town with my father and soon will return."

"May we wait for him?" Kitty asked.

"Yes," Luke said. "I will get you some water, or tea, if you like."

Matt looked at Kitty. "No, thank you. We're fine."

"I know this property of which you speak. Uncle Jeremiah once lived there with his wife and daughter, Sarah. He came here after they both passed."

"We spoke with one of your relatives, Mrs. Fletcher. I understand she's the sister of Jeremiah. That's how we were finally able to locate your family here in Strasburg. She said she had three other brothers . . . Matthew, Peter and James."

"What you speak is true. Matthew and Peter have passed. James is my grandfather. He, too, is still alive."

"May we meet him? May we speak with him?" Kitty asked.

"I will see." Luke rose and went into the house. Several moments later an aging elder accompanied him back to take a seat with them on the porch. "Grandpa. This is Miss Smallwood and Mr. Bodine."

"We're very glad to meet you," Matt said, smiling. "We're waiting for Jeremiah to return so we can talk to him. We thought you might have some information to help us."

James was more alert than expected. His teeth were stained from chewing tobacco and his cheek bulged from having a chunk in his jaw. "Luke says you want to buy the property in Deale. Is that true?"

"Actually, we're interested in the house and wanted to discuss several things with Jeremiah."

As James spoke, a second pickup truck drove up, stopping near Matt's car. Two occupants exited the vehicle, Luke's father, Samuel, and Jeremiah. They approached the porch, Samuel carrying two bags.

214

"Father. This is Miss Smallwood and Mr. Bodine. They have come to see Uncle Jeremiah."

Samuel acknowledged their presence with a nod of his head and proceeded into the house.

Jeremiah approached them and took a seat with the others sitting on the porch, while Luke followed his father inside.

"Why doest thou wish to see me?"

"Do you still own the property on the shore in Deale?"

"I do. It's not for sale," he answered, curtly.

Matt and Kitty were taken by surprise.

"May I ask, why?" Kitty responded. "We thought since it had been abandoned for so many years, you might consider getting rid of it."

"I have told you. It is not for sale." Jeremiah started to get up and leave.

"Sir. . . . Mr. Colison. Please. We've came a long way to speak with you. Can't you at least give us a few moments of your time?" Matt asked.

Jeremiah sat down.

"My friend and I have spent a lot of time locating you," Matt continued. "We've talked with your sister and others who knew your family when you lived in Deale. We've even spoke with Richard."

Matt could have bit his tongue.

Jeremiah's face showed a definite expression of anger. "I will not speak of him."

"Please, forgive me. I didn't mean to cause any ill memories. May we speak of other things?"

"Yes. If that is what you wish." Jeremiah's belligerent attitude slightly softened.

Kitty spoke. "We know very little about your religious beliefs and Amish customs. Please forgive us for being ignorant of them. I do have something I must ask because of this. Do you believe there is a spirit, a soul if you prefer, that transcends our earth-life?"

"There is a heaven and a hell," Jeremiah answered, without hesitation.

"But," Kitty continued, "do you also believe a troubled soul may exist in a period of indecision before reaching its next destiny in the life hereafter?"

"I do not know of such things," Jeremiah said. "What doest this have to do with your interest in my property?"

"Would you please excuse me while I get something from our car?"

Jeremiah nodded agreement, as Kitty moved to retrieve a paper bag and returned.

"I have two things to show you. I'd like to know if you recognize them." Kitty first removed the tea cup and presented it to Jeremiah.

He offered a slight smile. "This is the same as my wife used in our home." Jeremiah handed it back to Kitty.

She handed it to Matt and took the doll from the bag, holding it in front of Sarah's father. "Do you remember this?" she asked, rather defiantly.

Jeremiah's face turned to an almost horrified expression. "Where did you get that?"

Matt entered the conversation, placing his hand on Kitty's knee. "I found it in the house. I was given the tea cup by the spirit of either your daughter or your wife."

Jeremiah trembled and rose from his chair. "I shall speak no more of this." He rushed inside the house.

Matt turned to James who had sat silent through the entire conversation. "I'm sorry for disturbing your brother, but there is something very wrong from his past. Has Jeremiah spoken to you about anything to do with the death of Sarah, or the injury to Richard?"

"I, like Jeremiah, will talk no longer of this. I suggest you leave."

CHAPTER XXV

On their return from the Blue Ridge Mountains, Matt and Kitty weren't entirely displeased with their trip. They had realized ahead of time delicate issues would be probed when confronting Jeremiah and his family. The fact he had recognized the tea cup, and especially the doll, they returned feeling their mission accomplished to a degree.

Jeremiah's reaction to the doll, and his overt expression of distaste for Richard, opened new avenues of consideration.

Kitty spent the next week at work while Matt picked up a few odd jobs. She returned Friday around noon.

They spent the evening in a low key manner, having a dinner of their earlier catch, and watching a romance movie on TV. The following day, they got up early, had breakfast, and drove to Solomon's to keep their meeting at Dr. Perry's office. When they arrived, Beth was already there and in conversation with Richard's doctor. Richard arrived a short time later.

"Hello, Richard. Please come in," Dr. Perry said.

"Thank you, Charlotte. Can I have some candy?"

"You most certainly can. Help yourself." She took the lid off of a candy dish sitting on her desk.

Richard moved forward and took a single piece of chocolate.

"Why don't you sit down in that seat? Charlotte pointed to the only vacant chair in front of her desk -- Kitty, Matt, and Beth occupying the others. "Richard. Do you remember Kitty and Matt? They spoke with you a couple of weeks ago while you were working at the boatyard."

"I think so," he answered, without looking up, focusing on trying to take the foil off of his Hershey Kiss.

"Hello, Richard," Kitty said. "Do you remember talking

about how good you did your work?"

Richard looked up and grinned. "Oh, yes. I remember. You liked what I did." His face altered expression to a more serious state. "Can you do what I do?" he asked.

"Oh, no." Kitty smiled broadly. "I don't have the talents that you do. You're much better than I am."

Richard's face again beamed an even bigger smile. "I knew that. I knew that," he repeated.

"Richard," Dr. Perry said, getting his attention. "This lady you haven't met is another doctor, just like me. Would you like to meet her?"

"Yes. I will meet her."

Dr. Perry smiled. "This lady is Dr. Placid. Or, if you would like, you can call her Beth."

"Yes. I like Beth better. I don't like doctors," Richard stated.

"I know," Dr. Perry said, soothingly. "But, I'd like you to let Beth talk to you. Would you like that?"

"That's okay. What does she want to talk about?"

"Why don't you ask her?" Dr. Perry nodded her head toward Beth for her to take over the situation.

"Dr. Beth. What do you want to ask me?" Richard inquired.

Beth smiled and reached to get him another piece of candy. Richard accepted it with a huge smile. "Do you like to watch the television, Richard?"

"Oh, yes," he answered. "I like to watch the pictures. Sometimes I don't want to stop."

"That's very good," Beth counters. "I'll bet you really like Bugs Bunny, don't you?"

"Oh, yes. I like Tweety-Bird better."

All present smiled. Matt whispered to Kitty, "That's my favorite, too."

She nudged him as Beth continued. "Do you like to go to sleep?"

"Oh, yes. Sometimes I get very tired. I like to sleep when I'm tired. Do you like to sleep when you're tired?"

"I sure do," Beth said. "Are you tired, now?"

"No. . . . I don't know." Richard seemed confused.

"Well, could I try to see if I could make you sleepy?"

"I don't care."

Beth moves forward in her chair. "Richard. Please look at my face. I need you to look into my eyes and concentrate as hard as you can."

"I don't know concen . . . concentrate. What is that?"

Beth reached into her satchel retrieving a metronome as Richard sat looking at the ceiling, sucking on the piece of hard candy he had received from Beth. "Richard. Can you listen to me? I need you to watch the arrow on this machine." Beth put it into motion -- the ticking pronounced through the small office. "Are you watching the arrow and listening to the sound it makes?"

"Yes," Richard said.

Beth spoke in even softer tones. "You feel like you are becoming very relaxed. You have worked very hard and need to get relaxed. Relax, Richard, relax, . . . relax."

Richard's eyes closed.

"You can hear me, Richard, even though you are very relaxed. I want you to keep your eyes closed and when I ask you to open them you will not be able to do that. In fact, the harder you try to open your eyes the tighter shut they will become." Beth leaned forward to wave her hand in front of Richards face. "Open your eyes, Richard," she demanded.

Richard's face reflected his attempt to open his eyes, but with each effort his eye lids squinted more and more shut.

"He's under," Beth stated.

Kitty, Matt and Dr. Perry breathed a sigh of understanding and relief.

Beth referred to a notebook containing questions provided by Kitty. "Richard. Do you know how old you are?"

"No. I know I am very old."

"I want you to go back in time. I want you to remember when you were a baby. I want you to remember your mother holding you in her arms. You are asleep, and drifting back into your past memories. Your mother loved you very much. You are a baby in her arms."

Richard began to writhe in his chair, trying to form almost a fetal position.

"I don't want you to be a baby, any longer," Beth said. "I want you to grow slowly, until you are the age at the time Sarah

219

died."

Richard stopped the contortions and sat up in his chair. "Here, Sarah. I've brought you some flowers from your garden. Do you like them?" Richard slumped in his chair again.

"How old are you Richard?" Beth asked.

"Fifteen."

"Do you love Sarah?"

"Yes. I love her. She is so good to me. We love each other." Richard is still half-lying in his seat.

"Can you sit up, Richard?" Beth asked, as an attempt to establish her hypnotic control.

Richard immediately righted himself in his chair.

Kitty and Dr. Perry expressed facial amazement at Beth's ability to manipulate his state of hypnosis and the astute answers received from Richard.

"Richard. I want you to go to the day Sarah ran out on the jetty. Can you do that? Do you remember her being very upset at something? Can you remember what happened to Sarah?" Beth asked.

"No. No, Sarah. Please don't do this. Please. I love you. Please," he cried out, once again slumping in his chair.

Dr. Perry leaned forward and, in a whispered voice, said, "Are you sure we should continue? I feel he's becoming disturbed."

"Please, Charlotte," Kitty interrupted. "I must tell you these responses, under his determined mental condition, are literally new and unexplored in medical history. We are setting inroads to new scientific discovery. He's fine and won't remember any of this."

"Yes," Beth said in confirmation. "Richard is not in distress. At least, not at this point. I'm even amazed at what we've accomplished reviving his previously dormant long-term memory. Please. Give us the chance to continue. Kitty and I are both quite well known and respected in our fields and we would do nothing to jeopardize his health, either mentally or physically."

Dr. Perry nodded her acceptance and sat back in her chair.

"Do you remember what your birthday is?" Beth asked.

"No. I . . . Yes, it was in the cold winter."

"You can't remember the date?"

"No. It was too long ago. I can't remember."

"It's good that you remember Sarah? And I know you loved her very much," Beth said, prodding Richard to go on.

"Oh, yes. She was my friend. I love her. Where's Sarah?"

"She'll be here soon." Beth looked at Kitty, questioning how she should proceed.

Kitty nodded for her to keep pursuing the list of questions provided.

"No. No." Richard almost screamed his response. "Sarah died. She died. She can't come here."

Beth's voice became even more soothing. "Now, now, Richard. Please calm down. I know you tried to save Sarah. You were very brave."

Richard began to rock back-and-forth in his seat.

"You fell and hit your head on the rocks while you were trying to save Sarah, didn't you?" Beth asked.

"No. No. He hit me."

Matt's eyes enlarged so much it looked like they would explode out of their sockets.

"He hit me," Richard repeated.

"Who hit you, Richard?" Beth pursued her line of questioning.

"Sarah's father. He hit me in the head."

"Oh, my God." Kitty gasped, clasping her hand over her mouth, concerned her overt expression had caused interruption to the session. Whispering to Matt, she said, "Jeremiah knows one hellava lot more than he admitted to us. He's covering up something really horrible."

Beth asked Kitty to give her the doll from her case. "Richard. I'd like you to open your eyes right now, and you will be able to do that this time. Open your eyes, Richard. Look at me." Richard slowly opened his eyes and stared in Beth's direction. "Do you know this doll? Was it Sarah's?"

"Yes," he said.

"Is this Baby Sarah?" Beth persisted.

"No."

Kitty again expressed surprise at his response, as did Matt.

"Are you sure? If the doll isn't baby Sarah, who is?

"Our baby. Sarah's baby. My baby."

221

"Sarah had a baby, Richard?"

"No. . . . No. No! Her father hit her in the stomach and it came out dead."

"Aw, Jesus Christ," Kitty said, in distress. "That's enough. Get him out of this Beth."

"Richard. When I snap my fingers, you will awake and you will not remember anything that has happened. You will ask for another piece of candy and, until we meet again, at sometime in the future, you will not remember anything that you have said, or remembered." Beth snapped her fingers.

Richard responded. "Can I have some more chocolate?"

Dr. Perry smiled and gave him two pieces.

"Can I go now?" he innocently asked.

Dr. Perry nodded her approval to his request.

Matt offered to give him a ride home, but his doctor disapproved, noting that Richard prided himself on being able to come and go under his own effort.

With Richard gone, a summary meeting ensued. Dr. Perry began. "I can't believe what I heard and observed. Richard is sorely retarded, but you were able to broach areas of his brain and long term memory I never dreamed possible. I don't know what you gained from his recall, but I do know I'm amazed at what I saw and heard."

"Charlotte, I can't really express enough thanks for your cooperation," Kitty said. "Please forgive me for not being able to be more explanatory about the real reasons for this. I assure you what you've seen will establish a new insight to psychiatric medicine and the benefits hypnosis can mean in working with the retarded. Things happened today that even astounded me." Kitty stood and gathered her things. "If you'll excuse us, we'll be on our way. I do promise you we'll keep in touch."

* * *

Matt and Kitty rode in his car returning to Deale following the meeting. Matt smiled. "It's almost like a feeling of deja vu," he said. "We were doing this very same thing just a couple of weeks ago after seeing the ol' man.

"You're right," she agreed. "But, this time we know a lot more than then."

"Pardon my French, but ten seconds after we met Jeremiah, I

didn't like the son of a bitch. I knew he had to be at the bottom of something rotten," Matt said, with disgust.

"But . . . ." Kitty paused and gazed out of the window at the passing scenery. "You don't think he killed his daughter because she was pregnant, do you?"

"No. I don't. But, I wouldn't put it past him." Matt reached and patted Kitty on her leg. "Not sure, yet, but I think her baby is what it's all about."

"What if the baby was born and is still alive? Richard might be wrong. Could he still have the child with him at that farm?" Kitty paused to get her cigarettes from her purse. "I'm sorry." She smiled. "I'm just running at the mouth to hear myself talk. It's a way of thinking. Sometimes it helps."

"I know what you mean," Matt said, smiling. "If that's the case, it's my turn." Matt looked at Kitty and he winked at her. "As far as the baby still being alive, I doubt that seriously. Sarah would have certainly mentioned that in her diary I would think. From where they supposedly found Richard, after the so-called accident, he was evidently trying to stop Sarah. I figure Jeremiah was chasing after the both of them and in a rage hit Richard in the head with something. Sarah continued out on the jetty and either slipped, or intentionally jumped into the water."

Matt pulled into a service station to get gas. As he filled his tank, Kitty got them drinks from a coke machine. Shortly, they were back on their way.

Kitty opened both of the cans and handed one to Matt. "I've been thinking about what you said. As rebuttal to the concept that Richard was trying to stop Sarah, possibly from committing suicide, maybe they were both trying to get away from her father."

Matt pondered Kitty's appraisal for several moments. "I've considered that. But, if they were trying to get away from him, why would they corner themselves at the jetty. It doesn't make sense." Matt sipped from his coke. "No. I don't think so. I think the old man caught them together and went berserk."

"How do you feel about confronting Jeremiah with this?" Kitty asked.

"Sooner or later, I don't think we have any other choice. I'd like to wait a while. I've got the strange feeling we'll learn more before long."

* * *

Mentally spent from their morning experience, Matt and Kitty took a long nap in the afternoon without removing their clothes. Matt was the last to wake. A crash of thunder and lightning accompanied the harsh rocking of his boat in the water.

Throwing his legs over the side of the bed, he stood and went to the head. Looking out of the porthole, the sea was in a frenzy and rain pummeled everything without showing any mercy. Finishing his business, Matt proceeded to the salon and was surprised to find Kitty not there. Suddenly, he became uneasy and afraid. Rushing up the steps, he left the boat and sped to the old house. The rear door was sitting open. Instead of entering, he ran toward the jetty by instinct -- the downpour soaking him to the bone.

Arriving at the breakwater, Kitty stood on the rocks near its beginning at the shore. Afraid to call to her, Matt slowly approached. Kitty turned and screamed, "Richard. Look out." She then began to run toward the end of the jetty.

A ghostly mist suddenly appeared turning into Sarah's spirit merged into Kitty as she ran.

"Oh, my God," Matt cried out. "Kitty." He chased after her, nearly slipping and falling on the wet rocks. She reached the jetty's end, stopped, and stood facing the beating rain as it continued to drench her body. As Matt neared, she plunged into the water.

Matt screamed at the top of his lungs, "Kitty . . . Sarah," and jumped in after her.

She thrashed wildly, trying to deny Matt saving her. He was surprised to find he could stand on the bottom in water more shallow than thought. Subduing her, he quelled Kitty's rage and got her back to the jetty and to the shore.

CHAPTER XXVI

Matt sat patiently at the end of the bed watching Kitty as she slept. Drinking the last bit of brandy from his glass, he rose and went to the galley for a refill. As he turned from the counter, he was shocked in confronting Kitty standing behind him.

"Hi, honey. We sure had a nice nap," she said, yawning.

"Doc. Are you all right?" he asked with a desperate tone in his voice.

"Yeah, silly. What's wrong?"

Matt's mind swirled with thought about how to respond. "I . . . I just wondered if you slept okay?"

Kitty laughed. "Oh, yes. I really needed our nap. How long have you been up?"

"Since I brought you back from the jetty."

Kitty ignored his remark. "Is there any coffee left?"

"Yeah. It's not fresh, though. I can heat it in the microwave if you'd like."

"Please," she said. Kitty sat in Matt's recliner, pushing it back to its full lying position. "I sure understand why you love this chair. You know. I still feel groggy."

"Just relax," Matt advised. "The coffee's almost ready."

Kitty suddenly sat up, raising the chair to its upright state. "Oh, my God, Matt. What happened?"

Matt rushed to kneel beside her.

"Something happened, didn't it? I know it did." She began to tremble as if in a chill.

Matt rose and got the Afghan, returning to cover her with it.

"Was it a dream? I remember what happened to Sarah and Richard." Kitty began to cry and tremble even more. "Oh, Matt. Please help me." Her sobbing slowly subsided and eventually ceased. By then, she was in deep sleep, her skin tone still bluish as before.

After making sure she was comfortably warm, Matt got his rain jacket and ventured out into the dark stormy night carrying his flashlight. Arriving at the old house, he went inside and shouted at the top of his lungs. "Damn, you. What do you want from us? We're only trying to help."

Suddenly, the room began to brighten. The kerosene lamp appeared and the atmosphere again transformed before his eyes to yesteryear. The old lady sat in her rocker knitting. At first, she said nothing, ignoring his presence. Then, she rose from her chair, putting her knitting aside, and crossed the room. "Would you like some tea?" the spirit asked.

"No," Matt answered, emphatically. "I want some damn answers. Why are you doing this to us? If you want our help, tell us what to do."

"I'd like to have some tea," the old lady responded, ignoring Matt's remark. She left the room and entered the kitchen.

Matt followed her.

She went to the wood stove and picked up a tea kettle and poured a cup full of brown liquid. "I love jonquils, Richard. You should, too."

The apparition immediately faded. Matt was stunned.

* * *

Pulling into the Colison farm driveway, the place seemed deserted. Jason and Matt exited the car and approached the front of the house as Luke greeted them.

"You were asked to leave and not return," Luke stated. "You're not welcome here."

"That's tough shit," Matt said. "Get Jeremiah out here or I'll have the local police do it for me."

Luke displayed shock at Matt's vehement attitude. He quickly disappeared inside of the house -- two of his brothers and James accompanying his return. "It's best you leave this place," James demanded.

"No." Matt contradicted. "You either listen to what I have to say or I'll bring the authorities into this matter so fast your head will swim. We have proof your brother has broken several serious laws, possibly either manslaughter, or even murder. It's your choice, not mine."

James' attitude softened. "What is it you have to say?"

"We know Jeremiah was responsible for Richard's accident. It wasn't an accident at all. He attacked him and gave him a blow to the head causing his mal condition. We want to know why. If you won't let us question him about this, I swear before your God and mine I'll get all of the legal help necessary to get to the bottom of what happened and fry that bast . . . ."

Jason snatched Matt by his arm to cut him short.

James didn't hesitate. "I'll get him to respond to your query. Please wait a moment."

* * *

Matt's car arrived at the marina after dark -- Colison's pickup behind. All of them, including Luke, James, and Jeremiah left their vehicles, and proceeded to Matt's boat. Kitty greeted them on their arrival.

"Let's get this over with," Matt said. "I'm getting tired of all this bullshit."

As a group, they walked toward the house.

Without warning a brilliant ghostly haze encircled the structure which appeared to be vibrating -- all of the windows aglow as never before. A screeching scream permeated the night tailing off to a mournful cry as Jeremiah stepped onto the property. He tried to retreat -- Jason impeded his escape.

Matt realized Luke and James were oblivious to the apparition taking place.

"Wait here," Matt said, in a demanding tone as he approached the house and disappeared inside.

Brief moments later the eerie glow subsided -- the house back to its realistic state -- the familiar faint flickering light filtering through the downstairs windows.

Matt returned outside motioning the rest to come forward.

Luke and James led the way, followed closely by Jeremiah -- Jason and Kitty bringing up the rear.

Jeremiah made it a point to avoid going near the corner flower bed which was teeming with jonquils that, normally, only grew in early spring.

As they entered the back door all were privy to see the events transpiring. The elderly spirit sat in the rocking chair humming

227

her lilting tune.

All were shocked at the scene, except Matt.

The elderly spirit stood and moved to the table retrieving a single flower from its vase. "I do so love jonquils," she softly said, returning to her place seated in the chair while continuing to chant her eerie lullaby.

"What do you want, Sarah?" Matt asked passively.

Slowly the elderly form altered into Sarah's spirit. She glanced at him, started to resume her humming, then said, "I love you, Richard."

Jeremiah suddenly began to weep.

Luke shouted, "What is this happening? This abomination of . . ."

Kitty responded in like manner, "Shut up!"

James stepped forward to steady his grandfather.

As Jeremiah moved in s shaken manner toward the back door he motioned for Matt to follow.

Outside, James helped Jeremiah to the now almost barren flower bed at the corner of the house, a single jonquil remaining in full bloom.

Matt stood in the doorway and watched.

Dropping to his knees, Jeremiah began digging deeply into the soft dirt with his hands. Moments later, he lifted a metal container and carried it back inside of the house. He paused briefly, and then approached Sarah, kneeling next to her, and placed the tin at her feet.

Sarah reached down, picked up the container and laid it on her lap. She gently opened it, exposing the remains of an infant child.

Before everyone's eyes, the bones slowly transformed into the image of a just born premature baby.

Sarah cradled it in her arms. She reached to touch her father, and he crumpled to the floor.

Sarah glanced toward Matt and Kitty exposing a contented smile.

The vision disappeared.

The house became dark and current to its time.

Jeremiah was dead.

* * *

Inside Matt's boat salon, his dollhouse rested on the dining booth table completely finished. Slowly it began to alter in shape and detail to become an exact replica of Sarah's house as if it were in its first built state.

* * *

Lights flashed brilliantly from the emergency vehicles parked at the old house as a stretcher carried the body to an awaiting ambulance.

"What happened?" an officer asked Matt and Kitty, as Jeremiah's son and grandson stood aside.

They looked at each other and smiled.

"Nothing really unusual," Matt responded. "We were trying to make a deal on the property with the owner and he must've had a heart attack."

"Yeah," Jason added. "I think the old man had a real attachment with the place."

"If you need any more details, I suggest you speak with those Amish standing over there," Kitty suggested. "They're his kin folk."

Matt chuckled as they turned and walked away arm-in-arm. "You know, Doc. I could get used to this afterlife bit. In my next one, I think I'll come back as another Bill Gates.

They walked a little further.

"Tomorrow morning I'm going to call my kids and let them 'guess who's coming to dinner.'"

* * *

A light flickered in the upstairs rear bedroom window.

"THE END"

Copyright © 2006 by FictionWriters
www.fictionwriters.ws/Store.htm
FW: 622112
ISBN: 978-0-6151-3914-2

All rights reserved including the right of reproduction in
whole or in part in any form.